No Part in Your Death

Since his birth in the Gray's Inn Road in the borough of St Pancras, Nicolas Freeling has lived all his days in Europe. Fifteen years as a cook in expensive, and generally nasty, restaurants: thereafter, novelist. His house lies on a historic route from Germany through to France. It has been most things, and now has a future as a lighthouse. *Love in Amsterdam*, his first novel, was published in 1962, closely followed by his second and third novels, *Because of the Cats* and *Gun before Butter*, which were published in 1963. His other crime novels include *Valparaiso*, *Double Barrel*, *Criminal Conversation*, *The King of the Rainy Country*, *The Dresden Green*, *Strike Out Where Not Applicable*, *This is the Castle*, *Tsing-Boum*, *Over the High Side*, *A Long Silence*, *Dressing of Diamond*, *What are the Bugles Blowing for?*, *Lake Isle*, *Gadget*, *The Night Lords*, *The Widow*, *One Damn Thing After Another*, *Castang's City* and *Wolfnight*. Many of these are published in Penguins.

Nicolas Freeling

No Part
in Your Death

PENGUIN BOOKS

Penguin Books Ltd, Harmondsworth, Middlesex, England
Viking Penguin Inc., 40 West 23rd Street, New York, New York 10010, U.S.A.
Penguin Books Australia Ltd, Ringwood, Victoria, Australia
Penguin Books Canada Ltd, 2801 John Street, Markham, Ontario, Canada L3R 1B4
Penguin Books (N.Z.) Ltd, 182–190 Wairau Road, Auckland 10, New Zealand

First published in the United States of America by Viking 1984
First published in Great Britain by William Heinemann 1984
Published in Penguin Books 1986

Made and printed in Great Britain by
Cox and Wyman Ltd, Reading
Typeset in Times

Part One

'Me and Capablanca'

You and Capablanca, thought Castang; how did it go? Something about 'beautiful creepy remorseless chess'. Muddled somewhere in his memory with who? – Woody Allen? – catching sight of his face in the glass while cleaning his teeth, trying out a tough snarl, fleeing in terror from the resultant vision.

Perhaps he had bumped the driving mirror getting into the car: perhaps Vera had left it that way: it would take a cop to find out: it wasn't supposed to be reflecting his face. Put it straight.

The one outside the window was crooked too. Were he an organised man he'd have done it all before starting: he wasn't. Were it a slightly grander car one could straighten it from inside instead of waiting for a red light: it wasn't. Cheap small car, as most of his things were, except for his hats, his shoes . . . but most of the Commissaire of Police felt cheap, was cheap. He wasn't much good at beautiful creepy remorseless chess, neither.

A blowing equinoctial day in early October, with the side wind leaning on the car at street corners, the poplar trees streaming and losing their leaves, the willows yellowed and half bare already. A nice time of year and one he liked.

He himself was getting on for forty and feeling his age in traffic. He would still take his bicycle to go to work, but nowadays he looked out of the window first, at the weather.

The building where he worked was a massive and dreary block of the previous century, in the ponderous rectilinear architecture then thought suitable for schools, orphanages or madhouses; and suitably it housed some hundreds of functionaries supporting state bureaucracies of the sort whose purpose nobody can guess and whose meaning if they have one is carefully concealed. The Regional Service of Police Judiciaire is distinguishable from Youth and Sport next door by thick wire screens over all the windows on the street side, which trap all the available dust and send the lighting bill up. It is to be presumed that they also stop people jumping out of these windows.

As a Commissaire and thus a senior official Castang had an office on the courtyard side, where there are plane trees, older and rather decrepit horse-chestnuts, and a lot of parked cars. The offices are large and the windows can be made to open in fine weather. For no amount of promotion or money could he have been persuaded to work in the municipal services, who are housed in a modern block of minute boxes whose windows do not open at all.

The half-dozen department heads have supplemented officially provided furniture with objects to their taste and choice. Castang had a massive flat-topped desk of the same period as the building, in a wood said to be oak, and a bentwood Victorian hat-stand. Divisional Commissaire Adrien Richard, who commands the SRPJ, is both old and old-fashioned. He is also highly intelligent and has much force of character. When he retires, as he will be forced to any day now since he is past sixty, nobody knows what will happen. Castang does not like to think about it. Monsieur Richard has sought and encouraged a close personal friendship with this particular subordinate. Not very long ago, Castang, then a junior commissaire heading the Serious Crimes brigade, got fairly badly shot up. Richard managed to keep him on as chief of staff. He had learned to be patient and fairly efficient with the administrative detail.

Bits of the place are modern. The ground floor and much of the basement are full of electronics. We have learned from Germany that communications are the secret of modern police work. Mm, we have still a long way to go. There are numerous different police forces in France, and they all dislike one another intensely. Monsieur Richard believes (for himself) in a great deal of oldfashioned privacy and is guarded by a dragon called Fausta who had been startlingly pretty as a young girl and now – she must be approaching thirty – has matured into

6

considerable and serene beauty.

He believes too in leaving department heads alone, facing their responsibilities. It is Castang's job to pounce upon young inspectors who daydream of obscenities while picking their noses. But Richard likes to see all his senior staff every day, and face to face. Castang is first on this list. He opened his window, which the cleaning woman always shuts, turned the central heating down quite a lot, and spent a quarter of an hour with all the paper on his desk before going along the passage. He does not shake hands with Fausta: Richard has abolished this ridiculous French habit along with much else that is meaningless (one can do less with the quantities of paper from Paris, but one is a filter for the more preposterous instructions).

"Good morning," said Richard, who was making his daily tour of the flowers.

This isn't at all French either: they hate flowers. German and of course Dutch policemen are strong on horticulture. Richard's wife Judith, who most illogically is Spanish, is a tremendous gardener. For years and years Richard threw out all the plants with which she sought to humanise PJ offices. But he has learned at last to throw out the abstractions that sterilise French thought, instead. Like all middle-aged converts to a new creed he is even more Catholic than the Pope. Fausta says he now talks to the plants, but she may have invented this. He is meticulous though with his little scissors. A tall and quite elegant man, with that smooth kind of silver hair and a tendency to bow ties, he looks ludicrous pottering at those damned-geraniums-again. Do not think however that he listens with only half an ear. He knows all about the paperwork on Castang's desk; is adept at the difference between making a verbal précis and gliding over the surface. At sixty-two he is in excellent health and offensively spry. Castang does not know whether Paris regards this as an argument against retirement.

They went over current affairs in the usual way together, exchanged a variety of reports and dossiers. Richard saves up any surprises – mostly unpleasant – there may be, to drop them casually at blank moments. He calls this 'gingering up the soldiery'. Castang calls it self-indulgent dramatisation, but he'd better not say so in office hours.

7

"Paris has a new, and tedious, invention." Pause for coat-trailing, which one knows better than to interrupt. "We're going to join another club."

Paris is always doing this. There are plenty of fairly futile inventions like the Common Agricultural Policy, made more or less respectable by long usage. Ministers get together to chat about finance or fish, and there are interminable proposals to unify and codify one's attitude towards bombs or sulphur dioxide, instantly torpedoed by chauvinism and umbrage-taking. Recently, because of terrorists, there's been a lot on the judicial level. Ministers sign agreements: all the countries then refuse to ratify them, because of surrendering sovereignty. There's not one of us that has sovereignty over the seat of his own trousers, but simultaneous with umbrage-taken it's a thing they go on about. Democratically elected representatives of the people have this in common with elderly bigots: the less their virtue is threatened the more prudishly do they defend it.

"What's it now?"

"There's an Alpine Club for flatfeet. Austria, Switzerland, Germany, Italy. We've been hoity-toiting this for some time, but the place has got so full of gangsters claiming political asylum that Paris had their arm twisted. Dragging flatfeet suddenly full of enthusiasm."

"So the Quai des Orfèvres goes climbing Alps, and so what?"

"Totally mistaken, boy, this is you: don't waste your breath saying no: it's a decision."

"No."

"Out of my hands: I got designated myself, the sous-chef said I was too old, there was a wrangle, I was told abruptly to find a suitable substitute among the more intelligent of my senior staff; you're the most suitably moronic and that's it."

"Why here, dear God, why not Dijon, Lyon? Trust that old bastard not to pick Marseille, but – "

"Stuck a pin, no doubt; save your breath for the address you will be expected to deliver to the congress."

"About what for gossake?"

"Anything you like as long as it's not terrorism." This entry into international limelight gave Castang no joy.

8

"My work."

"Nonsense, you'll only be away a week. You do no work anyhow." This is called hardening the attitude, or sometimes heightening the tone; mulish or mutinous faces having been perceived. "And what there is, I'll do. You'd prefer that to staying here and doing mine.

"Do understand, you silly thing; I'm looking for some promotion for you and this is fertile terrain for acquiring merit."

"Grease marks."

"Rubbish, there'll certainly be some senior medulla oblongata from the Quai, with a watching brief for Paris, but nobody's asking you to carry his coffee cups for him, and now you will kindly put a stop to this arguing."

"Getting sent like a bloody parcel and I don't even know where to." Oh well, the police is supposed to be disciplined.

A couple of weeks later, and Castang found himself in München, a city called Munich by the French. It took a couple of weeks for oracles to pronounce and wheels to turn in Paris. Also for a German talent, that of organising details, to express itself in some beautifully polished paperwork with translations in several languages, like the Operating Instructions on a new coffee machine.

It had also to be later because of the Oktoberfest: nobody goes then, because far too many people do go then. It is the most colossal piss-up known to the human species. This conference would be a piss-up too, because as Richard remarked they always are, but there would be less folk, less noise, and less Bavarian bonhomie. Not quite so many ambulances in the street: the best thing that can be said for the Oktoberfest is that it kills fewer people than the Carnival at Rio.

Castang had also time to organise some sordid details of his own. It is all very well being invited to a piss-up and having your expenses paid, but when your wife wants to come too . . . These official or functionary kind of get-togethers are very oldfashioned, with a clubby atmosphere. There can easily be hearty laughter of a greasy kind; a perfume of the nightclub and the bordel in the cigarsmoke. Vera wasn't having any of this nonsense.

In the first place she is Czech, and Bavaria is more than halfway home: in fact it has a common border with home. Vera has not been home in over ten years now: it is no longer 'home'. She had a very strong family feeling, and the brutality of the break was to her exceedingly painful. She had said to Castang, immediately after the 'desertion' "You are my family now". Not being a total imbecile and having moreover no family of his own he has not done too badly, but that this has been a very traumatic affair indeed there is no doubt. Shrinks indeed had said – he hated shrinks and so did she – that her semi-paralysis, lasting some years, was hysterical in origin. Fell off the bars and hurt her spine? Yes of course, but guilt plays a rôle in this, you know. Leaving her half t'other side of the Curtain. She has cured herself. She walks, particularly since having a baby, as near as possible to normally: there is a slight limp. She had told all the shrinks to fuck off: there is fear of them as well as contempt for them. But never, never does she speak of this.

Was it then not a bit odd to want to go to Munich? Even a bit ominous? – sort of tempting providence a wee bit? She is robust about this.

"I like it, that's all. I'd like to see it again. Beer, and music, and the waitresses wearing boots, and baroque churches. They say the Orient starts at Vienna: well, Central Europe starts at Munich. I'll feel at home."

"Home is supposed to be where I am," jealously.

"Well, you'll be there too, won't you?" Childish answer to a childish remark. There is no more to be said. She is not jealous in any crude sense. She does not wish to keep him under her eye: she does not suspect him of wanting to sneak off and fumble flesh, overstimulated by fleisch in pots, or beer in more pots. She shows perfect trust because she is perfectly trustworthy. Whoever's tit gets lecherously eyed, it isn't Vera's. She manages this without any shadow of prudery. Strength of character, something seldom encountered in reality.

Financial fiddling has been called for. The plane ticket allowed by the administration has been turned into a train: the expensive hotel room laid on by the Germans bargained for a much cheaper one with no bath, and the Commissaire's bank account will have to be stretched. However, trust Vera, who in these circumstances isn't artistic a bit: hardheaded Central European housewife, all the way.

Strangely, he has never been in Munich before. A comment perhaps upon French provincialism, since it is no further from Paris than Marseille. A comment upon antique associations of thought, since after efforts at recollection he said 'Daladier and Chamberlain: François-Ponçet. The Men of Munich'. He will be charmed by the Feldherrnhalle, where those psychopaths had removed statues of rather un-martial-seeming generals and replaced them with utterly ludicrous SS iron men. This episode in Bavarian history will strike him as being more farcical than anything else. The inhabitants could say, like Evelyn Waugh after writing *Gilbert Pinfold*, "This was the time that we went mad": it is what happens when you put dangerous drugs on top of drinking too much. Paranoid hallucinations take one utterly over. The beautiful square is drenched in sunlight even when it rains: the sun of the Wittelsbachs, a generous tyranny.

We can't efface the twelve years of horrible abomination and we would not want to try. But Castang knows that when insane the human species commits appalling crimes. We can see them every day. The twelve years of insanity can be understood better in the perspective of several hundred years in the history of a city where the flowering of European civilisation can be studied with advantage; because it isn't any better anywhere.

There is another thing a policeman knows: it is always the people who have suffered least from a criminal action who are the longest rancorous and the least generous. A Munich beer-cellar is the best place in the world for telling Jewish jokes.

A bit of sleight of hand takes place in the Europäischer Hof, pompous hotel where Castang has been booked in; full as usual of Japanese Congressists wearing little plastic labels, and the loud voices of Conservative Members of Parliament, draped in the Union Jack and audible above all else. He picked up some literature, and a handy little map of the city. Walking back, he found Vera happily installed opposite the world's biggest beer hall. "I hope we get some sleep," he said. The music will in fact be rather pleasant and if anything, soporific.

11

They have arrived at five in the afternoon. There is time for Castang to change into his go-to-meeting suit and the most urbane of his hats, since the first get-acquainted session is at half past seven, and informal. Dinner an hour later, rather more formal. Time for a stroll, and to orient oneselves.

Can we come with you? asks Vera. Just to see your grand hotel, and to know where you are: humbly. Of course, says Castang amused: did you think I'd be ashamed? He has already formed a mental picture of several senior police officials in their Sunday suits, trooping pompously about, aghast at meeting their colleague on the pavement in the company of a limping young woman with a large straw shopping bag and a small child in a pram. For Vera with immoveable obstinacy has refused to leave Lydia behind. Judith (suggested Castang) would look after her while we're away; it's 'only a week'. Vera turned to marble instantly and said, 'Out of the question'.All those pavements – Munich is a large and spacious city – will tire a child of three, and the folding push-chair is added to the luggage. Leave all this to me, said Vera a little snappishly; only women know how to organise things, while men stand about helpless being embarrassed.

Lydia of course who has had an enormous sleep on the train is as fresh as a daisy and quite ready for explorations.

"Now just see to it," said Castang, being the captain-of-the ship, "that you've plenty of money and enjoy yourselves. We aren't short so don't begin the economising lark. If she wants an ice-cream give her one."

"Yes, Master," says Vera snidely, "we'll both get pissed." She was in fact looking forward to delicious dark beer.

The Central Station side of the Karlsplatz is horrible, nothing but sexshops and hamburgers. On the other side an immense and hideous fountain forms the frontier to pleasure, because all the streets are eminently walkable.

Fortune certainly smiled upon Vera since the climate hereabouts can be abominable and instead there was an Indian summer. This is a southern, indeed very Italianate town, one can stroll till midnight as in Spain: Vera stuffed her woolly in the shopping bag and hung the shopping bag on the push-chair, and stopped for all the street musicians. Castang escorted his family as far as the Isar and then it was time to go to that dread palace, parting under one of the numerous statues of the numerous Maximilians.

A discreet little arrow led him to one of the smaller conference suites where he was taken aback to find a good many more policemen in Sunday-suits than he had been led to count upon.

Typical Richard, or was it just typically French, being sloppy and not finding out things properly (too snobbish to read all the preparatory literature: we-know-all-that)? This wasn't just the Alpine Club, this was a milling mob. He was rescued by a busy bumble bee.

"Schumacher."

"Castang."

"Ah, the French colleague – great. Must add hastily, I'm not related to the naughty goalkeeper." Toni from Köln, who knocked a French footballer unconscious in the last World Cup, causing even more uproar in Germany than in France.

"It was an aspect of violence," said Castang politely, "but less worrisome than lots of our daily bread and butter."

"Oh you speak German, that's great. We've got sim-tran laid on for the formal sessions, and we hope to get by in informal discussion by pattering in English, but it's a help when . . . ja, of course, half of Germany's called Schumacher when it's not called Schiller." This plainly well-worn joke was equally plainly designed to defrost the chalkier sort of visiting cop.

"How is old Toni nowadays?" – politely.

"Oh he's just the same as ever – that's to say," hastily, "rather more subdued. But let me introduce you to some more of the colleagues – of course your comrade from Paris you know already."

"Not in the least."

"Heinrich," said a square frogfaced individual, but with something of a roguish grin about the chops. "Honoured, comrade," in German.

"Es freut mich," said Castang automatically. An Alsacien, of course! Also of course, the only one they could find in Paris who could speak a word of German. (It turned out in fact less dread than he anticipated. Commissaire Heinrich was totally

13

humourless, indeed alarmingly sentimental, about Alsace, but engagingly funny on nearly any other subject.)

"And our English friends – this is Chief Superintendent Elliott from Glasgow, and this is Chief Inspector Dawson," very Germanly punctilious over titles, "from the West Country."

The Chi-Sup was two metres high with a face certainly at least one metre long.

"My name is Little Jock Elliott," another well-worn joke, "and who dare meddle with ME?" This said in a funereal bass with a wooden face ending in fold upon fold of smile was indeed irresistible.

"Geoffrey Dawson," said the other man in a very soft voice, "and I hasten to add," – plainly he had overheard and relished the Schumacher episode – "no relation to the former editor of *The Times* but do come and sit down upon this comfortable sofa and what can I get you to drink?"

"One moment, who's the former editor of *The Times*? Obviously I ought to know about him. What's that you're drinking?"

"Ho, a linguist, that's great, or probably we'd say oh, that's very nice. He was one of the Men of Munich, a cause of great shame, but let's not go into that now, it might not be totally tactful. It isn't gin-and-tonic, I'm glad to say; that shameful English drink; it's vodka and something else which I didn't quite catch; it's rather nice; they've got some on a tray over there; let me pinch one for you."

These English speech rhythms: one had to listen carefully until one learned them afresh. But the soft voice was clear, and completely free from public-school affectations. There was what sounded like a very slight local accent: what the hell was the West Country: was that Wales? He took a terrific wop at the drink.

"I say," said Dawson impressed. "A hard man! Like ol' Jock here. Lucky I brought three."

"It's to get over shyness and help talk English."

"You're doing bloody well right now."

"Yes, well, if I get too uninhibited kick me."

"Nono, I didn't mean it that way. Jock's way ahead of all of

14

us: they've fantastic whisky here he can't get at home."

"It's this export nonsense," in the tragedy bass. "The Scot is starved and there's no slivovitz left in Jugoslavia either, I'll be bound."

"Gosh, here's old Spokesman round again; hush."

"Gentlemen! Pray silence one second. I note that we are now all assembled, and further with great pleasure that acquaint-anceship ripens rapidly, so may I suggest that if appetite is sufficiently sharpened we all go in to dinner. You will notice that by each place-setting there is a little name label. This is our wellknown German Tüchtigheit fussing about arranging everyone: you may if you wish disregard it and sit where you feel most comfortable."

"Make a dash quick," said Dawson grabbing three more drinks off the tray slick as any pickpocket.

They lost Jock who was slow getting unstuck from MacKinlay, but acquired Roberto Bonacorsi, a Colonel in the Carabinieri. Who spoke excellent English, much better than Castang's. Moreover, excellent company. Known at once as Bobby.

"Where's all the parallel police then? Aren't they following you about?"

"Police administration is as complicated and ambivalent in Italy as in France but invites less sarcasm."

"This is why," needling, grinning, "a mere commandant of gendarmerie gets named combined head of all the security services? The uproar there was!"

"Now let's see, Carabinieri are gendarmes too, isn't it, only with a fancy name and prettier uniforms? Ah, this explains the great expanded chest full of vanity and medals. But watch it mate, the Mafia is all around you." Bobby spluttered laughing.

"We had a wonderful conference," he explained. "At Assisi – Saint Francis you know, all about Violence. Nobody could even agree upon a definition. A very naughty professor suggested that violence began with the State, and that this might be a good place to start thinking about it. All the English Conservative M.P.s got very cross, resulting in a total fuckup. All ended throwing things at one another."

"You're looking at me," said Dawson, exaggerating guilt.

"The west of England is the chief temple of backwoods reaction. We gather at Stonehenge on midsummer morning, to pray for the gallows, the treadmill and the nine-tailed cat."

"I've been wondering where the West Country was."

"I'm from Dorset."

"Ho." Castang had heard of this: Commissaire Richard had had a metaphysical experience there the year before. "Eggardon."

"Yes, we take the uppity Bantus up there, for trousers down and a good stiff caning."

"Look out, old Schu's going to make another speech."

Delegates were again welcomed; he was happy to greet our brothers from Spain and Denmark. Bound to say, the list of titles submitted for papers to be read to the assembly sounded absolutely fascinating. This would all start tomorrow morning at the conference rooms set aside specially in the Polizei Präsidium. Bright and early, so while this evening's festivities should certainly end in the same spirit of convivial jollity that he was happy to observe at this minute (applause), might he jovially remind his listeners not to go on too long . . .

"There aren't any listeners," said Bobby sotto voce. "Let's have a drink in my room."

"No, let's go for a stroll in the street: lovely night."

"These English are always going for brisk healthy walks."
Castang supported Dawson.

"I've a wife and small child awander in the streets of Munich: we might meet them."

"I say, what a bloody good idea: how did you swing that?"

"I didn't I'm afraid; all hole 'n' corner."

"Should have brought them to dinner," said Bobby. "Not a single woman among us; a glaring flagrancy, can you say that in English?"

"Can't have women on these occasions. Their originality and total disregard for male shibboleths like logic, comfort, and only hearing things you know already would cause consternation. How old is your child?" asked Dawson.

"Three."

"Wopping down beer no doubt in the Hofbrauhaus."

"I should say more likely admiring the clockwork dollies on the front of the Town Hall."

"Let's go look; 's not far."

"Wonderful names the beer has; what d'you fancy, Lion-brew or Hacker Pshorr?"

But Vera had said firmly "Bed" an hour before. They'd had a lovely time. Nicest had been three absolutely serious people, violin, viola, violoncello, doing a delightful trio that was probably boring old Brahms but sounded liltingly Schubertian this far south and in open air – Lydia, throw this in the hat – and next nicest an equally serious girl seated on an orange box with in front of her a cymbalum? – balom? – that thing like a zither only with little hammers, and a boy accompanying her on a guitar: not in the least third-man. Lydia had got the message and said 'Give me a mark' importantly. They had eaten Greek, possibly Lebanese food (in that direction anyhow . . .) They had drunk beer. It was enough for one evening. Like Mr. Schumacher they wanted to be nice and fresh early the following morning.

"Your wife took the key," said the night porter, smilingly. As long as she hadn't locked the door and then sunk into coma. But no, the policeman's wife was trained to husbands coming home late, their breath smelling of beer rather, and was out of bed to the softest knock.

"It's going to be a good day I think: there's that nice haze. Be sunny later."

"If it is we're going to make for the English Garden."

"And I'm stuck with that boring old Polizei Präsidium – but I'll walk with you that far. Let's say you pick me up there at five? Damned if I'll hold out longer than that. At least, we'll spend the evening together."

"Right, I want a socking big dinner, and with you. We'll just be lunching off a barrow."

Castang is listening, intermittently, to an exposition of police structures in the Federal Republic of Germany. On the blackboard are little squares, neatly drawn. Within are acronyms, formed from the initials of official bodies, sounding minatory. They lead, by way of arrows, to other little squares . . .

17

"The Bundesgrenzschutz ... The Bundeskriminalamt, or BKA for short ..."

Geoffrey Dawson sits beside him. The two men have slipped into an easy relation; are on the way to friendship.

"And we must write it all down on our slates," he is heard to murmur.

"The computers come within this orbit. INPOL encloses pretty well every aspect of a criminal affair. PIOS was created with the specialist mission of drugs and terrorists." Nobody has yet yawned.

"Now more recently, BEFA-7 was given a wider area of reference, and this has attracted criticism. It has been said, only semi-jokingly, that anyone happening to step on the same commercial flight as a suspect would find himself logged thenceforward on BEFA-7." At this moment Colonel Bonacorsi does yawn.

"Which brings us to the point under discussion," pretending not to notice. "How far can we extend data storage without threatening liberties? Put it another way: access to this information is strictly limited. Is that the best safeguard we can invent, towards the preservation of these liberties?"

"A damned hypothetic question," said somebody loudly.

"Before entering on general discussion" – the chairman, cosily – "perhaps we should round out the picture a little with the structures in France. Commissaire Heinrich."

A deadpan manner; useful for bouncing off ironic interruptions.

"For the reason just heard, the decision to computerise information was delayed. Further delay has been occasioned by interdepartmental jealousies," looking over his glasses. Sniggers rippled through the meeting at a phenomenon known elsewhere.

"An excessive fragmentation of different services . . . A proliferation of committees and study groups. They have tended to invent long complicated titles for themselves, the acronyms for which I propose to spare you."

Come, thought Castang, come, he's not all that bad.

"Numerous specialised subsections, all jealously guarding the liberties and prerogatives of their own computer. However, the decision was taken to stuff them all in together, into the extensive basements of number eleven, Rue des Saussaies, and build up a central unified command post, similar to the big block here in Wiesbaden.

"It was then discovered that no one computer was compatible with any of the others." A pause to milk the laugh. "When this minor problem is sorted out we will reach a situation comparable to that of the Federal Republic. Voices have been heard to say: ten years late as usual . . .

"It is to be hoped – I for one hope – that we will benefit by experience acquired. This is what we have come together for."

That is bold, thought Castang under cover of shuffling and coughing. In a French official that is really unusually imaginative. Since as a general rule, it is well known, we produce our own immensely complicated invention and then try to impose it upon everybody else.

As for suggesting that the F.B.I. (in the Rue des Saussaies) would cooperate for a single second with the C.I.A. (very haughty, Rue Rembrandt in the 16th arrondissement) – that is downright audacious.

"Oh God," said Dawson beside him, "here's Jock."

Chief Superintendent Elliott wasn't having any Glasgow accent this morning or jokes about the Procurator Fiscal.

"English or Scottish police structures are more decentralised than those the last speaker described – I notice however a remarkable similarity in the anti-terrorist measures taken which are decided by the Parliament at Westminster. We are in general ruled by the Prevention of Terrorism Act, a legislative measure much disputed and probably useless."

"Good ol' Jock," audibly.

"We have a computer known as the National Joint Unit: you notice that we share the French liking for prolix and meaningless titles. We have Special Branch. It isn't enormous. Maybe fifteen hundred of the wee lads across the whole country. We have also a specialised subsection: I don't know whether it's the sixth or what; the public just calls it the bomb squad. And so do I; if I view it at all I do so with the greatest reluctance.

"In close parallel to France we have the Direction of

Intelligence, which used to be called M.I.5 and deals with the interior, and the Secret Intelligence Service which used to be M.I.6 and covers the exterior. I know very little about either but ye can always try reading the books of Len Deighton.

"We have this horrible dread of a government being taken over by the military which is a constant in our history so we don't have any gendarmerie: it wouldn't be popular there in the village. Inside the army there is this high-flying outfit they call the Special Air Service, which is like the gendarmerie's intervention group. An assault unit. Probably an Indecent-Assault unit. And that's all."

"This might now be a good moment for a coffee break," suggested the chairman, "before going on to the experiments and results of other countries."

"One moment." It was the same voice as before – was it Dutch? "May I? The smallest word?"

"By all means."

"With the greatest respect, to the preceding speakers with whom I have the utmost sympathy, all this is quite irrelevant. We can fill a whole office block with computers, we can post heavily armed cops at one metre interval over an entire area felt to be threatened, the fact remains that at any moment, any point, a violent attack can take place with heavy damage and loss of life, which we find impossible either to predict with any accuracy or forestall with any certainty. We could spend millions if we had them and what guarantee would it give us?"

"That," said the chairman blandly, "could well set the key to the ensuing discussion."

Looking at the map Vera has thought that Munich is large and so is the English Garden; and walking both ways, with Lydia and the push-chair, a bit much. She plunges into the bowels of the Karlsplatz. First is the underground shopping arcade, and under that is the S–Bahn which takes one to distant suburbs where she doesn't want to go; and under that is the U–Bahn, a rapid transit system running roughly north and south, where the trams, which she would much prefer, seem not to run: they have more of a cross-town pattern.

There is a frightful smell down here; a shrill stink of choking dust combining with a total absence of ventilation. Ho, German technology is not quite impeccable. Lydia says loudly 'Es Stinkt' though luckily not in German. By comparison London is a High Wind in Jamaica, and Paris is a garden of violets. It is her first setback to joy and she will not repeat this bit of exploration.

The escalators disgorge them at a place with the charming name of Münchener Freiheit, and this is another disillusion, this one her fault. She has again been romantic. She had read too many books, and whenever she has read one about this city it has always been full of the wonderful things to be found in Schwabing, full of artists, students, jazz cellars, nice things to eat, and Happenings.

Well, maybe it used to be like this. She doesn't see much sign of it now. The boulevard is broad and lined with trees: the pavement is broad, occupied at frequent intervals by tables and parasols. On the tables are checked cloths, and the busy pleasant litter of a great many people taking their ease, and they won't all be talking money. Most of these conversations will be foolish and ignoble: some will be comic, intelligent, touching. It is all natural and unselfconscious, and Vera hates it. She takes a disgusted sniff at hamburger-perfumed air, and the first side street towards the park. She is not working it out in her mind, but it is all too like that other, even better-known Latin Quarter; the Boulevard Saint-Michel pretending to be a Boul'Mich'. Poverty and gaiety students still have; imagination and idealism; some honesty still and the longing to create. Cynical people with money have moved in, to make more money: surely they were always there, with the gangsters and the police spies? Perhaps they did not work quite so hard at the exploitation: it was a little less calculated? Words like spontaneity or innocence arrive upon the threshold of Vera's mind, do not fit, are rejected. It is a metaphysical question of the sort she likes, but she is not working at it. She is enjoying herself too much.

Castang, had he been with her instead of in the rather stuffy room at police headquarters, would probably have said 'Metaphysical, my foot: it's the smell of hamburger. Loss of identity; are we in Detroit or Seattle? Or it's those damned check cloths: put one of those down behind something green and dusty in a wooden box and it must be Hampstead. The place where it's real starts to look like a copy of the place where it's phony.'

She seeks solace in the park. Not called the English Garden for nothing: if Schwabing is really Kensington this is equally unmistakable.

She is happy in simple ways. To walk the push-chair or stroller without knowing where she is going. To have nothing to care for. People who accept no responsibilities have no holidays, for theirs are made up of the same dreary enslavement to pleasures that have become insipid.

She is one of those women that change like the sky: she can be both tall and small, both frail and sturdy, chunky or lanky. A long shapeless skirt and a man's shirt, Italian sandals with lowish platform soles, a woolly knotted on the bar of the stroller. Colourless hair of the sort that can be fair, brown, or plain mud, is always thin and fine, and invariably tumbles down no matter how you pin it up. The eyes can be small, with odd angles at the corners, and suddenly simply huge. A pale face which flushes patchily under sun. She has been out of doors quite a lot during the summer and had tanned. This has faded but under the autumn sun she is showing blood under a skin that is tanning again. She looks healthy, because she is happy.

After a while it gets too hot in the park and a litle boring: there are not quite enough people. Lydia has had to be sat behind a bush to pee, and she would rather like a pee herself, and a cup of coffee. She tacks towards the buildings: it is cooler under the trees and there is a pleasant little waterway. Lydia, detecting with a child's deadly accurate instinct that Ma would like a drink, starts to complain of thirst; will soon begin going on that she doesn't want to walk and doesn't want to sit in the stroller; wants to be carried. Vera starts to look for a nice terrace. There should be something, though these streets are all very bourgeois. A nice enough place to live, but horribly expensive. They have worked down quite a long way along the dreary Königinstrasse before finding one.

Must be down as far as the university level, for besides notices about the riding school (she has seen horses in the park and there is the pleasant manège smell of straw and horseshit) there is a thing about the school of veterinary medicine, and there are a few students neglecting their studies over a beer in the sunshine. She goes and has a blissful pee and a bit of a wash, comes back and sits without a care in the world. Coffee please and a glass of water and a fruit juice for the tiny-one. She thinks she would like a cigarette and hunts in her handbag.

Running feet. The handbag is Italian, capacious, full of all the necessary objects Castang describes as her rubbish. There ought to be two or three bent ones in here somewhere. Concentrated upon this task, sleepy from sunshine and well-being, she does not look up when the feet come close, stop suddenly. She can hear the sobbing breath of someone who has run too far, too fast, but if she thinks of it at all she thinks 'Some student'. The rickety metal table lurches slightly.

"Lydia, stop that." The answer is unexpected.

"Can I sit with you, please? Please!" Words wrung out by something stronger than breathlessness. Vera looks up almost with alarm at the figure standing right over her. The handbag slides and she catches it by instinct. There is a sharp smell of fresh sweat. The woman is holding herself up by the wrists on the table.

Vera looks quickly at Lydia, who sits with large round eyes and there is fright in them because there was fear in the voice. She has to make up her mind quickly.

"Sit down," she says, rather more sharply than she had intended. The woman throws herself upon the free chair, buries her face between her elbows. Lydia huddles a little closer to Ma. Vera tries to collect her wits. She is no longer used to large cities where odd things happen.

"Thank you, oh thank you." The woman looks up and round wildly, tossing her long hair, catches sight of the woolly. "May I, for just a minute?" She catches it and throws it across her shoulders. Sticking out of the shopping bag is a chiffon scarf; one never knows in autumn, when there might not be draughty corners.

"Please? Anything to alter my appearance." Vera hands it across without a word. Lydia is quite prepared to believe that this stranger will also take her little jacket. The woman shakes the scarf out and has it across her hair in a quick female gesture,

23

tying it under her jaw. Vera by now is looking with alert, police eyes. Older than herself, mid-thirties. Navy blue trousers, an expensive black pullover of thin wool. Brown skin very tanned, but she cannot see the features in the down-held face.

"Hadn't you better explain?" she says quietly in her sharp, Czech-accented German.

"Please – please, help me," in a hissing whisper. She puts her elbows on the table, snatches Vera's waterglass, pretends to be drinking from it.

Along the Königinstrasse, across from where Vera is sitting, a white Mercedes station wagon is driving slowly. Blue curtains are drawn across the back windows. In the front seats are two men who look busily from side to side as they cruise slowly by. Their eyes upon the café terrace. Vera picks up the flattened cigarette pack and holds it out in the familiar gesture: Lydia who likes to see the flame pop up scrambles to fumble with the lighter and Vera helps her, laughing, to get her thumb on the catch. The tiny scene is reassuringly domestic, and the car has driven on.

"Whoever they are, they've lost you."

"For how long? They'll think I got into the park and will search there." But she is reasoning now, able to argue with herself. "No they won't. It isn't that important to them; why give themselves a lot of work? They think they'll pick me up with no trouble. And no doubt they're right," dully. She drew fiercely at the cigarette. Vera had to light her own again because the child let the flame go out too quickly.

"And who are they? Is it the CIA, or only the Russians?"

". . .My child, what am I to do about my child? And I came out with nothing. I haven't a farthing. I daren't go home."

This was a thickening plot.

"Perhaps you could tell me about it. If you want to."

"I can't stay here. When they realise they've missed me they'll come back."

"Look, you're hot and sticky; go and have a wash. I'll call a taxi." There really had been two men in a car looking for somebody; it wasn't just febrile imagination. Perhaps her own imagination was beginning to overheat, thought Vera, paying the girl, asking her to phone the rank; the crowded town centre is more cosy? We're nearer the man, in case of need?

She was having an adventure! It would make him laugh.

"What about you, Bobby, don't you have computers?"

"Mafia's the biggest computer there is, mate. Learn everything that way."

"Colonel Bonacorsi – might we have your impressions?" He coughed a few times, fiddled with the mike of the tape-recorder.

"Sorry about that . . . Gentlemen – and why are there no ladies? I say, this mike's awfully old-fashioned. I mean the Americans have them now in cigarette filters, the heads of pins. Worrying themselves sick about industrial espionage, and no Congressman now dares accept a bribe for fear he's getting set up by the spies from the Treasury. Sorry, must keep to the point.

"Fact is, I'm not very interested in all this talk about technology. I'm frightened myself to take any bribes . . . No I'm not trying to be funny or paradoxical or what is it called. I think we should concentrate much more upon human problems – that is more our job, it seems to me. Leave the technology to take care of itself. The computer terminal in my office interests me, and worries me, but I'll be honest; the bacteria in the garbage chute at my apartment worry me a good deal more . . .

"However," scrabbling in his pocket for a torn press clipping, "here are my thoughts upon computers, just imagination.

"I disregard the stuff you're all familiar with, like road and weather reports; book your own theatre tickets. And the obvious idiocies, such as telediagnostic, of which the example given is knowing how to fix a breakdown in what this loony calls the domestronic sector . . .

"But in amongst all this crap there are a few that give me the cold creeps up my spine. The televote; described here as 'electronic democracy'. A thing called Big or Bim, acronym for what is prudishly translated as an Individual Genetic Badge. I'd like you to think about that one because as we've been told several times recently, fingerprints are the steam age.

"And lastly, one that is pleasing a few people no end. Example,

25

banks or insurance companies who own luxurious residential blocks. Example, factory owners, the kind that insisted workers asked permission before going to the lavatory. You will think of other good examples, like urban police commissariats. It is entitled telecontrol and the explanation given of this scrap of jargon is 'the localisation of individuals'. And you aren't going to tell me the fellow's been reading George Orwell. The justification given is of course Security. And you and me and all of us are no longer the peelers; we're security-enforcement-agencies. So is this the way we want it?

"Upon that, I rather think, it would be nice to break for lunch."

Castang and Geoffrey Dawson found a Brauhaus. Scrubbed wooden tables and a placid atmosphere; menu full of Munich folklore, all the weird names for concoctions woven of permutating and combining the pig. All good but needs courage sometimes, said Castang. And detective skills, added Dawson. There was a motherly waitress.

"Two beers, dear."

"All right for a beer, but if you're thinking of eating that table's reserved."

"We'll move."

"They're all reserved; got a bus load coming in about ten minutes."

"Oh bugger; we'll have to piss off then." She was back already.

"Here you are," slapping the beers down and licking her pencil. "Don't jump out of your knickers, love. Fit y'in somewhere. See the little table in the corner? – old boy getting his hat? Tuck y'selves in there. Soup's never eaten as hot as it's cooked," bustling off with a double handful of mustard pots.

"Fish, I think, I love fish. Can't get it at home; always stale and madly dear."

"What, in France?"

"French peasant hates fish. Germans eat it – lovely halibut."

"Ochsenbrust I think. God, this beer's good. Needed that."

"All right love, let's be having you," licking her pencil. There

26

was a shocking pandemonium from the bus load installing itself and shouting.

"Four beers."

"Six beers."

" . . . and two more beers," finished Castang. "Can't get proper bread in France either." He was watching the party, with a professional interest in the waitress's crowd-control technique.

Plainly this included getting the corner table fixed before giving undivided attention to the mob. Suddenly there was soup in front of him.

"Not forgotten the beers?" Gone again. The trouble with a corner is being isolated.

Beers arrived with the main course. Wop. Wop. Wop, wop.

"Hab' kein Schuld an Ihr' Tod – I've no part in your death, man," slightly exasperated.

No doubt she had a quiverful of these readymade expressions, to be launched upon such occasions: the *'coup de feu'* was her excuse for being short. But the arrow stuck in Castang; barbed, remained there. In years to come he would remember the scene in every minute detail.

The bus load engulfed its grub and became torpid.

"Was it good?" reappearing behind him and whisking away plates.

"It was super," sincere. "But you were wicked to me."

"Wicked? Me!"

"You had no part in my death, you said. Like I was some horrible alcoholic. I'd only had one beer," self-pitying.

Aghast, she put her arm round him, gave him a hug.

"Oh, love. It's a phrase. Wasn't meant wickedly. I was short like, account of them over there shouting."

"I know that," hugging her back.

"Forgive?" troubled. "Truly?" Geoffrey Dawson delighted at this maternal scene. "Okay then. Coffee?"

"Right." Mustn't drink any more or they'd be going foggy in the middle of somebody's closely argued interpellation: it wouldn't do.

Vera was stuck with her biddy. She was on holiday; she could truly have done without all this. But she had accepted responsibility and could not shuffle the woman off. Adhesive anyhow, clinging: the woman was both interesting and a bore; strange how few things are the one without also being the other.

To induce calm and coherence something to eat was indicated: Lydia was hungry anyhow, and herself ready to press down; they had walked a lot.

They found a Brauhaus too, in the Residenzstrasse; not as nice as Castang's, having that selfconsciously rustic look that is designed for the bourgeoisie who, dressed of course in dirndls, occupied the place. The pea soup, thought Vera, was not as good as that she made herself, but was nice because she hadn't had to make it. There was good red plonk from the Sud Tirol, the alcove was quiet. She took her shoes off under the table. Lydia, engaged happily with chips, gave no trouble. The story, bits of which had been uttered in the street in jerky disjointed phrases, was beginning to make sense.

The woman was Norwegian, or from that direction. Vera was not sure but did not want to interrupt. The only importance of the fact was that she had no family here in Germany. There was a husband. They weren't divorced, just separated in vaguely amicable fashion, which worked out well enough because he was an engineer, the sort that is always pottering around obscure corners of the world with generally unpleasant climates. He would reappear now and again. Absorbed in his own interests, finding it pleasant that the flat was aired and smelt nice, instead of closed and dusty, he welcomed her presence when he made a landfall.

And after all she did quite well out of it. He paid the rent, and God knows rents are high. Left at liberty for at least nine months of the year she could get on with her own affairs. She wrote a bit of fiction, did a bit of journalism. It wasn't much of a living viewed in financial terms, so that she was grateful for there being no need to worry about self-support. But the big argument against divorcing was the child, a boy of eight. One had to make a home for him and keep the atmosphere as harmonious as possible.

A dull and sloppy performance, thought Vera, with both sides letting themselves slide into acceptance of it – but who was she to criticise? One did such things, out of fear and lassitude, clinging to one's little comforts. Could she be sure she would do all that much better?

And it was a nice face, well drawn, narrow at the top and broad across the cheekbones; a bit of that Finnish Magyar look perhaps, not especially pretty but with large good features. A fine neck; Vera collected necks and her fingers fidgeted slightly for a pencil. She kept them still: the important thing was to listen. There was some wine left in the jug. Lydia played happily enough with the things to be found on brauhaus tables, ashtrays and beermats and toothpicks. Birgit; a conventional name, like her own, reassuringly dull. What had precipitated the crisis? She was still vague as to what the crisis was.

Mum. Mum and Dad. Elderly couple, on the verge of retirement. (Like Adrien and Judith Richard, thought Vera hazily: hadn't drunk too much wine, had she?)

Rich; with a decidedly gaudy flat over in the respectable suburb of Bogenhausen. Dad is a Rechtsanwalt, a lawyer: there are too many. Years of exposure to police business had taught Vera that if there is a chance of doing justice somewhere the lawyers are there to prevent it.

Listening to Birgit, Vera saw this one as no worse than most. They sounded the sort of people who are kindly, balanced and tolerant; for as long as they continue to get their own way. Catholic in the traditional South-German manner; finding the bishop over-liberal. Finding the administration soft on Turks and pacifists; the populace as a whole soft on honesty and soft on fornication.

And sorry, said Birgit, I suppose I don't judge people as harshly as I might. I don't cause scandals, I don't pursue flagrant adulteries, but hell, there's a man in my life from time to time. Their son Mathias – I can't call him my ex, can I? – knows better than to fall upon local girls out there in Bolivia. But sure as hell falls upon a lot of wives of the earnest American colleagues.

Neither of us has hard feelings about the other, Birgit could say. It's a modus vivendi, no? But Mum is that infernally self-righteous sort, and can see no speck upon the shining figure of Sonny-Dear. Makes up for that, by being mighty censorious if the furniture in the flat isn't kept well dusted. I had to be a daughter-in-law she could feel proud of, and I never have come up to scratch: if it isn't my clothes, my morals or my appearance, it's the way I bring up my child.

Dutifully, Birgit had brought Francis over to Bogenhausen every second Sunday afternoon; pains taken with manners and appearance. But on the pretext of taking an interest 'with the child's father so much away from home' Mum had taken increasingly to pottering in and out. And while realising it to be a caricature, Vera thought these bourgeois biddies must be hell. Bridge and the hairdresser doesn't occupy them. Sit (in the Café Luitpold, on the MaxPlatz, no doubt) and wind one another up to interference. If there isn't a dentist, an antique dealer or a decorator to play with, there's always a daughter.

She'd come into the flat and pretended there was a smell of pot. Birgit didn't smoke pot, or if she did it was seldom, and then not in the flat, and then only good-class stuff, and how did Mum pretend to know, anyhow?

And by now Vera inclines to a distinct belief that Birgit is tedious. What should one do to unstick adhesive females? Am I tiresomely moralistic, she wonders, to believe in cause and effect? As one makes the bed, so one has to lie upon it. Lydia is getting cranky too.

She has taken on a responsibility, even in allowing it to be thrust upon her; and then there is no stopping her. Castang lectures her on rigidity and she speaks in derogatory terms of compromise. Puritanism ... Moral cowardice ... Eyes glare. Somebody will throw an ashtray shortly.

The police have spent the entire day compromising upon moral issues, but then they never do anything else: it is this mixture of arguments in German and in English that has fatigued Castang as much as anything.

"Hallo, you've come to meet us, how nice. Geoffrey, posso presentare my wife – this is Mr. Dawson from darkest Dorset, a great stay in our afflictions. What gives with you then, duck?"

"Oo, I've had a day. And I'm not your duck."

"Right, well, what we all need is a drink . . ."

" . . . So Ma 'n' Pa managed to turn some mild eccentricity into being unfit to be in charge of a minor, and by bribing, presumably, some commissaire of police get her committed to the psychiatric thingy."

"Right, immorality not being an infraction of the criminal code that's always the handiest let-out. Is this the way to get rid of inconvenient relatives in England, Geoffrey?"

"It's been known. Need a couple of tame pill-pushers. That's no problem down our way."

"So two characters in white coats turned up, but she was robust enough to kick one in the balls and the other I don't know" – Vera always literal – " and fled, into my arms as it happened. No bag, no keys, no money, nothing. Can't get back into the flat and is frightened to try anyhow: now sought, presumably, by the police."

"So the police are now asked to cope with this phenomenon," said Castang sitting comfortable with Lydia on Pa's knee and allowed a sip from his glass. "What d'you say, Geoffrey?"

"That I much admire Vera for being gallant."

"Stop making love to my wife. Where is she now then?"

"I took Lydia back for a rest, so suggested a wash and a bit of a tidy, and lent her a clean shirt. Left her having a kip on my bed, and blowed if I'm going to leave her there all night."

"No, quite: we've got to get rid of her before dinner, and what will the Police President of Munich say if he hears that I'm meddling in his administration? So we better go sort her out. Will these domestic entanglements interest you, Geoffrey? – hardly."

"I feel quite interested and I'll come along if I may. Illegality wouldn't worry me as much as a turn up with the more rigid attitudes of German bureaucracy."

Castang didn't like the sound of it much. The Rechtsanwalt would have been careful to observe legal forms, and one has no wish to try bucking the bourgeoisie on their own ground. The white coats, meeting with rebellion, would simply signal a dotty-missis to the police. Remained Schumacher, a great pourer of oil upon troubled waters but his eyes might go glassy on hearing this tale. The police president – he's rather too grand. There's an adjunct, Geoffrey's last remark was pertinent. The fatherly talking-to seemed indicated.

Vera went and got Birgit while we played with the child, who took one of those tremendous little-girl's fancies to Geoffrey.

The French Police Judiciaire gave some good advice. A couple of people arguing that one is sane, as against a couple more arguing equally woodenly that one is in Need of Care, will get nobody much further. We cannot in any case interfere with due-process-of-law, which only a judge can correct or reverse: what's the word? – set aside.

So you do the sensible thing, which is to submit. Agreed, a disagreeable moment. Looked at dispassionately, not that dreadful. The point is, in so doing you put yourself in a strong position. First thing will be a professional shrink interviewing you and seeking points to lead him to a diagnosis. You tell him you're as sane as he is and probably a great deal more so. Sane being the french 'sain' meaning healthy: we're all very unhealthy but how well do we balance that? Your calm and reasonable submission is a powerful argument for balance. All psychiatric clinics are overcrowded and he'll be relieved to order your release. You're a charge of about a thousand marks a day upon public funds, a fact worth pointing out.

Birgit showed herself as obstinate as Vera would, in such circumstances. That all sounded very well.

"It sounds all right," said Birgit. "As long as it's somebody else we're talking about." You've a point there, thought Castang, not saying so.

"Look, we're adults, no need to dramatise. The fellow's not coming there with a needle, all sly crooked smiles and sadistic delight."

"No," she admitted. "But it's easier to get in than out."

"They won't do anything at all. You get the chance to talk quietly, to explain yourself. Listening is what they're trained for."

"Maybe, but I know doctors. They're in no hurry to contradict a colleague. Even if they think a previous diagnosis ignorant, they cover up. Once you're there – you're helpless." Her voice beginning to rise again to the jagged, shrill level.

"I'm on your side," said Castang patiently. "So is the shrink, basically. He has no reason to be otherwise. Make it easier for both of us, will you?" She focussed her eyes upon him. Good-looking eyes. Maybe a bit too close together. But steady; no hysterical glare. A good, open look. But don't read anything into that.

"All right," she said. "Assume he agrees. I'm adjusted and everything: great. But the opposition gets maintained outside. Backed up by legal talent and there's plenty. Believe me, I know that old swine. At school with half the judges in the city, and lawclass-mate with the rest. And if he decided to show malice, it'll be tenacious."

"No," advised Castang. "Pleading malice is a bad argument. Can be made to sound paranoid. 'Look, she has this persecution complex.'"

He could understand. She felt helpless. She didn't have the sort of friends that she felt would stand by her, against official frowns.

"I'm giving you nothing but grief," said Birgit dolorously. "I'm grateful as hell, I appreciate it very much, the trouble you're taking. Vera's been lovely to me. You're patient. I'm all right now, really, now I've had the time to quieten down. I can handle it. Only – going back to the flat though," pathetically.

Of course he could see it. To her it looked like putting her head in the lion's mouth. But he was getting bored. He sighed, a little.

"I've given an opinion, no more. Don't have much to add to that. You're perfectly free after all. Disregard it. It's only advice. Geoffrey – what can you think of, to add?"

"Not much. Summed it up pretty fairly, seems to me. What I might say, is ask what choices you've got. The alternative seems to be to flee, and where d'you flee to? And what good does it do? And if you'll listen to a cop point of view, what chance have you, if they start looking for you? A room in a hotel? Catch a train? Get money from the bank? They know where you're vulnerable, you understand, and that's where they pick you up. When you're sitting on a pin I don't want to be the one to hammer it further in. We'll go home with you if you like: moral support."

Vera, who'd been saying things like this all afternoon, kept mum. One didn't hire a dog, and then keep on barking. Two dogs in fact. She liked Mr. Dawson. A sense of the comic is the most valuable contribution the English have to offer anywhere.

"Well, I suppose that if it has to be, it has to be," said Birgit bleakly. "If you come with me I promise I won't yell and fight." She had to go back, for clothes and toothbrushes and stuff. The police know all about the little bag that has to be packed.

"But how are we to get in?"

"You'd be surprised what gangsters like us can do when we try."

A conventional house of the former-villa type; the space to one side with a couple of flowering bushes apologising that garages have been thought more needful than a scrap of garden.

"Push the button," said Castang smiling at the big fearful eyes. "There might be someone there."

"That's what I'm afraid of."

"Whoever it is, it won't be dragons." The door buzzed and clicked, and she stared at it nervously, a Papuan suspecting witchcraft. "Confront them, shall we?" Now that he'd come this far . . . "Which floor?" ringing the lift down.

"Top." The door rumbled open and they stepped on to the landing.

The flat door stood open, and in the opening stood a woman.

He didn't know what he had expected: a cop, whose profession is to be unsurprised, never expects anything, but Ma-in-law is expected both to be a dragon and to look like one. She paid no attention to him, as though he did not exist, but smiled pleasantly at Birgit, who stood not knowing how to get into her own flat. It was a mistake for him to have come. She would have done better on her own.

"There you are, dear child. I knew you'd be intelligent once you'd thought things over." The voice was clear, calm, pleasantly posed in the middle of the register. Musical? – Castang wasn't musical. A woman in her middle fifties, who has neglected none of the arts available to money that can preserve natural good looks.

Birgit had pulled herself together and walked in, the older

woman standing gracefully aside. She looked at him then, as though seeing him for the first time.

"I don't think I know you, do I? You must be one of Birgit's friends."

"More a casual acquaintance." She lifted the corner of an eyebrow at his funny German.

"A foreign gentleman?" smiling. "But you must allow me to thank you. I feel sure that you gave Birgit both help and good advice. Have a drink. No no, I won't keep you from your own affairs. Just for a moment. I've been packing for our little boy, you must forgive the untidiness. You look like a man who drinks scotch. Icc?"

One of the drawbacks to being a cop is the journalistic wish always to know a little more. But Geoffrey Dawson would be looking after Vera. He took the glass, admiring the professionalism of voice and gesture, the control over the neat and elegant body.

"I am Frau Rennemann – if you hadn't gathered," pouring one for herself. Birgit had gone on to what presumably was her bedroom.

"Castang," bowing formally.

"Castang. A French name," smiling and raising her glass to eye level. Shrewd long greenish eyes. Nothing of the femme fatale, everything of the well brought-up and always well behaved young women, with neat blonde hair and regular conventional features, in so many Alfred Hitchcock films, who have hairbreadth escapes from calamity without an eyelash getting displaced. From Madeleine Carroll to Grace Kelly; one never could tell them apart. Strangely lifeless. The clothes were in excellent taste, the jewellery subdued; the perfume barely reached him. "You look like such a sensible counsellor. I'm sure Birgit hasn't been drinking. It wouldn't create a good effect."

"I haven't played any rôle at all, Frau Rennemann. If she kept her head, which I'm sure is a good one, she should have no difficulty at all convincing everyone of her sound health."

"You are a medical man, Herr Castang? No? I'll hazard the guess that you're not a jurist. But there's something professional about you."

"Just the chap from the escort bureau."

35

"More interesting than that, I think."

"He's a police officer," said Birgit rather too loudly. She had come back into the room and stood with her hair tossed back and her strong jaw thrust forward. "And at his insistence, I should say, insistence I am behaving as though this comedy were serious, for a second."

"Really?" looking for a cigarette in a leather box pretending to be a book. "I'm afraid my vulgar curiosity is getting the better of me. Just a tourist, in Munich?" coming towards him for a flame.

Why hadn't Birgit kept her mouth shut?

"I'm sure you'll forgive me now." He looked at Birgit, he hoped a bit acidly. "I've no intention of interfering in anyone's affairs. Common courtesy ... Delighted to have met you, Frau Rennemann."

"Oh dear, what a hurry you're in. Has this silly girl embarrassed you?"

"Perhaps the circumstances embarrass me a little," still nettled at the indiscretion. "And I'm afraid I've a taxi waiting which will be madly dear." The silky performance had ended by irritating him. "My German is inadequate. But she's as sane as either of us, any of us; I always get these pronouns muddled. You or me."

"I fear that here, Herr Castang, your opinion, however valuable, might not carry quite the weight it no doubt does at home. Let me thank you again, and say perhaps au revoir."

In the lift, Castang could not feel quite sure he'd heard the last of this now decidedly unwelcome interlude. The foreign-gentlemen were here in Munich to talk about how poorly police forces reacted nowadays to matters they had not yet properly understood. Yes. But not, decidedly, to do any more than talk. And in the intervals to enjoy themselves. With plenty to eat and drink. The taxi, which had clocked up a fortune, hardened him further in the resolve to forget this and other annoying episodes, and dropped him at the restaurant, amiable and easygoing (as distinct from phony French ones) he had picked on and where he'd left the others on the way up. Vera and Geoffrey Dawson were giggling a good deal over drinks; he felt vexed, and resolved to catch up quick.

* * *

The medicine worked to such good effect that Castang forgot the whole thing. It returned like a thunderclap towards lunchtime next day. Not that Mr. Schumacher's blend of the genial and the pompous held anything more ominous than a slightly heightened colour and a faintly fussed expression.

"My dear Castang, a word with you, if I may ... apart perhaps, I beg you to forgive me an instant, Colonel ..." Bonacorsi and Castang were chatting but it could only be called desultory: Bobby loafed off in search of someone to tell a joke to. "You must really forgive me, Castang but something has come up." Mum – Granny – no, these appelations did not suit that elegant and coolheaded lady: but she'd been up to something, he knew at once. "It doesn't concern me at all, and indeed I know nothing about it. For a virtual certainty, some stupid misunderstanding of no importance. What I feel, and I hope you'll agree ..." This boiled down after awhile to a suggestion (more really than a suggestion) of a chat with Herr Pohl. Herr Pohl had something he wished to discuss in confidence. He said okay, feeling slightly less relaxed than he had.

Herr Pohl isn't the Polizeipresident, but he's something close, with one of those peculiar German ranks, a Kriminalrat or suchlike, that has a Königlich and even Keizerlich sound to it. Geoffrey, who was amused by him, said that he looked like Evelyn Waugh: pressed to explain said Englishly 'Florid ... not quite so strong on the cigars and claret ... behind the glaring irascible eye is concealed perhaps an altogether different and perhaps surprising personage.' Perhaps he was about to find out. He decided that perhaps he had been slightly indiscreet. Nothing reprehensible. And it might be a good moment to suggest that Mother Rennemann's stories should not automatically be taken at face value.

The thunderclap made itself felt fairly fast. Herr Pohl sat in his private office (large, commodious, expensively furnished) behind a nice desk (high-class reproduction antique) in a well cut suit of aggressive check pattern: they are a bit given to this in Germany. The face was florid, the hair thin, the eyes glaring behind the steel-framed glasses, but the voice was slow, quiet.

"Please do sit down," he said politely, but there were no further preliminaries.

"Mr. Castang, a complaint has been made and passed along for me to look into; naming yourself. Leastways," a slight smile, "it does not seem probable that another French citizen with your name should be hereabouts passing himself off as a police officer. Well," making a note on the paper in front of him, "you are of course a police officer, so that this phrase 'passing self off' with its pejorative suggestion of a masquerade, is pointless as well as tendentious.

"This is clearly an embarrassment, isn't it? It would help me in the handling of it, as well as in limiting any side-effects, if you told me with perfect frankness whether there's anything in it, since so far," turning back a page and reading, "it's fair to say that the claims made seem unsupported by independent testimony."

Whatever might be said about Mr. Pohl, he was scrupulous about the exactitude of words; their content, their meaning.

"I know about it, naturally. I'm only surprised she should make a complaint; my attitude didn't merit anything of the sort. That's an unsupported statement likewise: it will be for you to form an opinion about that. Before going further, perhaps I should know the nature of the complaint; I'd be better equipped to answer."

"She?" enquired Pohl, seeming puzzled.

"Frau Rennemann; I may not have her name exactly right. I'm taking it that there isn't a complaint I got drunk in some pub and broke the furniture."

"Good, I've understood. The complaint was formally lodged and signed by Doctor Rennemann: you might not be fully aware that he's an eminent jurist, a man highly placed in our society; his word carries authority. Not a man to quarrel with, Castang – speaking for a moment as man to man off the record. You seem to me to have been ill-advised. You can speak quite frankly to me, you know. We're alone here, this is informal; nothing taped or whatever. Had you had a few drinks? I think that very probably the matter could be arranged with no further ado, and the complaint withdrawn, if you would consent, lets say, to some form of apology. I'm sure I could work out a form of phrasing you'd agree to."

"Forgive me, are you perhaps misreading, or is she misrepresenting the matter? Am I supposed to have insulted her? We had three or four minutes casual conversation pitched in friendly tone and she offered me a drink."

The slight smile this time seemed to be suppressed.

"Shall I perhaps give you a brief outline of the whole incident? It is exceedingly trivial, save that for the person concerned – I'm not speaking of myself – it isn't trivial at all."

"By all means, by all means; I've time; I've time . . .

"Tja, Castang, I scarcely know whether to tax you with indiscretion or naiveté. I never knew your wife was here, and nor did Schumacher. However, you're the guest of the government, as such entitled to consideration, which can be said to cover Frau Castang likewise.

"No doubt of it, it is disconcerting – disagreeable – to be accosted in the streets of a foreign town. We can cover that. There's in any case no formal complaint there, merely a suggestion," reading "'that attempts were made to hinder or evade agents charged with the execution of a judicial procedure.' In your own case it's stickier. 'Attempts made to interfere with a judicial order made in due form, and to abuse a pretended official position in so doing.' Strike out pretended; in fact strike out that entire clause, since from what you tell me you did not name yourself as a police officer; I give you credit anyhow for knowing better. It's plain that the young woman attempted innocently to reinforce her position by claiming some official status for you."

"You can I think strike out the whole thing – malevolence can there clearly be shown. Any lawyer could, within ten seconds, but I don't want any fuss, any more than you do."

"I agree. On the basis of what you tell me, and the young woman's tale repeated in the hearing of Mr. Dawson, who'd be held to be an unprejudiced witness, I'd throw this out," tapping the three pinned-together typed sheets of a complaint.

"It's delicate, because the gentleman in question, I must tell you frankly, is in a position to make things stick if he chooses to press them. I could add that if he were to go down to the local commissariat and prefer a charge that X had stolen his gardener's bicycle, he's in a position to make that stick too."

"I've no wish to get involved in anything political," said

Castang, "I'll point out that my wife could not possibly have known that, when appealed to by an obviously frightened and harassed young woman in the street."

"As I've already remarked, I appreciate that," said Pohl a little snappishly. He took the sheets and laid them aside. After a moment's hesitation he took another pair of clipped sheets – of a different colour – from the side of his desk; laid them in the exact centre before him. Took his glasses off and laid them on top. Began to rub his face and eyes.

"Unfortunately," Pohl continued, the words muffled by his hand but came out quite clearly, "there's a sting in the tail, of this."

There'd been a little rain, and a few faint mutters of thunder in the distance. One has come out from underneath one's tree, which one was in any case not very happy with, trees being not recommended during any electric disturbance, while offering some shelter against mere rain. The storm, one may safely say, has passed. A few drops of rain upon the face and no more, so that we stride out confidently into open countryside.

Of a sudden a bolt of lightning strikes no more than a field ahead. Simultaneous comes a colossal clap of thunder right overhead, and the rain comes down in torrents. Opinions are divided upon what one does next.

"You are not aware, indeed you could not be, that a communication – verbal, I repeat only verbal – was made to the officer who registered this" – a slap at the papers now lying aside. Pohl sighed: this was heavy going. The tone alerted Castang; he focused all his attention.

"The suggestion has been made that among this young woman's associates are people who might, it's only a might, be thought of as not politically reliable.

"I think – again off any record, again man to man – that this may be what lies behind the decision, on the face of it shaky, to order a temporary internment and a psychiatric examination for this young woman. As you noticed, making a snap diagnosis based on your observation and experience, she's probably as sane as you or me. And should have no great difficulty in demonstrating as much to any doctor trained in psychiatry who makes a thorough examination. That much would be clear, wouldn't it, to Doctor Rennemann as much as to anybody else?

"So, might it occur to us to wonder why this gentleman chooses to adopt such a procedure? Does it strike us that it would serve a double purpose? Perhaps to isolate, as it were disinfect this young woman for a brief space of time? Giving an opportunity to take a quiet look at her friends and associates? While dissociating the person concerned from oneself and ones family. We could use the word discrediting and we wouldn't be far out, for if you suggest that X is not quite right in the head, however unfounded that proves to be, you do discredit him; as the Russians are forever doing and we get examples every day.

"We can say, I think, that something of this sort passed through the officer's head when Doctor Rennemann presented himself at the commissariat last night. There's a bit of smoke, he thought, discommoding a fellow, and where there's smoke there might be fire, concerning this notion of people politically unreliable. So he makes a note. No names have been named, with the sole exception of your own.

"In a case like that the instruction is clear enough and the procedure simple: put through a trace to Wiesbaden asking whether this rings any bells. Just a positive or a negative, that's all. And lo and behold, your name comes up positive.

"Two points here. First there's been a lot of discussion about the merits and demerits of computerised data, and you've been intimately concerned with much of this, right here. We all admit that people, it happens every day, can ring up a positive on the data bank without this indicating the faintest guilt, even by association. The other point is that rain or shine I have to do my job, and if any little red lamps light up I can't just shuffle them under the carpet on the pretext that so-and-so is the guest of the government. Even in cases where he might be personally known to myself.

"You agree?" he asked Castang.

"Of course I agree."

"It was therefore incumbent upon myself" – poor old Pohl, he had to have justification every step of the way: damn it, the guest of the government is also a senior official of the friendly neighbour nation, and a PJ cop into the bargain – "this morning, to attempt such verification as could be made on such short notice. And my terminal spews this out. These print-outs are confidential by definition. So far, my eyes only. Nor have I mentioned this to Kommissar Schumacher.

"It is possible, indeed probable, that here is the sort of fragmentary thing that gets on to a computer and sleeps there, perhaps for years, to be neither proved nor disproved until it comes up in another context, and then, of course, an effort has to be made. Again, you agree?"

"I agree."

"We talk a lot – I've been following it while not a delegate personally to this symposium. About justice. Well, here's a case in point. Got to be open, and no secrecy. So here's something, and I put it to you, and I give you the opportunity to explain yourself, and if you so choose you do, and if after listening to you I decide it's to go no further I've the authority to do so. I can't wipe it off the computer, but I can mark it dead and that's it. So it's up to you."

"What is it?" asked Castang, who knew already. But he had to gain a little time. Pohl was an honest, conscientious man who would like to cover for his colleague and not just to save himself a lot of trouble. If the German government were vexed at having its attention drawn to something it preferred forgotten, it might vent this irritation upon the Herr Kriminalrat, asking crossly why he hadn't kept his stupid mouth shut.

Castang, if asked whether he were a chess-player, would have answered that he knew the moves. There was a bold kind of move called a sacrifice, in which one placed, temptingly, a major piece *en prise* for the sake of positional advantage.

At the time, now two years back, the German government had shown no zeal for knowledge: still less, apparently, for action. That it possessed knowledge was now manifest. Herr Pohl had paused to clean his glasses on a paper handkerchief, to blow his nose on the same, and dispose of it in the wastebasket.

"The Frau Baroness de Rubempré, a French citizen, disappeared under suspect circumstances from German soil. Subsequent enquiries into her movements in the hours preceding

42

established the continuing presence of an individual – purporting to be a police officer charged with a matter of national security ... We seem to possess a good description of this individual, amounting to an identification.''

One can always *bétonner*; whose literal meaning is 'to pour concrete'. In chess or football, a system of closed-up defence behind an army of pawns. A tactic at odds, even when sound, with his temperament.

"My memory of the occasion is vivid.''

"Well . . . I must give you marks for frankness.''

"The print-out you have there; a bit sketchy? Holes here and there?''

"It seems adequate for the purpose.''

"I mean only – I've no right to pry – perhaps some coded instruction or notation?''

"The usual. That the file is classified; access restricted. If need be, Herr Castang, we call for it.''

"Might have been something, papers been sent to Bonn, or to that effect.''

"Don't fence with me, please. Without offence, don't put up bluffs. You were going to be frank. It would be preferable.''

"I said I had a vivid recollection, not that I had total recall. Couldn't. Too much I never knew, and still don't.''

"I must emphasize that I cannot recoil from responsibility before a vague hint of diplomatic privilege.''

"I was under orders, you know.''

"Is that a disculpatory argument?''

"Oh God, it's that familiar dilemma again. No, I don't claim that being under orders is the justification for being immoral. I'll try and help you. Yes, I did something pretty bad, yes it was illegal, yes I'm ashamed of it, no, I wouldn't want it brought out into the light. And quite frankly, it's a sleeping dog others besides myself wouldn't want stirred up. I've no pressure to apply, though.'' Pohl looked at him steadily, in thought.

"What exactly did you do?'' bluntly. The sudden departure from guarded, cautious, official circumlocution startled Castang.

"There had been a kidnapping on our territory. A strong hypothesis that the Rubempré woman had aided and abetted if

43

not actually instigated that. Plenty of evidence but insufficiently direct to apply to a judge for a warrant; and a probability she would enjoy political protection, at a pretty high level. I did not resist the temptation to pay her in her own coin. I had her pinched from the French Army Headquarters, in Baden. Not a place with diplomatic immunity, like an embassy, but if there was any fuss the Army would prefer to keep things in the family. And – it's no more than fair comment, so take it as such – the Bundesgrenzschutz, when they got to hear of it, would think twice before creating a political turmoil, in Bonn or Paris. There was more, of course. But that's the bones of it."

And nothing crossed Pohl's face; neither frown, smile, nor even twitch.

"It might be as well to examine the options. Reaching a number of hypothetic conclusions . . . A case exists, you admit it and that's sensible, for a charge to be laid, a criminal instruction pursued. A modus operandi you say would not be welcomed in unspecified quarters and probably you're right. I lay that one aside, for the moment . . . We cannot arrest you or imprison you without a specific charge. If convinced that circumstances warranted such a step, I could have you declared persona non grata and escorted to the frontier, which could be done without publicity, and your colleagues told you had been taken ill. And if there were diplomatic consequences, which I take leave to doubt, there's enough in reserve, here," pointing.

"Hm, this isn't a trial," he went on. "You don't have to speak in your defence. In common courtesy . . . you have opinions to express? Further considerations to offer, perhaps?"

"The zero option, no? Masterly inaction, or simply doing nothing. The good Herr Rennemann's effort isn't worth the paper it's written on. The other thing, I can tell you, caused no prejudice to German interests: in fact the contrary. You need not take my word on that; you can pull the file. Probably a private explanation was called for, accepted, and no further steps were thought necessary."

"They'd hardly have sent you here, would they, if there was any mark on your file."

"To be quite candid, I don't imagine anybody even looked. It wouldn't be anticipated, let's say, that any trouble would arise." Pohl's faint smile had not been seen for some time.

"We are colleagues."

He had stopped tapping with his pen or playing with his glasses. Senior government functionaries are often prosy. The well-rounded periods indicate that a decision has not yet been reached. Afterwards a different man is heard.

"A concept of personal honour – is that meaningless?"

"I sometimes think it's all we have."

"Yes. True. In accepting a situation: or an order: there's a threshold: as with pain: some have lower tolerance than others . . . Can you give me your word of honour?"

"In return for?"

"True; there are two formulae to find. Let us say; I daresay I could – no; those are conditionals . . .

"I'll engage myself: you've my word you'll hear no more of this. Doctor Rennemann can be persuaded to withdraw his complaint – in toto. This other affair we'll agree to disregard. Following a personal interview with yourself, shall I word it, I am satisfied that grounds for complaint do not exist.

"Your side – the condition for success – your word that you cease henceforth to concern yourself. Totally."

"No."

"No?" Frown.

"If I do so, so does everybody else," replied Castang. "Putting women arbitrarily in the bin isn't on. Nor is intimidating cops, or the attempt to. I'm not speaking about me. Munich cops."

"I see." The by now wellknown smile, appearing. "On that point also, I'll give you assurances."

"That being so, you have mine. Upon my honour. Mark," said Castang grinning. "I'm not sure I could undertake totally to control private thinking completely."

"I think I rather like your formula," said Pohl not smiling at all – "that it's all we have left. Will you give my apologies to your wife – and I very greatly hope she enjoys her stay in our town."

"Perfectly beautiful town. So says she, and so say I."

Castang sat upon the terrace of the Brauhaus. Within a couple of days they had formed habits: sitting at the same table, by way of becoming a Stammtisch. The Polizeipräsidium, handily situated between the Street of the Augustinians and the Street of the Carmelites bespoke the devotion of earlier generations of Münchener policemen, archers of the watch or whatever they called themselves, to the excellent beer brewed by these reverend and holy fathers. Grey, Brown or White friars (Löwenbrau where the grub was good had inherited the cellars of the Franciscans) – great piss-artists all.

He was alone. Vera, a maniac for looking at pictures, had gone carting off to some goddam Pinacothek (Castang had small Latin and less Greek) to look at primitive Florentines, at whom he looked, if at all, with a dull thud. Even without Vera's denunciations of his crass imbecility he knew this was a hole in civilised-renaissance-man, but acted unrepentant.

Geoffrey Dawson, much keener (and much more educated) had been taken in tow. They had taken a great fancy to one another. It didn't worry Castang at all. He had many nightmares, but Vera-committing-adultery never had been among them.

Mr. Dawson had made a good intervention that morning. Serious and witty, altogether English.

"Here are people who speak highly of Compassion. It must be clearly understood that Compassion and the Cop do not go together: it is a contradiction in terms. Mitleid is shit" – a happy combination of German and English – "or if I may so put it, the compassionate-cop is Scheisse." Quite right; down with Mitleid. It had got him into trouble already around here: take that tedious Birgit and give her a rapid unconstipating series of electrochocs . . .

Castang had made the same point earlier.

"Looking at her with detachment," he asked Vera, "do you see us as meddlesome interferers in Birgit's affairs? Have I made a bad mistake? I won't ask you whether it might have consequences." She borrowed a cigarette, to think with.

"You always say that being sorry for people is a very bad basis for police work. But I'm not a cop. And I'm a woman."

"Pass for one, it's said."

"Don't be facetious," irritated. "You're an official, and a guest here, and you have to be on your best behaviour. And I'm here on sufferance, and in your shadow, so I can't . . . I'm not at home, am I?" Mixed feelings, and struggling to articulate them. "She's sloppy, and she did pour it all out on me, and she did exasperate me. But there didn't seem to be anybody on her side. Nobody to say she had a rotten time, with Ma obviously angling to get the custody of the child taken from her. If they bring her in front of a judge for a 'show cause' who is going to stand up for her and say rubbish, she's no more insane than the cat and are we all to be so holier than thou? Hasn't she the right to a woman sympathiser? But I can't be one, without dragging you into it, and I have already, and that's a mistake for sure."

"Don't go getting guilt feelings."

"Oh shut up," said Vera crossly. "The moment a woman shows signs of emotion the men are there sticking grubby little labels on her. Compassion might be shit, and so is being coldblooded and oh dear," comically, "I'm always falling over on one side or the other." He was amused: didn't that happen to men, then?

"I have to give you a police aphorism, though. As long as there is a judge, he has to be the one to judge. Ach, don't worry about it. I get a black mark: I'll survive."

The rest of the day promised to be tedious. The works of the Symposium had bogged down in earnest discussion of protection. Of presidents, of synagogues, of airports: going on and on . . . He felt little sympathy (or Mitleid) for these activities: the cop-in-uniform, picking his nose outside a consulate, induces a psychological feeling of security? . . . my foot. In fact Geoffrey, Vera, and he had planned to sneak off that afternoon, play truant.

And they had a date for dinner with Roberto Bonacorsi – "I am not northern enough to sit in the park all afternoon simply because the sun is shining" . . . suspicion reigned that Bobby would not be found either at this afternoon's Discussions. Nor, it should be added, looking at Florentine Primitives – Bobby was unpatriotic. Venice was not spared. "I don't want any more

47

Senates", (quoting Napoleon). "I will be an Attila upon the Venetian State. A Cossack," he said, "a Sabreur," (enjoying the word). Castang was looking forward to dinnertime. Meantime, drinking beer peacefully upon a sunny terrace.

What was it old Nietzsche said? – "Action is an illusion"? (Let it not be thought for an instant that Castang had read Nietzsche: his authority was Divisional Commissaire Richard; much handicapped – he said also – by education.) In a cop's existence there was some action – a great deal less than supposed by the readers of crime stories. It's about as welcome as compassion is . . .

The police: in no sphere of human endeavour is the bull in the china-shop less welcome. And this particular shop (surveying the city of Munich with languid gaze) has plenty of bulls of its own. This is not the Bavarian Backwoods, where opinion in general can be summed up as "Save us from the Communists, the juvenile-delinquents, the immigrant-labourers, and the Prussians." This is a highly sophisticated European capital. To be sure the government is rather more right-wing than some might like: to be sure the police is rather more heavily equipped than some would care for. More zealous too. In the first place the Herr Chief-Counsellor – Pohl's rank was Oberrat, which is high, and it was no good Geoffrey Dawson making those English jokes about Rat and Superrat – had shown a great deal less zeal than he might have. And in the second, one didn't have to look far to find governments every scrap as right-wing as that of Bavaria. Castang felt he had been lucky.

The sun shines. Upon the dark scarred brickwork of the Frauenkirche, upon the elegant green and gold facings of Walterspiel, upon the blue and white diamonds of the Wittelsbach flag. Upon a great many dead-and-gone Wittelsbachs in bronze, upon baroque stucco and upon the trompe-l'oeil painting that has had to replace stucco reliefs, destroyed by bombardment. Upon the chocolates and coffee and crystallised fruits in Dallmeyer's window, upon a million people and upon Castang. The sun is autumnal, delicious, generous; it ripens grapes, it supplies the arteries of this robust and energetic people. Castang sits on, his coffee gone cold. People at his table pay for beer and ice-cream and gather up their luggage and move on. Someone else comes and sits and he pays no attention.

"Monsieur Castang," says a voice, quite softly.

Sun and beer and white sausages have induced lethargy, but this voice is speaking French: the tonic accent on the first syllable of his name while Germans tend to place it on the ultimate. This last day or two he has worked hard at speaking German. At a level of concentration that now surprises him: he catches himself thinking in German, and it is laborious to straighten up and uncross his legs and make a half turn and take the cigarette out of his mouth. Plodding; both a mental and physical plod. People speak of thought, it occurs to him, when they mean no more than talking to themselves. The idea is no defter for being expressed in French: saying Who-are-you-then isn't very original either.

"Qui êtes-vous?"

"A friend of Birgit's."

"And who is Birgit?"

"Oh come off it. I've been using my eyes and ears."

"Very good work but I've no interest."

"Look it's important that I –"

"Lose yourself."

"Stop being so stupid for Christ –"

"Piss off." Turning away is easy, no more than slipping back to his former attitude.

People make this mistake of forever shoving everyone into categories – a very French attitude, thought Castang, though perhaps I say that only on account of being French. And there I go again; how French am I? No more than half for maybe one half of the time?

Like bright or stupid? People tend to go on as if it were tall or short, an unvarying constant. Well, I, Castang, am occasionally bright, rarely for any length of time. And the average person (who doesn't exist) is very dense, very thick, and makes up to the average (which is me) by being bright now and again. I am now being muddled; I've had a lot of beer and have been sitting too long in the sun: Richard would be giving me one of his looks. I'm trying to say that people thought of as bright are generally trained as a professor or a research scientist or whatever.

Intellectuals can be so damned crass. If there's a rule at all, then the brighter the stupider.

Or a cop. Isn't he supposed to be observing and deducting at all times, trigger-quick? My eye: my left foot. And since my attention has been drawn to my left foot it's gone to sleep. Sitting too long with legs crossed.

So this young man is "a friend of Birgit's." If there's any more of this the Munich police force will become highly uneasy. Do not worry, boys. I've only one word, and when I give it I try to see that it stays given. Furthermore Geoffrey Dawson's words about the Compassionate Cop are relevant. Mitleid with Birgit is piffle. The Bavarian police has a reputation for heavy handedness towards Youth. Brutality, even. There is of course no police force in the world exempt from both taints. An overuse of all that lavish sophisticated material . . . if I think that I'm just being envious.

Castang looked up, and saw Vera, looking sunny and satisfied from seeing nice pictures. Good! It was only at that minute that he realised that the young man was gone.

Geoffrey, looking a scrap fidgeted. Don't feel shamefaced, mate; I do not imagine that you are trying to get off with my wife.

"I had a case of conscience for a sec, you going off like that with Superrat, wondering whether I ought to stay. But oh they were boring, even worse than anticipated. Bobby will fill us in on anything we should know, he promised. How d'you make out with the Rats incidentally – no bother? Sorted out? Oh, good."

"We've had a lovely time, but oh my feet," said Vera.

"Have you eaten?"

"Yes we had hamburgery things while gazing – and you?"

"Sausage and whatnot, here. Let's go rest our feet in the park and Lydia can have a sleep. They're all going somewhere for a free afternoon. Weisse Rössl beim Wolfgangsee, no doubt, not our cup of tea? I thought not. Right, let's make tracks."

A funny thing happened on the way to the park . . .

There is quite a lot of green space on the far side of the Residenz palace. The Residenz garden, nice in a French gravelled-path formal way, but outside there are some large blanks.

Probably there were buildings there that got bombed, and have been cleared, but nobody has yet decided what to do now with all that space.

Beyond this is part of the inner Ring Road that circles the old city, a broad boulevard where traffic, everywhere thrusting, simply belts along. Before the pedestrian can cross here, he must wait for this ferocious spout to shut itself to a momentary trickle, blocked at a red light higher up, at the crossing of the Prinzregentenstrasse. The big BMW and the ubiquitous Mercedes take the broad swinging curve habitually too fast, tyres screaming in an ecstasy of technological egoism.

They were standing, dreamily waiting for the gap. A screech louder than the others alerted them like a siren.

Geoffrey Dawson, who had become good friends with Lydia, was pushing the push-chair in which she was having something between a sit and a snooze. Castang had taken Vera's arm in paternal fashion, for the crossing. This he habitually did with his good right arm, since the bum left arm was always wooden in its movements.

Dawson, more athletic than the studious bespectacled look gave one to suspect, picked up the stroller bodily and made a complicated jump backwards. Castang, grabbing Vera round the ribs, half jumped her half pulled her in a rightwards and backward-reaching arc carrying them both up on the grass and off the concrete verge. Nobody actually fell but they all ended sprawled with hands on the dusty grass.

"Whew."

"Bloody loony."

"Nothing to cry for, darling. Just a jolt."

"Sorry about that."

"Thank you for that!"

"We can cross now." A little breathless, they reached the pavement.

"Bloody clot. Tyres underinflated, you don't notice till you corner too fast. Heavy car . . ." Nobody had seen what kind of car it was.

"Moment," said Castang, going back. Had the car actually mounted the verge? Smooth slightly rounded concrete. Difficult to say. Dry dusty weather, grass at that spot completely worn away. Certainly something of the sort happened quite often; there were tyre traces right up to the gutter. Centrifugal force, he said sagely, and of course Geoffrey was right; tyre-pressures too low. The hot weather caused evaporation, a fellow had a drink too many at lunch time. The question didn't even arise. One could not stop oneself from putting it, nonetheless. Accident or incident?

Geoffrey was looking at him with cop eyes but said nothing. Vera, a perfectly good walker nowadays but not able to make sudden jumps (and never would be) was bent over spitting on a handkerchief and wiping Lydia's mouth: the momentary blubber had stopped as quickly as it began. There was a tacit agreement to say nothing more about the ridiculous incident. They strolled onward, the length of the Hofgarten and crossed the Prinzregentenstrasse with the green light. One had only to skirt the block of the Museum of Modern Art and dip into the park. Ducks attracted Lydia's attention. Pleasant mixture of shade and sun. The afternoon was really hot for the time of year. Persons of bohemian mentality quite often took all their clothes off on these occasions and strolled about with, perhaps, a not altogether innocent desire to go yah at patrolling policemen with an eye to Moral Conduct. There were numerous benches.

"Which bench, one wonders vaguely," asked Geoffrey, "did poor Unity Mitford sit on?"

"It interested me ever since reading about it. Not her, poor sad wretch – the dilemma," said Vera.

"Uh?" said Castang who knew nothing about it.

"She shot herself hereabouts," said Geoffrey who knew all about it, "with a tiny pistol given her by her Führer. It started as a game, being excessively Nazi, sucking up to ol' Dolf, telling everyone happily what a Jew-Hater she was. And then at last England declared war on Germany and it wasn't a game any more."

"And what happened then?" asked Castang.

"They put her in hospital and got her the best surgeon in Germany. He couldn't get the bullet out though – you know, those tiny twenty-twos – but the wound healed. And they shipped her home.

"She lived another ten years. Kind, quiet, gentle, a bit silly. A retarded child, smiling at people and pissing in her trousers, big and fat and affectionate, until a merciful meningitis swept her off. A sad story with its horrible side, because for those bad years in this city she was a horrible person, without really meaning to be so.

"Violence," said Geoffrey, "and at last no way out – turned in on herself."

"Sounds to be a classic of its sort," said Castang, half-interested.

"They're not very likely to have put up a little plaque, to commemorate the event."

"Not very."

It is as English as its name suggests, this park. Everywhere were little groups indistinguishable from themselves, playing with children.

"Vera looking happy," said Geoffrey.

"Immensely. Feels at home here. Not often she gets away from the grind."

"Has value after all, the get-together. Cops are the same wherever they find themselves. If you hadn't brought her . . . Not exactly the typical French couple, would you say?"

"Typical cop couple? Criminal couple!"

Did it all come together here, as it had for her, the sardonically named Unity? The irreconcilable opposites in every human being – let alone couples! The duality, dichotomy – whatever it was called – in everything: male-female, intellect and emotion, active-passive, free will and predestination. There was a specially German one: Dichtung und Wahrheit. Metaphysical; they are like that. This is a very metaphysical city; southern city, lot of southern blood, Latin blood. Latin and Nordic, the two don't mix easily, or well. Celt more than German. Funny people, Celts: I ought to know, one myself. Bloody funny people, the French. No wonder everybody else detests them. Not Nordic enough; not Latin enough either.

Dawson lying there chewing grass – very English-looking: funny people too, whether Celtic or Nordic; that damned island gave them a peculiar look, not just attributable to their funny clothes.

"Just supposing," said Geoffrey, spitting, "that fellow in the car had hit one or more of us; and gone on driving in a panic, classic instance of hit-and-run. Even if other people stopped to report it, they'd never have got the number, and where would the chap be five minutes from now? Cross any of the bridges, take any direction, needle in a haystack; not find that in a month of Sundays."

"Right," with enjoyment of these English phrases. A month of – how right and succinct for those long-drawn-out enquiries that got nowhere.

"Can't deduce anything in a town like this. Got to think metaphysically . . . What a bore to have to go back and be subjected to more of the remorseless logic."

"Leaving the real world, to plunge again into fantasy."

"That is of course so," said Geoffrey Dawson, too intelligent to laugh or pass it off as a play on words. "We observe as realities a vast heap of petrifying junk that is no longer relevant to present existence, while a number of elementary truths that have been with us for all time are dismissed airily as myth."

The sun began westering and the band with regret to head for the stable. Describing the Polizei-Präsidium as a stable, said Dawson; the definition is inexact.

Psychiatric institute, suggested Castang.

"If one's life – let's take a taxi, it'll be simpler – is according to some worthy fellow the book one writes, and given that we are police officers; how then would you define your book? A novel? Or what the bookshops call the Mystery and Suspense shelf?"

"Oh poor us," said Castang. "Ask Vera: she's the expert on art."

At the hotel there was a phone message.

"If you will come to see me at the Seestrasse tomorrow towards lunchtime it will be of value to you – R. R." That will be Mum?

"A woman was it, who phoned?"

"Don't know, I'm sorry, wasn't me who took the call."

"Never mind." He didn't mention it to Vera, anyhow preoccupied with giving a tired and filthy child a bath. He changed his clothes in a hurry.

"See you at the restaurant – hour, hour'n'a half? Make yourself beautiful for an Italian seducer." That deserved no answer, and got none. It was another lovely evening, with a splendid sunset of which one couldn't see much, but a benevolent serenity, distilled over the city. The oppressive sense of clouds gathering was nonsense, he decided, and so was the feeling of somebody following him across that smelly concrete labyrinth under the Karlsplatz. Elementary techniques exist for detecting anything of the sort, and this was excellent terrain for doing so. He could not be bothered. Birgit's scruffy friend again, no doubt. No intention of getting involved there, even without finger-wagging from Herr Pohl. He was certain that the law in Germany governing people-put-in-the-bin would be elaborate, with a great many safeguards. Rechtsanwalt Rennemann (was that what the double R stood for? – hardly!) was well placed to ensure that observance of the same would conform to every letter of the law while blandly disregarding the spirit: but that is what lawyers are for. Somewhere along the line, though, a judge would be involved, and if Herr Pohl was worth anything at all a grain of sand in the smooth mechanism could be brought to this judge's attention. Not in the courtroom, naturally.

"Ah," said Colonel Bonacorsi, "there you are. I got those photostats of the *Law Gazette* you asked for: here we are, *Gesetz über die Unterbringung von Geisteskranken und Suchtkranken*, internment thus of loonies and drug-dependants, I never can make much of this official German, what's Einschränkung?"

"Restriction I think, that's what it's all about, restriction in these circs of a basic constitutional right to personal freedom, family unity and the sanctity of the home."

"Ho," said Bonacorsi, "this I must read. I always did wonder how they talked their way round allowing me to rush about with squads of SS-men arresting suspects right and left: a lot I worry about the sanctity of the home."

"Where's Geoffrey, his German's far better; all this tends to be a bit opaque. Hoy . . . what we need here is 'translate with brief notes' and you've been to the university."

"Why is it always said in American books that they take notes upon yellow legal pads, when we just use scribbling-paper – come to that why should they be yellow?"

"Paragraph three, the lower administrative authority – that the cops? – can take steps in case of danger to self or another or an Offence to Public Morals. There's the usual catch-all: *öffentliche Sittlichkeit anstössig*. However, district court must approve of measures taken; only then is hospitalisation possible."

"We can rely I think on these regulations having been carefully followed," said Castang dryish.

"Para four, written applications, certificates, plus expert report from institute *but* para five, in urgent cases all that can be over-ridden: the director of the nuthouse must inform the court within three days, within one week maximum the court must legalise the deprivation of liberty by interim injunction."

"You see, dead easy, you can go on to the processes for getting your liberty back."

"You're released when you're no longer ill."

"Oh dear, that's just what I was afraid of. Well, let's go and have dinner."

"And be anstössig to the öffentliche Sittlichkeit."

It was a great success, that dinner. A small but good example of the famous harmony that Castang is always searching for, and for the most part so lamentably fails to be found. A table the right size, in a room full enough to be animated and not so full as to be noisy and overcrowded; in a restaurant respecting the ancient adage: a dining-room should be cool and the plates hot. A young and pretty waitress, who had herself achieved an admirable harmony between dark wavy hair and big black-framed glasses and whose simple and agreeable manners were as fresh as the flowers. Might one mention along the way that enormity in today's Europe, nice food at a modest price? One may not say "unheard-of" (others tell one of this remarkable experience) but why seems it only to happen to others?

That Bonacorsi should make a great Italian seduction of Lydia was a foregone conclusion: that he should make Vera laugh in continuous healing happy waves with tears running down her nose was a huger lovelier dividend. Allegro, Castang observes the gentle and innocent drunkenness of his wife. To use the word "indulgent" would strike a patronising, superior note that would do him an injustice.

Only once, and then only for a minute or so, is a false note struck in the reality of the evening. Geoffrey Dawson hits it, ordinarily so tactful. He is to be forgiven, for he is drunk too on this innocently gentle Sud-Tirol wine.

"There are moments when I wished I worked in Northern Ireland."

"What a peculiar remark, Geoffrey; do explain yourself."

"Silly, I agree. It's that Dorset is a very peaceful place. I am grateful, since it is one of the last corners left in Europe where the old Christian civilisation makes some pretence to be intact. However rickety . . ." Castang thinks of Commissaire Richard's little metaphysical experience a year ago – in Dorset! A sudden visitation of the realities (the esse?) of violence, alone on the top of Eggardon Down: Geoffrey, told of this, nodded, in perfect understanding. "But there's no conveying it to some."

"You're the real expert on violence, Bobby."

Colonel Bonacorsi has no wish to be reminded of it. Looks, a second, cross.

"Yes. We've always been inventive, haven't we, in Italy? True, Geoffrey. We're good survivors, we're loose, we work with bits of string. Perhaps you've read our history. Let's forget Rome, that rather tedious place. What's the best-known, to the English eye, Firenze one must suppose, Bernard Berenson and Harold Acton, and middle-aged English virgins of every sex thick as leaves in Vallombrosa, oh well, you're aware that the history of this place is as black with assassination and treachery as anything that ever took place in Germany, even in the Thirty Years' War. Cosimo would have had nothing to learn from Francesco Franco, any more than all those popes who are either Pius or Innocent would have learned from Gestapo Müller. I can't blame you; your English crooks, since the Tudor monarchs who can hold their own in any company when it comes to blood-drinking, are funnily squeamish.

"Good, Geoffrey," drinking his glass off and refilling it, "yes, I have to live with being frightened. My General, petit

57

papa Dalla Chiesa, died well, died fast, what more could he have looked for? The only question that really bears asking, is whether one is frightened to die. On first thoughts yes, oh yes, very; all the time. And on second thoughts no, because cowards die many times before their death, hm, Shakespeare, and that would really be boring as well as shaming, wouldn't it now."

"I am sorry, Bobby, I am much abashed and I do beg your pardon."

There came inevitably a moment when Lydia, overcome with exotic (not to say erotic, with meaningful looks at Colonel Bonacorsi) experiences as much as with strong drink, fell asleep suddenly (like the aged Somerset Maugham in similar circumstances). The men proposed that she be on the banquette "with leaves strewn over her": Vera said no. Bed. And herself too. No attention was paid to choruses of protest. There was much gallant offer of male escort, refused with the same polite firmness.

"You all seem to think I'm pissed."

"So you are."

"Able to wheel my child home, and myself too. Thank you. Perfectly safe and untroubled. Do stop it, Bobby, I'm feeling quite wonderful. How am I supposed to get into my coat when you dangle the sleeve there behind my shoulderblade? I'm going straight home and I don't want to know at what hour the drunks come straggling in." Struggling free of affections she made a good exit. The attentions of the gentlemen were diverted by the waitress with a pack of cigarettes, cellophane neatly peeled back.

"What's this?"

"HB." Pronounced Hah-Bay.

"Oh, dear child, and I asked for Kaffee. That funny accent of mine again."

Everybody was laughing; a shuffle-off-to-Buffalo. If accidental, spontaneous, then mildly funny. If Goldwyn really did ask "Who have you got for Scarface O'Hara?" – yes, it's funny. If fabricated, a form of humour the French are given to, then unfunny. A phrase misheard, a meaning misunderstood: we have too many already.

58

The gentlemen sat on, passably hilarious, for near enough another hour before calling it a day. Three experienced drinkers. More would not add to euphoria; make one a little silly, a scrap unsteady. As things were, tolerably exhilarated. Just short of doing something foolish which seemed comic at the time.

Castang left his companions by their expensive hotel in the Promenadeplatz and set off on the ten-minute stroll to his own quarters.

The Pacellistrasse is a gloomy little stretch full of high finance, the niceties of which always do exude a breath of boredom: the kind of street one never even notices. Nobody would ever walk there, let alone linger. As Castang crossed under the trees of the Promenade a police car slid softly past, seeing to the nocturnal safety of the bourgeoisie, and a hundred metres further he saw it parked. Rather a place for bored night-duty cops 'to have a smoke.

If not a smoke then to stretch their legs: the two had climbed out. One put a foot on the back bumper of the smart, clean BMW (Castang's interest was purely professional), swaying it idly as though not quite happy with a shock-absorber: the other stood as idly on the pavement, thumbs in his brightly-polished belt. Smart, thought Castang with approval of the forest-green uniforms. Rather over-equipped, dangling like Christmas-trees with expensive leather-cased accessories, giving them a Japanese look.

They turned to face him as he neared, giving him the same polite attention as to the gold coins in the burglar-proof (very) window of the private bank. The faces likewise over-equipped, with big neat moustaches and side-whiskers and tinted sun-glasses. He had drunk enough to be at peace with the world, would have given them a comradely wink but for it's being bad for discipline. As he came level the one lifted an arm, nothing aggressive: the other threw a chest slightly, as though to make himself a little bigger. No physical effort to bar passage, but Castang stopped obediently. The faces were calm, empty. Both sketched fragmentary salutes.

"Papers?" said the one gently, the soft voice and vague interrogative intonation making the order a request.

Perhaps they had a good reason. It was a time for leaving restaurants, like him: for wealthy tourists – not like him – strolling home to hotels. Perhaps one had been mugged and the car patrol alerted. Perhaps his step was a bit heavy with wine, and they'd thought he was making for a parked car and decided to check his alcohol level. Or perhaps they'd no good reason and were just killing time. But he had no good reason for refusing. He felt in his inside pocket, neither smiling nor unsmiling.

The cop studied his card carefully, holding it up to the light, comparing his face to the identity photo: pointed a casual finger at the open back door of the police car. "Im Wagen," he said, laconic and still soft-spoken. Wasn't that a little over-zealous?

"As you see, I'm a stranger. Going home to my hotel, five minutes from here. You can be satisfied, I believe."

A slight frown behind the glasses, as though of disbelief.

"In the car," a little more abruptly, pointing with the identity card in emphasis. Castang looked at him steadily.

"If you won't justify your order then, I'm afraid, I'll ask for your number. Just so's we understand each other."

There was a moment's silence during which the cop seemed to make up his mind. He stood immobile. Castang saw no grimace, no signal: it was the other who moved.

Very professionally done, without noise or gesture; as the elbow came out the wrist turned as smooth as a hooking boxer. Nothing too hard; no crude nor violent head-breaker; the merest flick of the pacifier (strictly an illegal object but most street-duty cops carry one and the practice tends to be winked at).

Certainly not designed to knock him unconscious; barely enough to stun and send him off balance, so that he put his hand on the roof of the car. The cop took him by the left elbow. The grip was not painful but it was his bad arm and a jolt of pain shot through him while he was still paralysed by the smack on the skull. The cop made a small bodychecking gesture and his limp body went into the car. Nothing more to it. The doors slammed; there was a cop sitting beside him and another at the wheel. There had been nobody on the street to see anything, but if there had been no one would have seen anything untoward. No struggle, no outcry. Before he had stopped rubbing his head and shaking his eyes back into focus they had whisked across the Lembachplatz and made a right turn into the Arcisstrasse, accelerating sharply up the straight empty street. The gearbox snapped between third and second; the car made two or three quick right-and-left turns on streets he was barely familiar with and which all looked the same: he was lost in no time. The tyres squealed on the ninety-degree turns; the sudden braking threw him forward. "Quickly now," said the one beside him, holding his wrist. On the pavement. Still that bourgeois quarter, still the serried row of heavy lowering apartment blocks, but no chance to orient himself: the one threw a blanket over his head, the other tugged sharply at his wrist: he could do nothing but fall or lurch forward so he lurched, stumbling on steps, panting through a doorway and along a passage. A police station? It didn't have the feeling of a police station but . . . what had they taken him for? A terrorist masquerading with tourist papers? He had not shown his official card with the tricolor markings. It hadn't seemed called for. He was whisked through a doorway and given another of those expert little bodychecks as the blanket was pulled off. The door closed behind him with a soft thump and a bolt turned. He was alone and imprisoned.

It was not a cell, being slightly larger. A waiting room. A bench ran round three sides, faced with thinly-padded plastic leather: there was no other furniture. The walls were plastered and painted, dark green to head height and beige above that: in the ceiling a cluster of three neon tubes set flush shed bright light. No window, but air from grilles in the top corners. The door was that of a cell; no handle, metal-sheathed, a judas at eye-level; another door immediately opposite, the same; leading presumably to some inner office or interrogation room.

It was time to be a cop. Vera would not be awake and waiting for him. She'd had enough to drink to sleep heavily. Even at breakfast time she'd be surprised, but not alarmed. Things did sometimes happen to keep him out all night. Here, she'd be – call it mildly astonished; she wouldn't rush about yelling. Nor would she think him out-with-the-boys, creating havoc among the whores . . .

Those two cops; they'd been waiting for him, they'd known who he was. He'd been mousetrapped, no doubt of it. Their

61

movements had been too rapid, too rehearsed. For an ordinary verification of identity they'd have phoned in, read the details off his card, waited for the duty button-pusher to get the read-out on his computer terminal. They'd known already, wanted to manoeuvre him into the car without fuss. Giving such credit as was deserved, they had kept violence to the minimum.

There was indeed a question whether they were cops at all . . . Professional security men; no doubt about that. Members of a uniformed urban force . . . he could feel more doubtful about that. Was it a bit pointless, fruitless, to ask the question at all? It raised the little matter of a car with official police markings, manned by two types in the uniform of authority. Oh yes, such things happened; he could think offhand of instances in both France and Italy.

This didn't have the feeling of a police bureau, here. Far too quiet, for one thing. Nor had there been any administrative procedure, and if there's one thing all police bureaux have in common it's the disposal problem, the getting rid of all the human clutter accumulated in the course of a day – or night. He looked at his watch; eleven-fifteen. They'd not even frisked him. Tolerance about cigarettes or a lighter is one thing, but they'd left him a knife large enough to be classed as an offensive weapon – they hadn't tapped him for a gun. Common law criminal or terrorist suspect or even a juvenile delinquent; they'll always look you over because one never knows.

Undoubtedly they'd known who he was. Monsieur le Commissaire did not just leave his gun behind out of common courtesy: he never wore one at all; had resolved, a year and more now, never again to use a weapon.

They'd left him now to cool off for forty minutes. He'd rather like to empty his bladder. There were other things he'd rather like, such as cleaning his teeth and going to bed. This wasn't much to ask. He gave the door a series of hearty thumps. Nothing happened so he did it again.

At last a faint movement outside. He was sitting quietly smoking when observed through the judas. The door was unbolted, reluctantly.

"You make a hell of a lot of noise," in a self-pitying voice.

Not a cop, nor any strong-arm sort at all. A wizened little man in his sixties, with red rims to his eyes, wearing a baggy work overall and woolly bedroom slippers, peering at him with disapproval.

"Lavatory," said Castang. It seemed a lot to ask; almost unheard-of. The concierge, or whatever, stood aside at last and jerked a grudging chin. The lavatory was in the passage, ill-lit and ill-smelling. He had a pee while wondering whether to push the fellow's face in. He didn't. They'd be expecting just that. And even if he could walk straight out on to the street it would not satisfy his now thoroughly-roused interest. And he wasn't going to push even the smallest and most toothless ratface in, ever any more.

Certainly it was the concierge – pointing with reproach at a squashed cigarette butt and saying, "You'll have to clean that up after you," before turning the bolt again on him. The October nights in Munich are cool, whatever the days are: they'd no heating on in here and he was glad of his pullover. He stretched out on this damn plastic bench, put his hat over his eyes against the glare of that needlessly powerful light (there might be a camera up there behind an air grille but he neither knew nor cared) and prepared for a kip: it was nearing midnight and what did he have to sit up for?

Asleep? As near as made no difference: dozing, it would be called. One can be asleep and perfectly relaxed; senses are still very much alert. He felt rather than heard the inner door open, was wide awake before the quiet voice said, "Well, Monsieur Castang . . ."

He took off the hat: there was too much glare from the lamps to see anything, so he sat up.

"You'll be wanting some information, I dare say."

"As a matter of interest, I'd rather a quiet night's sleep. As a matter of principle, certainly. You know my name," yawning, but the brief kip had done him good; his eyes felt rested, "so let's have yours."

"I'm the interrogator. I am not here to give information, but to collect it. So come through here, and sit down quietly."

True, there was little to be had from a conversation through a doorway. And when he sat he was aware that the bench was hard. He walked through. A room almost as plain as the other, furnished as an office: grey metal desk with a rather horrid veneer top of some exotic hardwood, adjustable office armchair behind and another in front. He sat in it; it was kind to his behind. Grey metal filing cabinets. Nothing on the walls but a calendar advertising Siemens. Nothing on the desk but a lamp which wasn't shining in anybody's eyes. Nothing anywhere of any interest but a third man sitting in a third chair, off to one side, an elderly man with silver hair, who looked at him incuriously, said nothing. His hands, loosely clasped in his lap, were as still as himself.

Castang took out a cigarette, noticing that there were only two left. After those, maybe he wouldn't be wanting any more. With a patient, almost indulgent expression the inquisitor opened a drawer, produced an ashtray, laid it on the desk.

"You have been interfering, Monsieur Castang, and it seems to be a failing of yours, in the private affairs of private persons. This, upon the soil of the Federal Republic. You have naturally wished to pass the matter off lightly, relying, it would seem, upon the reluctance of police officers to make difficulties for a colleague. You are given this opportunity of explaining yourself, but to a less indulgent listener: I make myself clear?"

"No. What are you? Judge, magistrate, prosecutor – what's your legal standing?"

"It will be wiser – this will become clear – to avoid procedural argument, confining yourself to answers."

"You seem to know that I talked with Herr Pohl. You're right in saying that that was informal, between colleagues. If that's not enough you have legal means of constraining me, I suppose, before a court. There's no intermediate stage."

"Perhaps then you'll tell me upon what legal grounds you based your sequestration, and forcible interrogation of Madame Alberthe de Rubempré. If you now claim to have been waylaid, or kidnapped?"

"Where responsibilities lie at my door, I accept them."

"This much is thus clear: you have and accept responsibility for illegal acts of violence upon German soil. Bearing that in mind, Monsieur Castang, I enjoin you to answer me very fully,

64

very frankly, upon your relations with Frau Birgit Rennemann."

"I can only repeat what I told Herr Pohl, that my meeting with her was casual and accidental. She appealed to me for help; I gave her what I regarded and still do as good advice: I maintain that."

"You'd like to repeat this good advice?"

"There's no secret about it: I advised her not to try to resist the duly constituted legal authority, but to contest the assumption that she needed psychiatric treatment arbitrarily imposed."

"You set yourself up as a judge of the medical treatment a person needs, on the strength of what you tell me is one casual meeting?"

"That is not what I said or suggested. She felt alarmed and harassed. Her balance was disturbed as a consequence. I had no reason to suppose anything else."

"But you contest the decision of the authority making the order. You know more about psychiatry than an experienced clinician."

"That's nonsense; I contest nothing. I have no interest in the matter beyond giving momentary comfort and reassurance to a woman met on the street who was in a state of anxiety."

"For which you are professionally competent and qualified, no doubt."

"One needs neither for the circumstances I describe," determined not to get nettled. "My competence is no more and no less than that of any experienced police officer. One tries to avoid putting people in prisons, which are excellent schools of criminality, and the same applies to psychiatric institutes, which fabricate insanity in large quantities."

"I see. You maintain thus that this meeting was isolated and fortuitous."

"Exactly."

"You have no contact with or knowledge of the lady's family or friends."

"I have said so. A moment's social conversation on a doorstep with a lady I was given to understand is this woman's mother in law."

"Then perhaps you will explain this." He had opened

another drawer, taken out a photograph, passed it across the desk. Large, clear, black and white. Taken from close by. Castang had not noticed: if he had he would have paid little heed – tourists will photograph anything.

He was sitting at the 'stammtisch' in the street in front of the Brauhaus, apparently in animated conversation with a young man of strongly marked features and with longish straight fair hair. For a second he wondered who this was before recollecting "being accosted" and his half-glance round before replying.

"You seem bereft of speech," said the inquisitor.

"As I recall he spoke my name and I said, I think, 'Piss off.'"

"So? How would he have known your name?"

"It isn't a secret. It could have been anybody. I recall the occasion. I'd just had a conversation with Herr Pohl, which had disturbed me, I've no reason to deny. He asked me for discretion, very reasonably. I was getting a bit fed up with people accosting me in the street. Understandably, as it now appears."

"You claim thus that you don't know who this is."

"No. Who is it?"

"He is named Dieter. His antecedents, and his acquaintances, are not what one would wish. We have had an interest in him for some time. He is the type of person one leaves alone, in order to see who he leads to. Among others, to the young Frau Rennemann. And yourself."

"I'm sorry; that is as coincidental as the first and presumably a consequence of the first, but I know nothing of that."

"That is your word."

"I have only one."

"Unsupported, as it happens?"

"A pity."

"As you say. You see, Monsieur Castang, there was the attack upon Madame de Rubempré. Now this. We are wondering whether there is a connection."

"That would be rather a lot of coincidence. Unless you – or this silent gentlemen here? – are friends of hers."

"You prevaricate. It is foolish. When Madame de Rubempré

66

was in your hands, and helpless, you had means at your disposal for persuading her to give you information. You are now in a similar situation. You have for example an ingenious electrical machine, known laughingly as *la gégène*, with electrodes you attach to the genital area. Or so I have been told."

Castang had sometimes wondered what, if he were ever to find himself in a situation of this sort, he would find, within himself.

"We have other notions. For example this." He reached again into one of his drawers, put a thing on his table Castang recognised as an ordinary disposable plastic syringe: a packet of hypodermic needles went with it.

"There is a chemical product which by intramuscular injection produces severe pain in all parts of the body for a variable length of time. Very severe pain."

"I think I've heard of it. Wasn't it used in experiments by Nazi doctors later condemned for war crimes?"

"The product is similar. The usage, if indeed usage is made, is not similar. Your remark is intended to be insulting, but may prove futile."

"I will make a short statement."

"Do so."

"I made up my mind, a year ago, that officially or unofficially I would have nothing further to do with violence. That's as you say a futile remark. I'm in no position, nor shape either, to show you any tough acts.

"Priggish too," drawling rather as he sometimes did when finding himself a prig. "I have never tortured anybody. I have upon occasion ill-treated people, and if it's my turn then too bad for me. What I said I have said, and I've nothing to add."

The inquisitor fixed him with a stony eye, keeping it fixed while the man in the grey suit, who had not stirred the whole while, leaned forward out of his chair and said a word in his ear; finally nodding.

He got up abruptly, pushing his chair back and smoothing his clothes as though ruffled. Standing up he looked smaller than sitting down. Still looking at Castang he drew a large white handkerchief out of his pocket and blew his nose at some length.

"I'll be in my office," he said. Heavy footsteps sounded in the waiting room. Castang wondered what the trick was for getting the door open.

There was silence for a half minute. The man in the grey suit stood up and arranged the furniture, pushing away the inquisitor's chair as though fastidiously disliking a seat cushion warmed by an official backside. He opened the desk drawer and shovelled the objects lying around into it, using his sleeve as though they too were untouchable. He brought his own chair to a point off-centre, where he could sit sideways and look both at Castang and at the wall. There was nothing on the wall at all but he looked at it as though there were a window upon a pretty view, to look at which would rest and refresh him. Sometimes he looked at Castang, studying him from the new angle, a little as though when ready he would pick up a pencil and begin to draw. The silence continued. Castang, who had looked at many people across many desks in the course of professional duties, thought the technique a good one, though he'd never be able to keep it up himself that long.

The face was distinguished, with a strongly-developed Y of prominent bone that slanted over the orbits of the eyes, met in strong concentration at the centre of the forehead and continued down the hard high-bridged nose. The eyes were a palish blue and healthy. The skin was fine-textured, stretched and polished. The man was a good sixty, but there was no loose or pouched flesh on him. Untanned, but neither bleached nor pasty. His suit was well-cut and conventional; his silvery grey tie had a layout of little scarlet diamonds.

It could as easily have been a French face as German, but nordic, Frankish, a face to fit a medieval helmet of polished steel with the visor raised.

When the voice came it was deep and resonant, musical, and beautifully modulated. A courtroom voice to be sure and why had Castang not guessed quicker?

"I am Dominic Rennemann. You are fatigued, Herr Castang, but I will ask for your patient attention a little longer. It will not be of great import whether it be two-thirty or three-thirty in the morning, but it will be of import that we have a thorough understanding of each other. We are not likely to meet again.

"There is no reason for any fundamental obstacle to this understanding. One has opinions, emotions, largely formed by instinct; guided, it is to be hoped, by reasoned intellectual convictions. Yours as I gather are of the nature termed liberal and progressive, coming under the generic cliché of left wing. Whereas mine are of the conservative and traditional flavour called right wing. These journalistic political labels are trash and with your permission I will disregard them. We are men with more in common than might appear. We share an attachment and a respect for the *res publica*.

"So that, Herr Castang, I am not worrying myself about conceivable communist sympathies or affiliations of yours. And for my part I should feel obliged if you could shake off lazy worthless thinking about fascism or reactionary élitism. Can we agree upon that?"

"After my experience of this evening – with some difficulty."

"That is to be expected, and that is why I suggested to the gentleman who has left the room that he do so.

"He is not, incidentally, as bad as he appears. He is a minor functionary, earnest, not very intelligent. He is a criminal Kommissar with a security function. He is not a torturer nor even a bully. That foolish theatrical trick with the hypodermic needle is just that, a foolish trick. Had I known of it I should have warned against it. I think it possible, in passing, that you have yourself had recourse to techniques of intimidation –on occasion.

"We have no Geheime Staats Polizei, Herr Castang. We have no private armies, no sinister militia. But we are careful, nervous people, and we suffer from over-anxiety.

"Nothing illegal has taken place. The two policemen who arrested you did so upon authority. It was thought necessary to sound you, your thoughts, your motives. The excess of zeal is imputable directly to your own excesses in the past. You are free now, and may walk out directly it so pleases you. You have a little time for me still? I am glad of it.

"You had a fortuitous meeting with a woman – I refer of course to Birgit – who is also a little over-nervous, over-anxious; and foolish. You were on your side a little over-ready

69

to take her at face value. The combination has led to some mis-fortune. You have been taking an interest in the *Law Gazette*. Die *Unterbringung von Geisteskranken*. And, Herr Castang, *Suchtkranken*: addicted persons. I did not believe that my daughter-in-law was addicted to a dangerous drug but it was necessary to find out. Her behaviour has sometimes been uncontrolled and embarrassing, her associates discreditable. A clinical examination under clinical conditions was thought needful. Once more, there has been nothing illegal. No excess, no abuse. By tomorrow morning she will have regained her liberty of movement.

"Unwittingly, you have encroached upon my personal affairs. She has thrown discredit upon my son, who has put a distance between them but who treats her generously. Her child . . . this is also my grandchild, and I have duties.

"One more thing, before we call a taxi to take you home. Two, my presence in this building, which is simply an office annexe used for security duties, is due simply to a position I hold, advisory and sometimes supervisory, on account of a wide range of experience and a certain eminence in my profes-sion. A security check came up against your name: that, and a certain unwillingness to embarrass your friends over there in the Karmelitenstraase.

"The point I wished to raise, and for which I should like you to show generosity of spirit,is this. This is my town. I am proud of it. Bavaria is my land. I am proud of it. In the late twenties and early thirties events took place here of which I am not proud. We acquired then an evil reputation, remnants of which still cling. This helps sometimes to engender a certain neurosis of behaviour, which we like to ascribe to the Föhn or other trivial pretexts.

"Will you allow me to offer you my apologies as well as regrets?"

"If you will accept my own."

"Where there is understanding there is respect. You will allow me to call a cab – you won't wish to renew your acquaint-ance with the car patrol."

"On the contrary; I should rather like it."

70

"You are after all a policeman," said Rennemann smiling for the first time.

Might it have been the smile that did it? Those people whose job it is to be professionally horrible, the businessmen and the bankers and the policemen, take pains to leave no cracks showing. Their dread is to appear vulnerable.

For a moment Castang saw him stripped of that dreadful grey suit (it is hard to imagine any male dress at once more dismal and more downright ugly: it is the more astonishing to recall that the basic style of this idiotic get-up has scarcely varied in a hundred years: the two stupid tubes and the ill-proportioned block balancing uneasily above them). Munich is a city where one sees both men and women wearing one of the few types of traditional costume to look natural in modern surroundings. They are not all Sunday-suited peasants up for a spree. The bourgeois wear it too. Since one of the advantages of the bourgeoisie is to be taller and slimmer, inevitably more graceful in movement than a peasant, it looks good upon them. They themselves look better. Suddenly human. Until they flee back to their star-wars get-up.

"Your wife invited me to lunch."

"She did?" Herr Doctor Maître looked puzzled; then amused.

"She found you interesting, I should think. I'd go, if I were you. She'll give you a good lunch."

"At Walterspiel?" smiling.

"I should think it very likely. You'd enjoy that? We owe it to you, don't we? I'll tell her so. Hm, I'd join you. But there are good reasons why I shouldn't . . ."

In the back of the patrol car Castang felt the side of his head, which was not more swollen and tender than one need expect. There was no comment, though it was certainly noticed, in the big rear-view mirror. On the Sonnenstrasse they got out politely to open his door for him.

"Sorry about that, chief. All in the day's work, you know." He was a cop too. How often had he not said the same?"

"Were you rather late last night?" asked Vera, seeing him swallow aspirin with his coffee.

"A little." She took pains not to look reproachful.

"I like your Carabineer."

"Yes." Bobby had summed it up well enough when she put it to him with female directness. "What is there to fear?

"One would be frightened all day. Anywhere. Here too, perhaps there's a bullet waiting for me. Plenty of eager characters anxious to plant a few in Colonel Bonacorsi. Life-insurance man rather tight-lipped, huh, if asked to write a policy for Roberto. Wife like you, finds it too much bother, finally, being frightened all day. What is it your man says, Geoffrey? 'Cowards die many times before their death.' Would be too great a bore, being frightened. Nurse knows that, nicht? in the terminal cancer ward, watching the old ones go. Her own turn's coming. Assume it, accept it. Good art has this inevitability, no?

"Once or twice in my life, seen Giulini conducting Verdi. You understand then, the pattern. Ah – he's doing Falstaff in the spring, in Milano. Must try for that. Be a jostle – have to try finding somebody to bribe. Verdi: right man to have around.

"All those chaps – like the Swiss – want to live for ever, building deep shelters, get down there when the phone rings to say the rocket's on the way. Terrible nightmare, phone rings the day I'm in New York screwing Morgan. Such a loss to the world . . . whereas shit, a colonel of Carabinieri shot – what, Another! – rates three lines nowadays, halfway down page twentyfour, next door the curate that got caught feeling up the Boy Scouts."

"A day to go," said Vera finishing her second cup. "Cloudier this morning but it might just hold out long enough for us."

It was the last day of 'seminars'. They'd been better than he'd expected. It was the smaller and poorer countries, as usual, that were imaginative and inventive. Paul Brady from Dublin and Pass from Sevilla (both decidedly outspoken on the subject of the Church; causing slight unease in the ranks of the Germans, whose relations with churches were upon occasion delicate). He had tried to be very cautious himself. Commissaire Richard would not be enthusiastic about anything oddball, and he'd felt old Heinrich's eye heavy upon him. Be funny if you like and if you can, but depart at all from the script and I'll scorch the

72

britches off you, the second I'm back in Paris.

The French, it was true, were fond of suggesting some ridiculous contrivance at international meetings, in order to invest themselves with a cloak of virtue when everyone turned it down as preposterous.

His own official intervention thus had been on the solid side and the title 'Bourgeois Mystification' taken from Gramsci had been more exciting than the matter thereof, quite correctly left-wing but fairly unadventurous.

He had mentioned his adventures of last night to nobody. Vera, who had gone for an orgy of baroque churches, thought he was having lunch with the others: the others, that he was with the family.

He had his business suit on. A darker grey than that of the Herr Rechtsanwalt, but then it was the only one he had, chosen by Vera not to show the dirt too much (dry cleaning prices, like most things, being a racket), of excellent material and sober cut, rather heavy for a hot day but it had to do the whole year round; assumed at home mostly for funeral, or at least funereal occasions. If she really did take him to Walterspiel it would assure him a respectable anonymity. It is part of bourgeois-mystification: senior police officers are supposed to look like Functionaries, even of the financial sort. As a cop-on-the-street he'd worn jeans and a pullover like everyone else – there a jacket was indispensible, because of that infernal gun you have to wear. With a few more steps in seniority he had allowed himself more eccentricity.

He'd like a Bavarian costume himself (not here, naturally). He was not really tall enough, but those knee-breeches, those lovely waistcoats with silver buttons were a temptation. Alas, one would only be able to put it on (he hesitated, wondering whether to be economical. No; if one was going to lunch at the Vierjahreszeiten it was no moment for economy. He set his face resolutely against that horrible U-Bahn and took a taxi.) in the privacy of one's bedroom. Exactly like those senior functionaries, doubtless including a few commissaires of police, who get home and dress up in women's clothes . . . He had – again – urged Vera to buy a dirndl, but she had been hardheaded and Czech about such foolishness.

The Seestrasse, sinister as ever. And why should it be so? he wondered idly: a haven of gaiety and innocence by comparison with so many he could think of, wrapped in soft and silent velvet – it cannot surely be only the bourgeois taste for conspicuous ugliness. A block of workers' municipal housing is just as ugly, even though not of their choosing. The silence! Vice needs adequate soundproofing. In that workers' block, everybody knows everything, right down to how many times the plug was pulled during the night. But above all, the fear. Enter any block inhabited by the secure and the wealthy; the smell of fear, the miasma of mistrust, takes you by the throat.

The archaeologist, sounding these ruins, some centuries perhaps after the extinction of life there, will be charmed; less by the treasures buried in every cranny and cunningly-contrived hollow (to him virtually worthless) as the delight of turning these pages, of this secret book. It will be fitting should it be the bourgeois bomb, tender towards material interests, whose poisoned particles shall have rotted the bones down to heaps of dust while leaving every squirrelled hoard intact for the searcher's delight; and perplexity.

She had the apartment door open as he stepped out of the lift; smiling, looking young and yes, wearing a dirndl. Damned good she looked in it too. the blonde hair was lifted, not into the sculpted pile he recalled from last time but into a soft puffed-out crown, an Edwardian fashion that suited the full skirt. The legs in patterned white stockings were young, the feet in low silver-buckled shoes danced lightly in front of him into the living room. Much tidied up, he noticed. She patted a velvet cushion as she went past towards the drink tray, inviting him to sit.

"Shall we be Spanish and drink sherry? I thought we might go to Walterspiel – you're my guest, naturally. But we've lots of time."

"What does the R stand for? – I've kept wondering."

"Renate." Flashing smile. Charm-school-trained, but fresh as the embroidered, very slightly starched blouse. Lawn, the stuff is called.

It was not the sherry which Uncle Penstemon called 'grocers stuff'. Not perhaps as good as Alberthe de Rubempré had given him (a long time ago, but fresh in his memory this last day or so) in the library of her château. That room had been full of sun-light. And whatever Alberthe's vices, or dottinesses, there had been nothing bourgeois about her. But there wasn't much wrong with the sherry; nor Renate. She was an experienced woman: there was no crude seduction act. She sat down across the room, crossed her legs to show how pretty they were, but who was going to complain about that?

"You see, it isn't just that I want to apologise; bit over hasty, jumping to judgment like that. Made myself unpleasant. My vanity, I suppose, wanting to leave you a better impression. And I've understood more since breakfast this morning – the subject came up!" smiling.

"I've understood a lot more myself." Warily. When they set out to charm, there's something they want. Two hours of time and a good lunch – that is an investment. But nobody had ever seen him as a good investment.

"Well – to get that over with – I was worried, and anxious. You appeared intrusive – but that wasn't your fault." Kein schuld – the phrase had a familiar ring, a resonance, striking a note he couldn't place for the moment . . .

"I'm afraid I'm a professionally nosy person. I have to apologise for that . . . And small things have momentous conse-quences," bringing out this portentous cliché as though he'd just invented it. A couple of drinks, and I'll feel a little less stiff.

"You've heard the men's side of it. Dominic – my husband – let fall . . . he's a very guarded person," laughing. "But he did give you some idea of a long-standing irritation – and worry – that's been nagging him this long while." Fishing a bit; there was a questioning intonation. Professionally prudent even with his wife, the Herr Rechtsanwalt. And I'd better be the same.

"I understood as much."

"There's a woman's angle too. I'm fonder of Birgit than perhaps she realises. Well. I'm saying this badly. You were sen-sitive to her troubles on brief acquaintance – not that I'm going to bore you with mine . . . Another? – I've my little car outside. You can drive me if you prefer: some men feel unhappy being driven by a woman."

"Not me," getting up to fill the glasses. "I still feel a bit pre-occupied. She's being released I gather. Been, perhaps."

"Oh yes, I was talking to the chief of the clinic on the phone, before you came. I don't quite know; the court has to cancel the order, some legal formality, it might take an hour or so longer. But today in any case."

"So she wasn't hooked on anything?"

"Dear me, I didn't realise you knew that."

"I guessed," not to give Rennemann away. "We meet that sort of thing at home too, pretty often."

"Yes of course – only pot I think and however stupid and reck-less that is there could be worse, as I imagine. Maybe she'll be home by the time we're back, if you want to see her again. It is her home after all. I've been here with my apron on, trying to make it a bit nice – sort of welcome, you know? and no rancour – I hope."

What is she getting at? Only a matter of giving herself a good conscience? Is there more? I almost think I'd like to see through to the end of this – since she invites me.

"Anything urgent this afternoon?" she asked idly.

"I'd hardly call them so. I daresay you know all about these conferences. Seminars, and round tables, and a lot of rather inconclusive discussion . . . being too negligent might appear impolite," he added a bit hastily, as a safeguard. She giggled, as though his being just a scrap impolite to a good if pompous soul like Kommissar Schumacher tickled her.

"Get my coat then, shall I? On second thoughts I don't need one – lovely out. Toss up, shall we, who's to drive?" A bit of merriment, and neither of them heard the key in the lock. Perhaps Renate had not quite closed the apartment door. The living room door was open; Birgit walked straight in.

She was dressed as Castang had last seen her, in black trousers and a thin pullover top, but she looked a lot madder. In the English sense, not the American. Maybe he was exaggerat-ing? Dotty? distraught? – or simply that I didn't know her well enough . . . She looked straight through him.

"Hallo, Mum," with a heavy emphasis on the mum bit. She was badly made up, with lipstick running over the edges, and her brown curling hair looking combed with her fingers. Not all that clean either. Renate was wearing quite a lot of perfume, but

76

there was a dusty sweaty look as though she could do with a shower. And the eyes looked funny, or hadn't she been sleeping well?

The two women kissed, Renate as though she'd have made a thing of it, but Birgit was, without exactly pushing her off, perfunctory.

"Don't you recognise your friend Mr. Castang?"

"Yes," said Birgit, with no enthusiasm and she wasn't embarrassed.

She'd a soft squashy handbag under her arm, held as though she'd forgotten it was there. Probably she'd put the overnight bag down in the passage. She looked around the room as though not sure she recognised it.

"I tidied a bit." Renate was embarrassed. "It's so hateful, coming back to a messy house. Uh – I wasn't sure when to expect you. I don't want to be in your way. Mr. Castang and I were just going out.

"Perhaps you'd like to come." Birgit seemed not to have heard. "It wouldn't take you long to change." Birgit responded with a dulled gazing around, oddly stiff as though her neck hurt her.

"What I want is a pee." Loud, dogmatic.

"But don't let us stop you," trilling with unnecessary laughter to cover the small coarseness. "I think I will wear a coat after all, Mr. Castang, in the shade it's not all that –" The coat was over the back on an armchair. He moved with her, grateful for the social mechanism, however trivial: the best place to be was out of here. He picked up the coat and held it for her.

Renate turned in front of him to slip her arms in. Flustered, she showed an uncharacteristic clumsiness.

Clumsiness is contagious, and Castang's left arm at the best wasn't much better than a coathanger. It was all highly un-cop-like.

Birgit's movement was so unexpectedly agile for a start. One moment she was standing there – she hadn't moved since entering the room – like a log washed up on the mud and stuck there. Brought by floodwater, and needing floodwater to carry it away.

She said. "You took my child," in a completely toneless

voice. She had slipped her own bag from under her arm. She took a pistol out and pointed it straight at Renate. "You don't deserve to live anyhow." She fired it; went on firing until the magazine was empty.

Castang had too many thoughts and all confused, and he was tangled with the coat and all he did was trip over himself.

Technically, for a beginning. In any kind of roughhouse and he had known plenty there is only one rule; be it gun, grenade, or flowerpot, be first. Than the Gurkha kukri, than the curare-tipped dart; you must be faster. Over the years he had been quite good at this. He had been, in his younger days, a fair gymnast. In more recent years, had got slower, decidedly. Besides a number of close shaves he had collected two gunshot wounds, the second a really bad one. And contrary to a popular myth the scarred and experienced veteran is not a better soldier than the raw recruit. Collectively he keeps his head down; individually he's likely to be gun shy.

More technicalities. Bloody Birgit hadn't done any of the things that women are popularly supposed to do with guns. She hadn't left the safety catch on, she didn't try consciously to aim the gun, but pointed it as naturally as a finger and fired it in the same movement, which is the right way to hit people with it. It was a small automatic, a six thirty-five probably, the vest pocket kind of model women – years and years ago – used to carry in handbags. Practically an antique nowadays. By terrorist (or police) standards a ridiculous toy. But it kills people for all that. It is smooth all over, snubnose with no barrel or sights. Nothing to catch or snag; it slips straight and easy into the hand. And it's not only small in itself but carries a small cartridge with a tiny charge: the effective range is about eight metres, say twenty-five feet. At a distance of three to four metres it is lethal. There is no noise or kick to frighten the holder. The report is a sharp pop, that of a paper bag blown up and punched.

And if it's an automatic it goes on firing. Things of that calibre are five, maybe six-shot: with a full magazine and one in the breech you can expect that many. It's a lot. Even if two or three miss, which they often do, even at close quarters.

Castang was gun shy as hell. The difference between this and being downright cowardly is small, and tends to be academic.

He shrank in on himself, paralysed and grateful that Renate was standing between him and that damn tiny pistol.

"I have to tell you – don't know how one says this in German but in French we say 'déjà vu'; been-here-before. The ghost of Alberthe de Rubempré. I don't mean she's a ghost. She's alive and well, I hope. I haven't laid eyes on her since. There was never any trial. They took her off – do I say 'too', 'also'? – for temporary insanity.

"Alberthe killed a man before my eyes in exactly the same way. Practically with the same gestures, taking a gun out of her bag I never knew she had. I was behind her then. I didn't intervene then either. The fellow – oh well. Waste no time with justice but he was no great loss. Anyhow; my instincts, my reactions, my thinking were altogether different at that moment. I make progress, huh?

"Alberthe – she's been following me around. She's been omnipresent. I came over here, well, that was in Baden-Baden, miles away but you know what I mean. It seemed necessary then as well as clever. Terrorists? – tchatch, I know nothing about them. I did wrong, and I couldn't get rid of Alberthe. Patterns; you can't get rid of the past, you can't snip an episode off like the cutter in a movie, it's there even when it's gone, the past is the future, and this . . .

"I'm talking so much I must be bloody shocked. No I don't want any stinking pills, tell the shrink to eat them. Give me another drink, yes, of course I'll get pissed on an empty stomach, I was diddled of lunch in Walterspiel, no well, I won't get pissed of course. One doesn't.

"Poor Renate. A calibre that size doesn't knock you off your feet of course but like a hell of a punch in the midriff, she must have taken two or three. Two? Will they save her? The resuscitation team they have now on the fast ambulance is marvellous, no other word for it. Right, I know something about that, the equipment, the techniques: still, it's the people they have, in the long run. All the way round, people count. Not their stupid fucking technology they keep boasting about. You don't ask the computer how to cope with cardiac collapse. Nor bullets in your belly neither.

"She had her arms out for the coat, and she clasped her hands together and tucked her elbows in – I half fell over her. Birgit didn't do anything, just stood there stunned with the thing in her hand. You've the tape running, I suppose? She looked at me, rather a nice expression, I'd call it kindly, and she said. 'Her death wasn't your fault.' Kein schuld . . . it's a phrase that's been following me around.

"No no, I'm not saying anything like that, merci, I'm not any sort of expert and I've no opinions. State of mind isn't my pigeon. Any more than it was with Alberthe. There are men who get intoxicated with violence, right, it's a drug readily available anywhere without prescription, you can pour it straight in, main line, into the vein. Like any other drug it gives euphoria. Bang him down, smash him, give him the business, kick his face in, he's a Baddy, he's got it coming, bash him before he bashes you.

"But a woman? – no, I don't believe it. If she was high on some speed pill or worse then yes. Otherwise insanity every time. I don't accept that a woman finds violence natural to her. Against her biology, her psychology, everything. Physically and metaphysically she has to do herself extreme violence before she'll use it.

"Birgit – her behaviour was very odd; I thought she might have been excitable there in the clinic and they'd given her a shot of some tranquilliser, maybe over heavy but people show funny side-effects now 'n' again. But a section sixtyfour whatever you call that here.

"I don't know exactly what my words were. 'You daft cow' – I really meant it literally. Put her in the bin on a slightly cooked pretext, and she turns round and gives you a real cause, no kidding, straight up the arse.

"I'm sorry. I just don't seem to stop talking, do I? I went for that phone to call the ambulance rather faster than I've moved since getting here – I've told you all this. First aid, there isn't any for a gut shot, haemorrhage is internal, you don't even move them. And I thought then to phone you. Birgit sat down good as gold when I told her to. Keeping the gun on her lap like a dolly. Give me some more whisky. Where's my wife?"

"Waiting for you," said Herr Pohl, tranquilly.

*   *   *

80

"When you didn't come back from lunch," said Geoffrey Dawson, "I naturally thought you'd been carried away by a tall blonde."

"Geoffrey!" said Vera.

"Well, I didn't know about Renate. Lunch in Walterspiel – pity you missed it."

"I have a good idea," said Vera. "We'll go there for dinner, shall we, and get rather pissed?"

"I'm pissed right now."

"And I'd intended to draw a veil across that."

We didn't, in fact, Vera reflected. We had a sausage instead. We didn't really have enough money left. Geoffrey helped me put Henri in bed, in his rather grand room in the Bayerische Hof, which was paid for anyhow. He had a sleep, and woke up starving. We had a nice evening. Geoffrey had saved some money, and wanted to buy his wife a dirndl, and asked me to come and help. I bought a rather nice apron, and some bedclothes for Lydia with horses on; she loves horses.

Why is one so touristy? I'd like one of those lovely suits for Henri. I saw a nice one, a lovely soft olive green with silver embroidery, no suède to get rubbed, really good wool all the way through. But when would he wear it? he says, and he's right. The men get drunk and exaggerate. I'm not drunk. I don't really get drunk, I think I've hollow bones. Actually one doesn't, because of having Lydia by one. Not that Geoffrey would try to make love or anything: he is gentlemanly in a way I thought no longer existed. I can hardly say as much for Bobby Bonacorsi. But he just accepts things the way they are. Very realist, those Venetians. "She doesn't . . ." and he is intelligent, and sensitive, and sheer Nice enough not stupidly vaniteusement to play macho: he is both terribly macho and not in the least and work that out and thanks, we get on fine.

We have been invited to come and stay in Venezia. I will draw and draw and draw. there is a smell, and the Adriatic is dead. But one must. It is dead, but so is all Europe. Simply in Venezia one notices it first. Geoffrey keeps saying England is dead. Oh dear – well, I've said come and borrow the cottage.

Alberthe . . . Henri got so worked up I think he forgot I was there, I saw it, I know her. He did *not* take her to bed. I do also

81

have a firm conviction, even after a gluttonous lunch in Walterspiel and about three bottles, he wouldn't have taken Renate to bed even if she'd been rather subtle about it. He is the world's greatest pest and fraud. But after thirty years faking, he understands how to take responsibility. Bless him. When you can handle women you can handle anything.

I've a pair of those waitress' boots: to wear in the kitchen and remind me of what was once my home. I'm glad we came.

The train, going home. For me, a wonderful enrichissement, a magnificent holiday. I have seen superb pictures, a superb town. I rather like the Feldherrnhalle. It is so beautiful, it has survived all that war, those stupid Feldmarschallen, those appalling generals, Tilly and Wallenstein . . . And the SS. People say the most awful things about the Herr Minister-President: Geoffrey Dawson was rather cutting, Bobby Bonacorsi downright crude, that elderly Scots gentleman whose name I have forgotten was quiet and sensible and had real penetration, it seems to me. The English have that woman who is their Minister-President. They have a lot of rather sour jokes in consequence, about Bayern, about Land-Of-Hope-And-Glory, about Military Glory and ReCapturing las Islas Malvinas, about SS-in-a-skirt. I don't have any opinions about this. Zal wel wijzer zijn, as they say in Flanders. She won't last forever: the English are frightful isolationists but they have so much sense.

We are alone, in this compartment. Lydia is asleep, not snoring. Henri is asleep, snoring. I'm awake. I've stayed awake, to see France. That, for better-for-worse and very much for worse ninety per cent of the time, God help me, is my country now. So I've been looking out, ever since showing the passports and whatnot, at the border in Kehl, for the first signs of home.

Alsace isn't France. They don't know, there, which way they're pointing, but since the beginning of time (kissing the Romans' arse) they've always been the same.

There are the Vosges. Tears come in my eyes a bit and how bloody stupid. I'm Czech, and will I be anything else? But with God's help one leaps over the wall.

There they are, in a line ahead, Geoffrey Dawson gave me a

lecture, about Matthew Arnold – who the hell is he? One more
again of those lousy cockass Victorian poets who suddenly got
it right in one perfect line like a line by Georges Braque, by
Giotto, by Vermeer, by those horrible South German wonderful painters I've been looking at in Munich. It explains all of
England. Quack, quack quack, the unplumbed, salt, estranging
sea. Estranging . . . And to that I add the line from the Big
Sleep.

The solid, uneven, comfortable line of the foothills. The
Santa Monica Range? No: the Vosges . . .

Part Two

'By the Brook'

Autumn ended, and police routines continued, with a series of long-drawn-out extended chords. People met one another on the street and uttered words of wisdom such as "The days are drawing in, aren't they", greeted with much sage nodding.

Nothing much happened. Prices rose, and so did unemployment. the balance of payments got worse. Politicians mouthed quite a lot, because elections of some kind were in the offing; but then they always do; they always are.

There was no call for Capablanca. For the Police Judiciaire, beautiful creepy remorseless chess was right out, but so thank God was scrambling around in the pitch dark barking one's shins on the same piece of furniture which had somehow got itself into both ends of the room at the same time; probability-defying, metaphysical, and most unfair of it.

The weather stayed serene; still and sunny. The difference was that half the time you didn't see the sun because of fog.

Castang went to the office, where Commissaire Richard behaved as though he had never been away. After a talk, of a boring nature, about work following the same paths, Richard did at last utter, "Munich," before falling into one of his comatose states.

"Produces beer in large amounts," said Castang, to be helpful.

Richard seemed to be thinking about this: like a good policeman he offered at last a deduction.

"Consequently urine in large amounts."

"That is correct. There is likewise Siemens, the Bayerische. Motoren Werke. Art galleries. Publishers . . . Policemen." But Richard had apparently learned all he had wished, about

Munich. Just as well: Castang had decided to volunteer no information about extra-curricular doings; least of all to say anything about Alberthe de Rubempré. Should Richard decide to go to Germany for any reason, and perhaps learn that he too attracted agitation on account of a black mark with the computer in Wiesbaden, no doubt it would gather his wits together, a thing he was always telling others to do.

As mentioned, work was as usual. In the doings of the Police Judiciaire is not much novelty, less excitement. Particular kinds of criminal or anti-social behaviour become more fashionable: as a rule one notices this a year later, when it has become a statistic.

"Let's go and see Roger," said Vera giving the French pronunciation to the name. This singling of a particular Roger, as though they were acquainted with a dozen, is quite unnecessary but is part of the personage, who is and remains very English in looks, voice, and behaviour in spite of (in cases like this it is more generally because of) having lived for many years in France. More English still is the fact that his name is not Roger at all but William, and as William Riderhood he is a passably well known name in the catalogues of English-language prose fiction. He gains, he says, a living by the sweat of his brow. He would always be called Roger, and as frequently, by editors and such critics as have heard of Dickens, Rogue. To complete the picture he lives by the river, mourning the fact that he has no sluice nor lock to drown people in (editors or critics for preference).

Castang thinks that he does know two or three more Rogers and can call as many more to mind. But these are not friends. He and Vera have few friends. The reason is simple and was put succinctly by the poet Georges Brassens.

'Mais les Braves Gens n'aiment pas que

L'on suit un autre chemin que eux' . . .

'If you choose a different way

All Nice Folks you shall dismay.'

Which, both as a private person and also as a police official, is exactly what he does.

Roger and his wife have no greater number of friends than

they. Large quantities of writers live in both England and France: he chooses to know none of them and it's a very dubious proposition, he says, whether any of them would want to know him. His books sell well; he is well off; in the literary circles, however, of Paris or London he is by many heartily disliked and possibly even hated. He is, upon occasion, and himself admits as much, abominably rude.

They do not see one another often. One reason for this is that Roger lives quite far away.

The geography of the district should be explained. The provincial services of the Police Judiciaire hold sway over large, ill-defined areas separated, for administrative convenience, into lumps that may include three or four 'départements' but that cut across the traditional frontiers of the old provinces. Richard's and Castang's area is large and oddly shaped for much of it is mountainous, infertile, and thinly populated. Its biggest river, running roughly from south to north hereabouts, is torrential and eccentric in the massif, wandering among the foothills, traverses Castang's city at the juncture with the plain (from which point it was navigable in former times to smallish craft and shallow-draught barges) and gathers importance as it progresses, until it disappears over Castang's horizon, to become one of the major rivers of Europe but that is the concern of other PJ 'regions'.

A hundred kilometres beyond the city, over an hour by car, it is a broad and powerful stream traversing flattish, fertile grassland. It is a purely English joke to refer to it as Roger does as 'the brook'.

It can be formidable: at the melting of the snows in the massif, and at all times after the heavy rains that in southern and central France alternate with prolonged dry spells, it floods with great suddenness.

This does not worry Roger. The barges that brought wine down from the foothills (still do to some extent) tied up for the night at the bank that is now his; brought blocks of stone from the hillside quarries, revetted the bank. There was a quay then, a trading post: the river however uncertain in its ways made for easier communications than the muddy rutted roads of the time. The quay has gone, and so has the manorial right of the local

robber baron to levy tolls and make a general nuisance of himself. The 'château' has gone, the local town once thriving has
decayed to a little marketplace of two or three thousand souls.
It supplies his needs; one can drive to the city for any more
sophisticated want; even to Paris, double the distance north-
ward.

Where the quay stood is now levelled and terraced: a large
and beautiful garden, or would be. It takes much too much
labour and is mostly overgrown. The present house is post-
revolution, smallish and unpretentious in an honest and simple
style: modern additions make it appear lower and more rambling. It is damp, which Roger says he rather likes despite much
complaining about rheumatism (he is self-indulgent towards
English eccentricities) and trees that have grown up too close to
the house and which he refuses to cut down. The house has an
unpronounceable name in the local patois – not the Jolly
Bargemen; that's the neighbouring pub. 'Seekings' Roger calls
it, after John Masefield, for, "in that house I spent my
childhood", and sometimes 'Stinkings'.

Of Roger's wife more anon. He refuses to answer the
telephone so she, patient, does this for him: if she's not there it
doesn't get answered. She was there; told Vera they would be
mightily welcome, that she would get something for dinner, that
Roger was in a bad mood but would cheer up on seeing
them.

There has been a long dry spell this autumn and there is no
flood. The far bank, across from Roger, floods so often that
nobody builds there and the farmer who owns the fields does
nothing much with them. Pasture, trees, tatty hedges stretch
away in an unspectacular but quite sightly view to low hills on
the horizon westward, where there are nice sunsets visible from
the riverside terrace, "when it isn't raining which is never" –
nonsense of course and typical-Roger; but it is true that there is
no shelter from the prevailing wind. Sunsets are luxuries and
must be bought.

They parked the car behind the house. It has no front door,
because the rooms inside have often changed their function.
There are no servants nowadays: even if one could pay their
wages one would break one's neck on the social-security con-

tributions, and much as though Roger would like a devoted-elderly-couple of faithful-retainers (he is a dreadful old fascist) Marlene has to make do with a cleaning woman who bicycles up from the village when the spirit moves her.

Her name really is Marlene. She was born in the Thames Valley, so that local damps and rheumatisms do not affect her beyond measure, at a time when girls were quite often christened Marlene. Her second name is Philippa, which mysteriously does not translate in the feminine into French, and her third name is Victoria, for her father was patriotic, with an attachment to the Hanoverian royal family. Roger calls her Madame Victoire. Louis Quinze had a plain, dowdy and obscure daughter of this name. Another English joke since Marlene is tall, statuesque, splendid.

She met them in the *entrée*: it isn't a hall, it's the kitchen nowadays, with an odd shape that allows it to be dining-room too; a meeting-place of most of the other rooms, the beginning of the staircase going upstairs and another down to the cellars, and still leave corners for muddy boots, damp umbrellas and Castang's hats. Tools that have no business here lie about; nothing that is wanted can ever be found; rubbish everywhere and dishevelment. Vera likes this house and so does Castang. It is too a writer's house and books hang about in every corner of it.

"Hi there – how goes?" says Vera. It has been some months since they saw one another.

"Just what I needed – la joie de vivre," Marlene answered. The two women do not kiss. Frenchwomen generally do, but they both incline to reserve. Castang kisses her and says. "Short on joy, then?"

"Oh – you know – a bit dull, a bit monotonous."

"What, with Roger around?" He finds her face thin. Pinched? Hollow? No; a bit drawn. "Aha, the pale and haughty beauty."

"Never haughty!" Plain truth; Marlene is a simple direct person and one teases her a little: he is fond of her. "Is it warm enough in here? Roger goes about turning all the thermostats down, except in his own room of course. I'm freezing. What would you like to drink? Tell me all the scandals of the big city."

Vera has noticed it too. Her eye is better than Castang's (he admits); her ear, she claims, no worse. Not very like Marlene to complain. And that slightly jerky voice. But she beams at them happily; she has a lovely smile.

"I can't imagine where he is, but it's lovely to have you to myself for a little." She pours in drinks, comes to sit beside Vera, touches her arm with an affection as straight and simple as a dog's. Vera cannot bear being 'fingered' but feels no dislike when Marlene does it. "We're going to have a lovely evening: I only hope I haven't made a balls of the dinner. Do Roger good too; he's been in a nagging mood all day. Let's drink a lot, shall we?" And indeed she has finished her first already. Pooh, thinks Vera who isn't averse to a drink either, stop picking at people. The woman hasn't seen anyone in too long; that's all. Castang is already slumped, content, upon the big shabby English sofa, playing with the dog. "Good ol' boy then. Bouh, you stink."

"He doesn't – he's just wet!" says Marlene indignantly. He grins at her.

"Ho." Roger who has been roaming aimlessly about arrives simultaneous, or nearly. "Has Lady Rachel Rougedragon bid you welcome?"

"Who?"

"He's been reading again," said Marlene in the slightly shamefaced tone used when speaking of deplorable behaviour in close relations: tolerance under strain. Goodness knows we try, but no one can stop Uncle George flashing at the village girls.

"What is it?" asked Vera, curious. Her friendship with Roger was comforted and stimulated by her quarryings in Eng. Lit., and his house was her best source for greedy indulgences, as it might have been playing bridge or eating cake. Castang would not say, 'Reading again', though often tempted to when he came home hungry. 'I've forgotten to put the potatoes on', guiltily dropping Anthony Trollope on the floor.

"She's a prissy old Jacobite lady in exile in France, in some slight demand for the chaperonage of young ladies. Preposterously named even for Sir Walter, sharing the pages with a Redgauntlet and a Greenmantle, thereby I presume stimulating the imagination of Buchan, who turned her into a Femme Fatale off the Orient Express." This literary explanation, Chinese to the police judiciaire, was satisfactory to Vera.

Roger was fifty-odd, a tallish man who had been slim when young, now florid in the face and with a considerable bow window to the figure, attributable to drink. In Mitfordese a fat fair, with that droopy corncoloured hair that whether cut short or long looks always awful. With little to boast about in the physique he boasted that he was neither grey nor bald: Marlene retorted tartly that either or even both might look better than the reality, compared unkindly to steamed ginger pudding with sticky custard poured over it. An unexportable English simile, Chinese even to Vera.

"Come into the parloir and have a drink." The living room thus named was as English as its squire; full of shapeless lumpy sofas covered in dingy chintz, found comfortable by the dog. Like every room in this house, lined with shelves filled with books. Roger specialised in what he called unreadable-books. His collection of the forgotten famous, 'lions invited to dinner by Lady Cunard', was remarkable.

"A corrective to vanity. Curative and carminative properties." "What was carminative?" asked Vera.

"Medicinal device for getting rid of wind. You belch, or fart, as the case may be." When in the house she was to be found sitting on her heels, from which she found it very hard to get up, with three or four books on the floor beside her, 'dipping into Hugh Walpole', and doubtless testing the medicinal effects.

"I've reached page hundred and nineteen of Hutchinson's *If Winter Comes*," after four or five visits.

"Get out, you smelly beast." Roger was as fond of the dog as Marlene was, but 'did it to pester her'. "They sit for hours staring at each other," she explained: "that dog writes all his books".

"Rather nasty Rioja? Tastes better in England. Why? – something they do with the air here. Water too. Tea from Fortnums, vast expense; tastes vile, great deception." Roger had mastered the art of the English living in France, which is to flatter all national vanities by unqualified abuse of everything both English and French. Objects neither German nor Italian found no favour; they come to pieces in your hand the first day. It went without saying that nothing fabricated in Japan, Taiwan nor Hong Kong was permitted. If told how inconsistent he fluffed up his feathers and flounced: why was consistency thought a virtue? – the refuge of bores, as patriotism of scoundrels.

Castang could maintain friendship with him because, said Roger, he's had the sense never to have read any of my books.

On the bookshelves hereabouts in a silver frame was a frightful photograph of Roger, drunk in a dinnerjacket, some years back – ah, that illspent youth – being crowned with Hawthornden or James Tait Black: some such literary custard.

"The only literary prize worth having is the Timothy Whites and Taylor. I've a Medicis-Etranger; very low in social standing."

There was also a photograph of Marlene, young and beautiful, in a ball frock cut very low, with camellias in her hair, known as Miss-Wienerwald-of-1931, of which portrait and appelation she was majestically tolerant.

She was a tall woman, as tall as Roger. Gone a bit hippy and bosomy from childbearing, but being tall carries it well. Has still long and magnificent legs, the ankles of a girl of nineteen, a most lovely walk. Has been a lovely dancer and perhaps still is. It is her great grievance that Roger in all these years has never once danced with her. She has two considerable burdens.

They talked about this while driving home. Vera said that the first burden is that of every woman whose man works at home. Musicians at least go out sometimes to concerts or whatnot even if all that tootle has to be soundproofed. But preserve us from painters and writers. No office to go to, the whole house has to be built around them, and worst of all is this permanent presence. There is nothing the woman can call her own. They think everything is permitted them: they lift the lids of your pots to criticise the food; they stroll into the bathroom and criticise your underclothes, or would if you didn't lock it, and then complain of that; they nag about noises from the washing-machine and the vacuum-cleaner though if there's a speck of dust or a shortage of socks oh, the hullaballoo; and then just as you sit after a damned hard day they come complacently boasting of how hard they've worked and say Oh, there's that agony in my back again, just massage that for me.

The second, as defined by Castang, is that Marlene has no brains at all. It is not easy to get this into correct proportion when one has oneself this terrifying bluestocking wife who reads and draws and all, because one can't compete with that amount of intellect but one must admit, Vicky is pretty dense. Okay, Roger is bright enough for two, she doesn't need to be bright, and she has qualities that are far more precious. If there's far too much stupidity in the world it's dead sure there's too much bloody intellect and the source of the more barbarous stupidities if you ask me, especially in France where being bright is so admired: the English have more sense.

"You're rambling."

"Yes. Good, she's kind, patient, sensitive and generous, besides looking good with a camellia above each ear. She must have a sense of humour to have married Roger, but one's never seen any sign of it. She's never been known to open a book."

"You mustn't take Roger seriously – less still, literally."

"Accepted. Good, it's sensible not to compete with the two of you. Hm, she's an excellent homemaker but is bored stiff by housekeeping and has no real outlet now that the children are grown up; always a dangerous situation. Even if she wanted one she can't take a lover because where would she find one? The old pasha keeps her in that cart rut all the time; she can choose between the dog and her horse. There's the gardener of course . . ."

"Stop being frivolous, this is serious."

"There are things wrong there. The jokes are getting edgy."

"Yes. Don't drive so fast; you've had a lot to drink."

"Yes. Say this for Roger, you don't get offered gin." (Castang had a well-developed taste for single-malt whisky.) "How far are you with *If Winter Comes*?"

"Page hundred and forty three: there's enough for another five years."

*   *

The doorbell rang.

Vera lived in a cottage. There are still cottages left, in odd corners of the outer suburbs where traces of village remain, obstinately clung to by old people who could remember when fields stood, here. They had bought it when the old woman who lived here died at last: tiny and tumbledown as it had been it was still very expensive, because of the rank neglected orchard behind – building land. Richard had fiddled it for them.

On the street side was a strong fence with a gate, and Castang insisted that she look, always, before pressing the release button. She did look: it was Marlene, in a raincoat and a silk square over her hair. The dog made a racket so she shut him in the kitchen where Lydia was playing on the floor; they could lick each other as unhygienically as they wished.

She liked Marlene. Castang saying she had no brains; a typically French remark, half right and more than half wrong. As though brains were important, as though one needed brains to think with! Herself she had her fair share, and rather despised them. Overestimated possession! Marlene had plenty anyhow, even if they weren't the French kind: a Czech woman could get on with them. She didn't know why Marlene had come (Marlene likely didn't know either). Did one need reasons then for doing things? Like the police?

Occasionally they had cups of coffee in the town together. The odd bit of shopping; trivial, leisurely, agreeable. Being female. Once or twice they had been to the cinema together. Vera would far rather have gone on her own (loathed sharing this type of experience with anyone); did not complain.

Vera made some coffee she didn't really want. Things stood about rather: it was a furniture-polishing day. She would have preferred to get it done with, and then go and draw, rather than listen to Marlene talk about furniture polish. But talking English was good practice. And she liked the woman! A straight person, a person with honour. It was what she hated most, in the world around her: from kings and ministers down there was so little. You didn't have to see or hear it – as Castang said you could smell it. Marlene smelt of rain, and her very well-chosen perfume (beastly scent manufacturers, if by any chance they find a good one they instantly stop making it), and expensive clothes well-worn (in both senses) and healthy woman who takes a lot of exercise. Her boots could do with a lick of polish. If Castang had been there he probably would have said, "Take them off and I'll do them for you" –a shoe-polish maniac, or do I mean fetishist?

"I do so like your house, always."

"The way I always like yours."

"Yes, I suppose I'm a country woman really, I'd never want whole-heart to live in a town even if I were stinky rich."

"I was too but never got given the choice. Don't marry policemen!"

Vera's father had been village municipal secretary, and agricultural every moment he got; her grandparents peasants both sides. Marlene's father had been a Royal Navy quarter-master: married late, retired early: she'd still been small when he got a lock-keeper's job. Next best thing to having a lock of your own, had said 'Rogue Riderhood', is to marry the lock-keeper's daughter. Marlene was still very handy in a boat, and swam like a seal.

She seemed absent-minded today, and nervous. Talked too much and was unusually disjointed. As Castang had remarked, there was something wrong there. But one could not interfere. Any more than the police – one had to stand in the street and wonder what went on behind those walls.

The weather broke that evening, in earnest. Just to show what it could do. For a month past the subdued but gleeful voices of National Meteorology had announced the death of sunlight and its imminent burial under Depressions off Finisterre, and obediently a mild westerly would bring a nice shower, lay-ing the dust and setting sparkles on Vera's dahlias, which went on and on blooming gladdening her heart. And invariably an anticyclone which the good souls had quite failed to notice (obsessed no doubt with meteors) chased the rain away: a com-placent sun reappeared beaming foolishly. Just as everybody decided that this would go on for ever the tempest arrived from a totally illogical direction in the south east. The meteor-man, announcing moderate to strong winds in the Gulf of Gascony as though reading figures off a gas-meter, was busted flat by a typhoon but nobody found leisure for sniggers because the whole of France was busted. The fire brigade, barely recovered from saving forests, got no sleep at all for several nights; the gendarmerie and the army rushed about with helicopters, rubber rafts chugged along main roads, cars were discovered upside-down a mile from where they had been parked, bridge-builders were in frenzied demand and the police judiciaire was in no demand at all. Nothing like the violence of nature to put the violence of out-of-work teenagers into proper proportion. Insurance companies talked very big about acts-of-God and the meteor men, abruptly demoted from divine status, made scuttling noises like mice in a wainscot. And for three whole days not a single minister found breath for making speeches.

Castang, with a rope round him and the other end round the chimney, frightened Vera by climbing all over the roof. Suppose the chimney gave way. As long as she only had dahlias to mourn for . . .

Placidity restored, flooded gumboots left steaming gently behind the kitchen stove, broken branches and (other peoples') rooftiles cleared off the street, Castang went back to work. There was as much paper as usual, even if there had been no crime, but at least it was dry. A holocaust of telephone lines, of junction boxes and buried cables made it unlikely that the telephone would ring, but ring it did.

"Castang," said a very loud voice in his ear. "This is Riderhood." He was going to think up a joke – there were few fresh ones left by then but the dead silence that followed stopped him.

"You still there?"

"Yes," said the voice at last. "And I need you."

Now the phone had gone dead. He tried ringing back, and a recorded voice said no calls could be taken in the sector.

What does need mean? A helping hand because a lot of tiles came off the roof? Some of those big trees ominously close to the house might have been shaky. Need a friend? He could readily imagine Roger being troubled by officialdom, and a friendly official might do him a good turn. Surely it wasn't a cop he needed: be it damage or pillage the appearance of a PJ-somebody would not sit well with the gendarmerie, with whom Roger would be well advised to pick no quarrels.

Maddening not to be able to find out. This word need . . . whatever it was it had to be taken seriously.

It isn't all that easy, reflected Castang. Someone rings up to say Mayday, but I'm not a lifeboat, I can't just drop it all and scoot out. There's an intervention brigade, and the criminal brigade. They do, but since the bum arm came my way scooting is no longer my scene. I am supposed to be in charge here of routines, details, coordinations, organising where need be; stuff that Richard cannot, should not, and in any event wont get himself clogged up with and tied down by. This everybody relies upon. He got me this job, where I would in most departments have got a small wound pension, a wooden medal, and work in the prefecture looking after aliens' visas . . . PJ work, however deskbound, would not have been considered.

Roger is a friend, and I have not that many. And if he's relying on me . . . excitable and neurotic he may be but he wouldn't ring me at the office for an electricity cut. Richard is a friend, and the best there is . . . outside the office. One can only go and see: nothing wrong I know of with the internal phones.

"Fausta, is the Divisionnaire visible?" Reassurance, in rose-petal tones: the head of the department is in a good frame of mind. He listened to Castang quietly.

"If I got a call like that . . . I think I'd want to go see. And there's nothing much on anyhow. If it were business of ours, would he say so?"

"He might not have had the chance; line went dead."

"Go and look."

The roads were passable, by this time. That particular road may be wider and better cambered and whatever, but it follows the same trace as under Good King Thingummy, and the people round here know about this river. It does this on a minor scale every three-four years. This bad, maybe every seventy. They just didn't build down there on the low bank. Roger's bank is higher but – well, they'd brought those huge stones specially cut, with great labour, precisely because they didn't want the bank to wash away at that spot in a bad flood: too much valuable stuff stored there. They knew what they were doing. He should be safe enough.

That river was quite something. Sheet of water a kilometre

wide in the valley. Wouldn't like to guess how many dead animals and tree-trunks are in there right now. And houses – in recent years dishonest promoters have sold quantities of building plots on unsafe ground outside the city. Poor wretches, on lifelong mortgages. Better you lose everything, mate, because the Bank won't lose sight nor hold of your ass. Water may flood riverside houses, but credit bank basements are aflood only with promissory notes.

He stopped three or four times to ask about things he saw. Lot of autos still to be hauled out of ditches; heavier stuff too.

Tcha, there didn't look to be much wrong with Roger's house. Couple of trees down but not dangerously. Make winter firewood for him. Some of these storms, better foresters than you'd guess, fetch things down that look safe and aren't.

Roger met him at the entry. One look sufficed – he'd been right to come.

"Marlene, who was so alive. Gone. Dead."

Drunk of course and in shock. If not technically hallucinating what odds does that make? Wild confused drunken stories making no sense at all. He'd been wandering about not knowing what hit him the whole night, half the morning, maybe longer. The house was a pig sty, as bad as though the flood had hit it. He'd broken things, thrown things about, in a frenzy of misery and fear and self-accusation. It wasn't the police he needed; it was a doctor first. It wouldn't be at all easy to get hold of a doctor: Castang would be his own; trust to common sense, experience, and a bit of luck. Try first to get one or two tiny islands of fact and certainty.

"How d'you know she's dead? Where is she? Gone where?" The river of course: only place she could be. He searched the house carefully, and the garden too. Can't rely on a word this fellow says. Her car was there. Her horse was there – suffering; he gave it food and water. When had this happened?

"Roger . . . Roger, listen to me . . . Look, I'm asking for no more than a moment's effort."

"I've done nothing but make efforts." And, no doubt, it was true.

"This is the last. I'm here, I'll look after you, I'll look after

97

everything. You let go then and rest."

"Can't rest."

"You will. I want a second of coherence. Has anybody been here?"

"Me. That's already too much."

"You called anyone? Bar me."

"Phone didn't work."

Has he already forgotten that he called me? The phone might have worked awhile before falling again into inconsequent silence; a thing that did happen. And not only to phone lines.

"Try and think back. Did you call anybody else? The gendarmerie? A doctor?"

"What good would they be?"

An open question. It could be checked. It was likely that he hadn't, for however overworked they would certainly have made an answer, and rather sooner than later they would have come. Even if they concluded upon a drunken fantasy. A crisis of this kind, breaking up the house, quite likely to set the place afire – they'd have taken Roger away.

One thing was for sure: Marlene had disappeared. Assume for a moment they'd had a row, a violent quarrel (Roger didn't have to be the only person to break things up) and she had stormed out in rage. i) she hadn't taken a car. ii) if she had packed anything it would be noticeable. iii) where would she have gone to? iv) Roger's confusion and instability was full, as always with people of his sort, of dramatisations and self pity, conscious or unconscious lies. As a witness he's worse than useless. I must get him settled, and rely upon observation.

"Come on, old chap, I'll put you to bed."

"No."

"Don't fuck about; you know it's the only thing for you. Upsadaisy."

"No . . . the bed's too empty. I'll keep waking up." And that, Castang could see, was perfectly true. Better; genuine.

"Right, I'll make up the divan for you in your workroom. You'll feel better there." It was no use to frig about over detail. Suitable pills of some sort there might be in the bathroom cupboard but the man was soaked in alcohol and there's nothing worse than mixing pills of any sort with whisky. A tisane-and-hotwater-bottle routine might help a little later if he doesn't sleep at once.

He was shivering violently in the last stages of physical fatigue as well as a fairly advanced level of nervous depression. But he submitted quietly to being undressed: lead heavy, but he didn't struggle or shout or fight: Castang had known worse patients.

The bed in the bedroom was unslept-in. Neatly made up as Marlene had left it. How long ago? The storm had lasted forty eight hours.

The dog was shut in the kitchen: its yelping and scratching had been driving him bats. It had of course shit all over the shop in its misery. Nice job for the police. It refused food but drank water. He shook up its blanket and coaxed it but it refused to lie down. He let it out – perhaps this would show where Marlene had gone. It brought him down to the river where it wandered about aimlessly, whimpering. Seeing the incredible amount of rain that had fallen, and the wind still high on the third day, there could be no question of scent: this was confused instinct. But it did look, indeed, as though the river was the answer. For that, one would have to wait until Roger had recovered. It was possible to think of a number of explanations. They had a little boat – it wasn't visible but was probably in the boathouse, a wooden shed with no window and a padlocked door and showing no signs of breakage. He followed the dog but its snifflings and searchings obeyed no pattern that he could see. Marlene was gone and the dog was unhappy. An animal sensitive rather than intelligent – that, at least, made a pattern that he might do well to try to follow.

Look, whatever this looks like – it doesn't 'look' like anything at all in any certain term – the simplest explanation is the last one thought of.

They have a row, a yelling row such as all couples have; he had such himself. Marlene bangs out into the storm, realises she's not going to get far in this, goes down to the village. Takes shelter with her cleaning-woman. Perfectly reasonable; many if not most housewives have a good and genuine friendship with their Putzfrau.

99

It's very easily checked. No need to start the villagers talking. Or not yet . . .

And in that case, she would shortly be home, ashamed at the outburst.

Castang didn't really believe in this drama. Roger's drinking bout, the busting up of things – he's a writer and exaggerates everything: even calling that a over-simple generalisation it would still be accountable in terms of temperament, temper, whisky, and plain profound unhappiness.

Castang did not want to muck about in that horrible squalid living-room. Having cleaned up the dogshit (if he had thereby obliterated valuable clues too bloody bad) he could sit in the kitchen and like it. Have a drink; have something to eat.

The electricity was still cut, might have been out all this time. More likely repaired and fallen out afresh – like the phone? It didn't matter. The fridge contained food – and beer – that had not gone rotten. It didn't look as though Roger had eaten anything: the place looked clean and tidy, as Marlene had – as always – left it. Roger, perfectly able to put his hand to housekeeping, could have cleaned up himself. Not when that drunk, though. One could see where he had sat for a long while, and passed out too, in the living room, in a litter of cigarette ash and smeared glasses – drunk a bottle of wine alone and then started on whisky . . .

If Marlene is dead, and in the river, that body will turn up directly the flood goes down, if it hasn't already. And that's police business. A storm plus flood this bad will always produce two or three deaths and as many disappearances, and it takes a week to knit the ends together. Normal routines, including those of medical-legal nature, get dislocated for a hundred miles and more around. A body might be washed that far downstream; the flood current has immense power. Or it might be washed out into some field or haystack where it wouldn't be found for a week.

But what would Marlene be doing by the river bank in a wind gusting up to a hundred and fifty kilometres an hour? She had lived by rivers all her life. And even though that type of semitropical storm is not seen in the Thames Valley she had lived here long enough to know about them – they can happen all over France, not necessarily of this nature, but with the same intense credulity-stretching suddenness and violence. It can be a tornado, it can be rain, it can be hail, but she was an adult sensible woman and not one to do foolish things.

A cop knows that the most sensible people can do foolish things, and sometimes fatal things . . .

Castang sat in the kitchen with the dog for company. The animal was as nerve-racked and fatigued as the master and, like him, consented at last to curl up on the blanket and sleep; reassured by a friend's quiet company. Placidity relative, he thought. He drank a bottle of beer. Long time since he'd done 'an investigation'. Criminal investigation? Well, some kinds of violence are obvious pointers. Find somebody bashed in with the blunt instrument, shredded by shotgun pellets, massively disrupted by explosives; you can reasonably conclude upon a criminal intent: the victim might not be the one intended but that is a different question. But if somebody has fallen from a high window . . .

He didn't even carry a scribbling pad nowadays: like a gun it was a thing he had learned to do without. He had a small memory-notebook, useless for the purpose. He got up and went into the living room, wrinkling his nose at the foul smell. The wind was dying; he opened a window and left it open. There was a lot of stuff in here that might interest police technicians from Identité Judiciaire eventually . . . what did that mean? In the event of what? Of a certain chain of reasoning showing as a probability? A possibility it is, right now. Mm, the police frequently break laws in their zeal for procedural rules.

There was a writing desk; he pulled open drawers, finding the usual débris of letters and household accounts. And a gun; the usual, a Luger – what was it about that damned thing that attracted people so fatally – the design? Well, some guns are works of art, but lying around the artistic ones are as likely to cause crimes as any other. He broke it open. Sten gun ammunition of English wartime issue: only two. It had not been fired recently, nor, probably, at all for many years; very dusty, and sticky with old blackened oil. He put it in his pocket with the firm intention of throwing it in the river at the first opportunity: Roger was not a person to be trusted with guns. Was indeed anybody? Himself?

He found writing paper and took it back to the kitchen table.

Three sheets: accident, suicide, homicide.

'Good with boats and excellent swimmer. In floodtime, at night, water running in strong current – whirlpools etc. – full moreover of large entangling débris such as branches, the second doesn't count for much and perhaps the first neither (check boat).'

'Overconfidence? Carelessness? Alcohol level? Body if/ when found and autopsied would give this sort of information even if much bruised & battered.'

Pushing someone in the river, at a moment like this, would be as fatal as pushing them under a car and the push doesn't have to be sinister: a wind gust of that force will push anything. Homicide needs no human wish or agency.

Can't rule out a suicide. Depressed and unbalanced when last seen by Vera. This means nothing; it never does. Not in character? – that means nothing either.

What Castang didn't like was the phone call. People like Roger act themselves (scarcely willing it, scarcely even realising it) into a condition of appearing far limper and drunker than they really are. So easy afterwards to say one was blind pissed and didn't know what one was doing. That way you can shuffle off a lot of responsibilities. It sounds normal and even reasonable to say that something dreadful has happened, you're in a horrible state, you need a friend. You imagine the worst . . . the drinking is post hoc or propter hoc? Appearing vague and woolly (Roger is neither) is a way of being dishonest with yourself. Phoning like that – rather handy too that the phone should have been working just then (possible to verify just how long the phone *had* been working?) – are you looking for a friend, or a confessor? – saying of course, "I've killed her" is simple hysteria and evidentially worthless.

Phoning a friend who happens to be a PJ cop, and at his office, has moreover a sinister resonance or is that professional deformation? You aren't ever saying so, but are you suggesting that a good friend will know how to efface any awkward little questions liable to be asked by the gendarmerie?

Sorry, this is pointless. Mr. Riderhood (my client) as well as having an active and vivid imagination, as I need not remind you, Monsieur le Juge, has high intelligence. With a little prudent foresight such a man can readily understand that close questioning, and we need impute no hostility, could very easily bring him into confused and self-contradictory behaviour. To have a legally trained friend standing by one would restore confidence. Innocence, Monsieur le Juge, (as I need not remind you) frequently appears far guiltier than guilty.

Castang was not being far-fetched: every criminal-brigade cop who has made court appearances thinks of what a lawyer will make of a situation.

An accident occurs, members of the jury, that through coincidental circumstances could be thought to point to suicide or even homicide. Your civic conscience makes you feel obliged to report the fact to a police official. I beg to point out that there is nothing in the least sinister in choosing an official who is also a friend.

Castang, you've a dirty mind.

He looked at his watch: time's a-wasting, Roger may sleep for hours and there's work to do. The rules for Coroners' Courts slid – jiggled – into his mind: any death which is sudden, violent, or unnatural.

It was necessary to have a word with the gendarmerie. They may be landed with an unexplained cadaver, and we want that body. If by any chance Roger had been abject dolt enough as to expect a cover-up then the exact reverse would come as a disagreeable shock. Now was this phone working or not?

"Police Judiciaire; pass me your lieutenant . . . Yes, I dare say he is busy, and so am I . . . Why didn't you say so? – give me the duty brigadier . . . PJ, brig, I'll read you off the name and address because we have to report a disappearance. That's right, death isn't a presumption – or not yet – but we're enquiring into it, so if you do get an unexplained body – yes, quite, and I've no intention of complicating your existence, I know perfectly how much work you have; rest easy, I'm not going to add to it."

Being tactful with gendarmes is a most important function of the PJ. A mighty, and in the countryside damn near almighty, highly disciplined and exceedingly competent force, the gendarmerie has a frequently justified concept of all other police services as a rabble in dirty raincoats.

It was a grave step he had taken. Having said that the PJ was enquiring into this death (disappearance is a good word) you are now obliged to enquire. Disappearance remains a good word because in the absence of Coroners a death, sudden, violent, or against the course of nature, must be reported to the Procureur of the Republic.

He took his car and went down to the village to the cleaning woman.

"Sorry to trouble you, Madame, but – "

"You're not the insurance man?"

"No, I'm the police. It's about Madame Riderhood." This is a name the French don't even try to pronounce: the nearest they'll get in all likelihood is to rhyme with Diderot and well, said Roger, that's a writer too if no more than fairly respectable. I do them up a Discourse on Method and they're quite happy.

Castang, doing the same, learned that Madame Arnaud had noticed nothing particularly untoward in Madame Marlene's behaviour, couldn't think where she might have gone but she did go away sometimes suddenlike.

Was concerned to hear Monsieur wasn't too well: that was a thing that happened quite often. Was most relieved to hear that she would not be needed to rally round in an emergency. Became voluble at this point, in relief.

"Well, y'see, there was a lot of damage – that's why I thought you were the insurance man – and my man's over his ears, y'see, he's the garde champêtre." Ho, the village constable: this was a handy thing to know, and explained why the lady was unperturbed by police – seen them before.

"So I have to stay at home really till things get sorted out – what was it you wanted, a statement signed or something?"

"No no, just the information. Nobody knows quite where she's gone, and Monsieur Riderot was anxious on account of the storm. She'll turn up no doubt; half the phone lines are still down.

"We got the phone back, but still no electricity."

"Thanks anyhow. I'll let you know if there's anything you can help us with. No, I won't bother your husband. Might be back to see him tomorrow, if she hasn't turned up, that is." A village constable in France has no great legal importance, but is a busy local grapevine; that's one phone line that is never down . . .

He left a note for Roger. "R – don't worry, I'll be back soon; got some shopping to do. I left the doors locked. Mrs. Arnaud cancelled, we'll see about cleaning up when I get back, make yr mind easy & get lots of sleep Yrs H." Drove home, mind turning. Flood water makes that turbine fly . . .

"Vera!"

"Tiens, surprise, aren't you in the office?"

"Exactly. Marlene's vanished, and given the flood Roger's got himself into the greatest tangle thinkable. Phoned me imagining God-knows-what-calamities. So I went out because he's off his rocker and totally pissed of course. I got him into bed. If she doesn't turn up, and I don't feel very happy about it, I'll have to take it seriously: the river's tearing past there like a train, full of haystacks and beehives and you can guess. Would you go out there until I get sorted out? There's plenty of supplies. I've stopped the cleaning-woman; don't want gossip in the village. Matter of holding the fort, and not letting Roger drink too much."

"I'd have to take Lydia – spend the night you mean? And the car."

"No bother, I'll take an official one."

"All right." She was a good coper. And a good policeman . . .

Monsieur le Commissaire entered his office, sat himself down at his desk, threw (crossly and quite pointlessly) a number of files about. Since he had been away all morning, three or four people came in with earnest expressions and legitimate business that was his simple duty. He had no right whatever to be irritable and sarcastic. Word spread that Castang, probably henpecked by his wife, was quite impossible today and better left unapproached. The door stayed shut and he returned to a state of simmer. The antique construction of the building meant quiet as well as a largish space around him. It was not like a modern office of four square metres and a door permanently open in the interest of team spirit. He could stand by the window and gaze sullenly out at plane trees losing their last leaves.

Human beings were well enough in their way. there were times when one would just like to go to, to, to a tropical island. There would be too many tourists. Well, one would have to be a detestable millionaire, that's all, fortunes founded upon ignoble trafficking in the black market. Corner a large piece of private beach. Keep a gorilla. If any bunnies approached from seaward with merry laughter, a clinking of bottles or other appurtenances of gracious living, the gorilla had instructions to shoot at them; no questions asked. Roger would feel like this. Pretty often. With himself it was a rarity and had better be: he'd be out of a job, short and sudden, if it weren't. Do it at home once or twice too often and one would be out of wife into the bargain.

Vera was tolerant, intensely disciplined by training and experience, full of antique virtues like humility and simplicity. She could also be very catty indeed. It didn't do to try any display of temperament on her: didn't wash.

It is justice that people with high standards of their own should be short with others' failings. One is shorter still when one has failed oneself to live up to high standards set. Now Roger can be a self-indulgent selfish bastard. He has also marks of his own, set high. And queer individual notions of his personal honour. I've some understanding of this; it's what makes us friends.

Honour: odd concept because unfashionable. Funny word; in many circles dirty word . . .

The door opened; hung half-open; creaked. Castang opened his mouth to scream "Fuck Off" before realising in time that there was only one person around here who tended to enter rooms in this devious manner; Divisional Commissaire Adrien Richard. Another complex person with recondite notions, honour prominent among them. It had not, strangely, stopped his getting and maintaining a high position in police hierarchies. The point was at present irrelevant: the door stayed open and nobody appeared.

"Come in and shut the door." Nothing happened. Was Richard talking to somebody in sign language? Just standing in the passage gazing? Anything was possible. Castang gripped himself and sighed.

The entrance when effected was in character: silent, flexible and somewhat mannered. Richard stared a long while at the desk, then a long while at Castang who was propped against the windowsill, fingers tapping the radiator.

"I was wondering," he said at last, "whether you were here." Flagrant coat-trailing, and nothing to say to that. He wandered over to the desk, pushed a large pink file, and sat on a corner to catch-up-with-his-foot-dangling. A thing Castang detested but at least he wasn't sitting at the damn desk.

Richard was over sixty and should by rights and rules have been retired. Some said he was under much pressure to retire and was being awkward; others said the contrary but being awkward either way. In person and movement far from awkward. Elegant hair now a beautiful silvery colour, a skin with an outdoor look: he was one of the few people who can play golf without being ridiculous. Odd blue eyes that should be cold and were hot, at times nastily so. Tallish, still wiry of figure. Bright. He should have got further in his profession; was sometimes lazy, possibly unambitious, certainly careless of what he said and did; at times 'mal vu' by the seigneurs in Paris. On occasion very much so, but had talent for getting out of the most horrible wasps' nest.

A friend too; the best friend Castang could ever hope to have. A wise person, who did not always behave wisely. Did he himself? Did anybody? Richard could also be a proper shit, having that much in common with everybody else.

He was now staring lengthily at the quite nice Victorian mirror which hung in the dark corner of the room (on that account) where sun never reached; with disapproval as though he suspected Castang of staring in it when alone while arranging his hair.

"I should like to know," amiably, "whether you have wasted your entire morning." Pause. "There shouldn't be two of us at it." Amiable-nasty.

"The woman has disappeared," for only facts were required, "and there's a strong probability she's in the river. Did she fall, did she jump, was she pushed? – a totally open question and when or if we find a body one wouldn't like to forecast how many questions Pathology will answer and with how much certainty. Remains a live person who won't or can't answer anything with any certainty. One, doesn't know his bloody self; two, is totally pissed; three, the line between fact and fiction is at all times vague at the best.

"I have reported the disappearance to the gendarmerie. Failing a have-his-carcass which could take a week judging by the state of the river, there's no official step you'd want taken. I've asked Vera to go look after the house and the fellow until he collects his wits. I've two eventual witnesses to circumstance whom I have not yet questioned and I hope not unduly alarmed. Is there any point in sending an IJ team out there after technical findings? – answering my own question I'd say hardly, unless you wish it. Summing it up I feel unhappy on several grounds. I don't see proper ground for sending any crim-brig people, and I see too much for making an enquiry myself – that I take it is the question you wanted an answer to."

"There was a fight?"

"By his totally inconsistent account a violent dispute. He threw a lot of stuff around. He was at the stage of accusing himself of everything and anything short of physically pushing her in the drink. Wait twenty-four hours and try again – tonight maybe."

"But technically she could have buggered off."

"Not so much where as by what means – and at the height of the storm. She could have got into the water somewhere else, and she could have hitched a lift or whatever. Not in character but how drunk was she? Against this is that once sober she'd have made some signal, unless of course she met with violence elsewhere. At present that would be turning over too many pages too fast. There'll be stuff to work on closer at hand."

Richard picked up the telephone.

"Fausta, find out what deaths if any have been reported on account of the storm, and whether there are wandering willies picked up with amnesia or pneumonia: all the stuff that should be on the telex and never is. Incidentally was a state of emergency officially declared or is the Prefect still havering about it?"

Castang took the phone.

"Fausta, we're looking for a middle-aged lady, tall, handsome, hair brown, face oval, speaks fluent French with English accent. The gendarmerie at Longueville have this but you might just check the obvious. Riderhood, Marlene, but a pseudonym is as likely."

"She has children?" asked Richard.

"One's in America and the other in Paris and it was the first thing thought of once the phones started working."

"You're a little too quick to my mind to assume she's dead. Planned or spontaneous, storm or not, she could have arranged for a friend to pick her up. Well, well, you know her and I don't."

"I never know whether that's less of a help than a drawback. You want somebody else to look at it?"

"The way things are," said Richard. "Vera's more likely to get at the truth than cops are."

Like the man in Dickens who disliked being seen 'in that bony light', Vera was far from seeing herself in any bloodhound aspect. There'd been an unpleasant row; things wounding and hateful and hurtful had been said, and if she thought about it at all she thought that Marlene had run off into the storm, very foolish but quite understandable; if something more tragic still had taken place it was none of her business and least said, soonest mended. One has quite enough to do trying to bring order into a disorganised house. Being a detective starts with finding where the dustpan and brush are kept.

"Why is everything broken?"

"People break things in a rage. Don't touch glass, it cuts. You do too, sometimes." Lydia acknowledged that this was so. It was cheering that adults should do so too.

The police might be cross and say it shouldn't have been touched. Too bad; she wasn't going to live with this mess. It is stimulating having to take hold of strange domestic patterns (finding a piece of cardboard to block the draught from a broken pane: finding scissors to cut it to size.) Marlene was often in a muddle, oftener slapdash, occasionally a slut. If anything more of a slut than Vera, but her house was much bigger and even with a cleaning woman far more work, and her man no such meticulous person as Castang but a leaver of things lying around, a liker of comfortable litters: the English hate things being tidied. She had to clean, and had to be careful not to overdo it.

Food was the next priority; plenty of everything and seven pots of mustard; a cupboard with a lot of weird cans and a deep freeze in a pigsty; things whose labels had come adrift. Marlene was a dashing and imaginative cook with a tendency to complications that didn't quite come off. Vera, either steady and careful or, when hard at work, capable of forgetting everything (putting a burned pot to soak and making do with sardines off the corner of the table) found something, scratched at it, decided it was navarin of lamb – from last spring? or the spring before – put it on to warm. Guest-room next; bedclothes: Marlene had done this and impeccably. There was a nice guest bathroom too and cunning arrangements, very English, for making ones own tea. Lydia trailed about fingering things, but that was no problem.

Roger was the problem. Still deep in alcoholic stupor? After putting the child for a rest and peeling potatoes – should be new ones with a navarin but not at this time of year – she screwed herself up.

Roger was on the daybed in the studio, covered with a rug. It wasn't cold out; the storm had been a warm one. There was no stench; a window was open enough to air the room – careful Henri. Nor was Roger a disgusting sight, but dozing quietly and it was not at all a mad eye that opened when she came in.

"Hallo. Have you come to cheer my solitude? That's nice."

"Would you like a cup of tea or something?" cautious.

"No no, I must get up and have a shower. Quarter of an hour, to become respectable. Okay?"

She had made tea, because in England it was teatime and a time Vera liked, particularly in November with the light beginning to fail. She cogitated on the best place to ensconce, decided on the living-room as obvious and natural. Nothing could be worse than ostentatious tact. One behaved as though nothing had happened.

Roger thought the same; appearing quite neat with damp hair, and informal.

110

"O, I like the dressing-gown."

"Rather Noël Coward but they're nice, at home. Tea!"

"Are they the right cups?"

"Yes, of course. Digestive bicky!" Why had she been frightened –? A civilised person, determined to keep perfect control of himself.

"I've lamb stew for tout-à-l'heure; I hope you enjoy that. What would you like to drink?"

"Shouldn't drink anything."

"Maybe but to do honour to me and Lydia you'll find something."

"What's the English for tout à l'heure?"

"Soon? Shortly?"

"Can't say 'I've lamb stew for shortly'."

"In-a-little-while?"

"No no, this is one of the things the language falls down on. Dinner will be served after the intermission!" It was perfect, and probably they would have spent a cosy evening languidly arguing about Proust or Anthony Powell ('Went on much too long about that boring war,' claimed Vera, 'why are the English so obsessed with war?') – but there came a lot of hearty banging on the door and Castang appeared (Vera claimed she could tell a police car by ear). Roger froze right up, instantly.

"You've found her?"

"No, we haven't found her. Is that tea too stewed to drink? We're looking at all the normal and reasonable things she might have done, made un-normal or unreasonable on the face of things by the storm. It's died right down, isn't even raining any more. This biscuit is stale. If only Marks and Spencers were nearer by. I hope you've made some proper supper, Vera."

"When the flood water goes down . . ."

"Roger, I'm an orderly person and I'm a good cop and trust me. It's what I'm for. And recognising that, very sensibly you called me. Now for gossake don't fuss. This tea's disgusting, I could do with a drink, Roger, haven't you got any red plonk and not that revolting Brit Bordeaux?"

"I thought you didn't drink at work."

"I'm exactly like you; I can go without for weeks and then I like to drink. In Munich I was slightly drunk all the time – felt like that, too. Did I tell you about that? Tja, I find the two of you all jolly, tinkletinkle the teacups and I come in and I'm the cold spoon in the soufflé, it isn't my fault." There was that phrase again haunting him. If Marlene is dead, who has part, guilt or share in her death? Technically – oh; *technically* . . .

The stew was good, and Roger managed to talk about Hermitage wine and everyone behaved as though Vera had cooked the stew and brewed up the wine into the bargain. Marlene was the cold spoon in the soufflé and Vera characteristically lanced the abscess: mixed metaphor.

"You were drunk at the time and emotionally very keyed up, and you have extremely vivid memories that will turn out to have been plain not-so. It will come back; you'll remember properly. Give yourself a chance; it's not even twenty-four hours." Roger was looking at her, without any expression. One couldn't be sure he was listening: the best that could be said was that he had an absent-minded air.

Is he beginning quite to enjoy it, wondered Castang. A good go of what the Victorians would have called brain-fever; sitting now convalescent, a bit shaky still but brave about it, with a kind nurse to look after him and everything. Castang thought Vera was overdoing the sweet sympathy a bit.

He killed her, thought Castang. She didn't run away; a friend didn't come and pick her up. She wouldn't have left her handbag sitting on the table like that.

Roger, in a padded armchair, Victorian, with wings to keep the draught off one's whiskers, uncrossed and recrossed his legs.

"All my life," he said, "I've been fascinated by a phenomenon – a trick of light, I suppose. Look out of a window, at twilight, with a lit room behind you; you see the whole landscape, with the clarity of detail – peculiarly vivid, even, in that lighting. And superimposed you see a reflection of the room behind, ghostly and transparent. And you see yourself, the face and figure of the beholder. Not more than half as a rule, I think; the rest stays in shadow. I imagine it's the base of most ghost stories. Too many Victorian gentlemen in dressing-gowns, carrying candles. Pissed very likely, or perhaps been sipping from those little bottles of laudanum. The image floats, on the surface of the glass . . .

I'd better go to bed, I think. Seems rude. Hope you won't mind. Don't feel too gaudy."

"Off you go," said Vera. He had not drunk much; hadn't eaten much either. No surprise, after that colossal overdose of whisky.

"I'll put the dog out and lock up," said Castang. "No worry, it'll all still be there in the morning."

"Yes indeed," mildly, climbing to his feet. It hadn't been, thought Vera, the most tactful remark possible.

"You think he did it," undressing in the guest room, a pullover covering her face.

"Feel sure of it," said Castang, "but being sure is never any good to a cop."

"His Doppelganger did it."

"Huh?"

"The one he sees, floating on the windowpane at twilight. No ghost but a reality: but what's reality?"

"Not the kind of explanation a judge likes," said Castang, climbing into bed.

Up at seven, and shave close at a quarter past, like Dickens's Podsnap. Why not? Whatever house you've slept in, the routines are the same when there's work to do.

Vera, washed, dressed, made the coffee because he had phone calls to make.

"Going down to the village?" seeing him in his leather jacket, twirling car keys on his finger. "Get some fresh bread. Milk, if there is any; I've enough for Lydia."

"Coo, you're an early starter," said Madame Arnaud, surprised. She was still in her dressing-gown, quilted nylon affair with large improbable mauve roses; and yellow plastic curlers.

"Yes," said Castang, not very smiling yet; hadn't even had a cup of coffee. "Be wanting a chat with you in an hour; thought I'd let you know."

"Well; uh . . ." This morning, the fellow looked a lot more like a cop.

"And I'll be wanting to see your husband."

"He's got a lot to –"

"Here," not taking any no for an answer, "or at the mairie?

Eight-thirty on the dot, and making it official."

She thought about that.

"Here," she said. "That secretary at the mairie is right nosy."

"I'm easy. 'S long 's it's understood."

"'S long 's I can get my shopping done."

A kilometre further, in the 'real' village, there was a good smell of bread, but no milk yet. It would be there any minute: supplies were back to normal: well, more or less . . . Roads clear enough, but those fields . . .

"Staying with Monsieur Riderot?" asked the baker's wife pleasantly – even the tiniest scrap of fresh gossip makes the day smoother. "Your turn to get the bread?"

"That's right – keep me two milks then would you? – back this morning some time."

"He's nice. Always got a joke," hopeful. Castang smiled encouragingly while feeling his pockets for change, but had no jokes. "She is nice too. The English," in the voice of an acknowledged expert, "either they're very nice, or they're bloody awful."

"Not like us?" suggested Castang, putting the bread under his arm, "we're all pretty awful."

"Gotto take 'm as you find 'm," said the good lady with village philosophy. "You in the book business?" He grinned and said nothing. An accomplished fisher, but she hadn't heard anything untoward about the Riderhood family. So Madame Arnaud had kept her mouth shut.

Out of obedience, or had she reasons of her own for discretion?

Roger was dressed too, when he got back. A little pale and puffy still, but normal enough in looks and behaviour.

"No news I'm afraid," said Castang slapping the bread on the kitchen table and ruffling Lydia's hair. "It's early still." Early in the enquiry, or just early in the day? "Ought to get something today, I think. Things are back to normal, pretty well."

"Are you thinking –?" began Roger but Castang cut in.

"'M I allowed to dip my bread in the coffee, Roger, in your house?" – false genial tone meaning not-in-front-of-the-children.

"Disgusting habit," said Vera, slicing the loaf held against her chest in the old peasant way. "Good country bread, this."

"In England you break bread if you've any manners." Roger sounded normal too. "In Ireland you cut it, rather odd."

"How d'you go about cutting Mother's Pride?" objected Castang, "it's like chewing-gum."

"Always liked Tom Sharpe's phrase for the Irish gynaecologist – a pussy-prying Paddy." Relevant to nothing, but sounding more like his usual self.

"What did he do to the pussy?" enquired Lydia; it cheered them all up.

"Be back for lunch," said Castang coming downstairs after doing his teeth. "I'll arrange with the Putzfrau's husband, Roger, to look after the horse, as long as that's needed."

"Oh good; I hate going near that beast. Sidles at me in a nasty menacing way."

Roger and Vera stayed sitting over another cup of coffee.

"If you want to work," said Vera, "pay no attention to me; I'll just potter on with the housekeeping."

"I can't work. I'd rather sit and talk. If you don't mind."

"Not a bit."

"And the hell with the housekeeping. And the cooking. Deep freeze is full of stuff she was forever shoving in it and nobody ever ate."

'She', is it now?

"I'd rather be in my own room."

"The child will follow me about."

"She doesn't worry me."

The house sat on its low bluff, long and plain like a big barge, lifted by flood and left there when the water went down. A more baroque building, with gables and visible beam-structures (Norman say, or Alsacien) would have had a stern gallery for the admiral: this more utilitarian vessel had a pilot-house for the captain. The sleeping-cabin with its austere bunk (Vera was pleased to see the bed made up neatly) had many cunning little shelves and pigeonholes built around it – no fake-nautical treasure chests but thick, silky, hand rubbed teak and brass from a real boat; childish may be, but justly Roger's pride. A big airy space with a wide desk, and all his navigational instru-

115

ments grouped neatly to hand. From here a kind of companion-ladder led up to the bridge, where he could pace to and fro, and take a celestial fix. In earthbound terms he had wanted more light and all around instead of merely behind his back from the existing window. Instead of putting mansards in the roof he had had the ceiling broken out and penthouse windows made on all four sides. A wooden gallery within gave him access to the higher bookshelves. It all made a very pleasant studio for man: a woman, thought Vera, would and certainly did complain about the amount of glass to clean – some of those charming panes were difficult to get at – but when did a man ever worry about things like that? Double glass too for insulation; wind blew hard up here when it was exposed, and would wail dramatically, providing romantic comforts for the captain safe in bed as his ship affronted the gale.

Roger sat in the captain's chair, a splendid thing of black but-toned leather that swung to and fro, and tilted. Like Divisional Commissaire Richard's, back at the PJ command-post. Vera got into an armchair, tucked her feet in, leaving her knees stick-ing up; a comfortable position for women if (as Castang pointed out severely) bad for the back posture.

Perhaps she was looking around with some disapproval, because "It's not as bad as it seems," said Roger. "You were thinking, 'Oh, men', weren't you?"

"Not as directly as that but perhaps, a bit."

"The male donjon, to which he retires when in dudgeon to cosset his vanity with toys and junk. What Americans call a Den. Truth in that here, I'd have to admit. But at least it's a genuine work room, and I'm not a total phony. A writer does truly need a place for quiet and concentration. The work really is terribly hard."

"But I know," nodding helpless as the flow swept her aside.

"I forgot, you're a painter, or you draw, there's no difference. I could work with artificial light – but I've had too much of that. I was young once too; Leni and I were poor. I've worked in every kind of damn corner, wherever there was space enough cleared to put a portable typewriter. Children up to here, and the doorbell ringing. We had children too once," breaking off

116

because Lydia appeared. Roger took an antique vase off the desk, full of pencils and ballpoints and letter-openers, and gave it her; reached for a pad of scribbling paper. She got down on the floor and was happy.

"The radio used to play all day. Leni was one of these people who can do nothing without the radio on. They're all like that now, but I was brought up in silence. You learn of course to block it out, you can block anything out. Learn the hard way. Did work a lot better then than anything I do now. After forty-five or whatever, y'need a place like this; the little patterns and routines help you climb into your other world. Like Simenon sharpening his pencils every morning. You need the crafts-man's manual contact with tools.

"Don't think I kept her out. When I was at work – that's natural: even the tiniest interruption can plain paralyse you once you're on the trip. But I like working in the early hours. Kipling has a phrase somewhere, about the southwest wind just before the dawn, that was always favourable to him. Leni liked to stay in bed. An evening person. But –" he pointed to the television set and the magentoscope beside it, on the swinging side table – "she could always come here if she wanted, any time after midday. Can't have the thing in one's living-room. Kitchen's the place for it really but she wouldn't have that; 'keeping the housemaid happy' she called that: only justice I suppose since she did nearly all the cooking.

"I like music, too: but Leni's idea of music ... Richard Tauber singing, 'You are my heart's delight'."

"I'll stick up for what is called housewife's music," said Vera with warmth, "and without that sort other sorts are meaningless."

"Agreed, agreed, I don't want to sound snobbish, but I want to listen; I want to concentrate upon it and respect it, whether it's a Goldberg Variation or whether it's 'Malvina, Malvina, Du bist mein Apfelsine' – not have somebody singing and humming and taptoeing. Dancing: poor Leni, she loved to dance. Great grievance all her life that I would never take her dancing. Tall, you know, and flexible, and beautifully balanced. That lovely port of the bust and head, that wonderful walk. And a very acute sense of rhythm. Too tall and big in the bone for pro, but to

117

watch on the floor: which is why I liked watching. Anyhow I move like a sack of potatoes."

"Roger, why d'you keep saying 'was'?"

"She's dead. Henri pretending the contrary is to kid me, and if he really thinks the contrary he's kidding himself. Silly. She's dead and I killed her.

"Oh, don't think I've brought you here to sob out confessions. Not that way; I didn't push her in. Henri might think so but it's not my style. Vera, I'm sorry, but I need a drink."

"If you can't manage without, I'll get you some. No, I need movement; I mustn't stay too long immobile. But don't drink whisky any more."

"Bottle of red then; that Rioja: on the right in the first cellar."

"And you must share it with me – you mustn't just get evilly drunk."

"No, that stuff I can drink all day and just be gently oiled. All writers are soaks, and all drunk writers are bloody useless. The stuff looks good at the time but next morning it stinks and one knows it."

"I see," after the journey, "it's impotence we're on about. Hell, I forgot the corkscrew."

"Never," said Roger opening a desk drawer and producing a big brass one, part of the ship's furniture. " 'Captains Courageous' – bad book as everyone knows but full of good things, never toshy. Uncle Abishai – fishing boat full of criminal old villains all permanently pissed. Boat leaks like proverbial sieve; little dancing swell on the water, she meets a wave and goes straight under. Me. Leni. Happens very suddenly. One moment, writer, wife, nice living, respected by all save people who can read, but hardly anybody can. Next moment nothing there. Run under. Seams worked open, and neglected the pumps just that bit too long."

"Roger, forgive me, but I think you're attitudinising."

"Sure I am. They never do anything else. One set of attitudes for journalists – special one, witty and elegant, for television interview. 'Nother for the crew, bloody editors, sales managers; all those necessary technical folk. Humorous and forgiving, for cattle like reviewers. One has them by the balls, you see, because they're all failed writers!"

"Roger, you're boring me!"

"Bore everyone. Bored Leni. Bore myself. You're nothing special."

"No. Yes. Do stop!"

Country people, still called 'peasants' by surprisingly many people in France, from which one can often conclude that whoever does so is sensitive about his own beginnings, are not easy to interrogate. 'The working class', and that is a phrase more often heard in England, likes a direct approach as a rule; if there ever is any rule. The bourgeoisie are devious because they think of everything as property. Information might seem harmless but has to be dragged out of them. The motive is mostly fear that you've come to take something away from them, catch them at some disadvantage. And add their fundamental training; give nothing away without calculating what you can extort in return. the peasant's attitude is much the same but the motive different; more an ingrained dislike and distrust of interference. Suspicion: give them as much as the time of day they'll interpret that as 'fucking me about'.

Castang was no worse at the job than any other cop.

He found Monsieur Noel Arnaud seated at the kitchen table immersed in football results. His face had rich tints of brick and carmine, whether from an outdoor life or alcohol it would be hard to say; but say both and you won't be far wrong. His hair was straight, stiff, iron-filings colour; he was tall and broad; his massive hands rested placidly on the newspaper. His blue eyes were calm, bright in the coloured face, neither watery nor bloodshot: cirrhosis had not yet laid claim to the muscular body. He was in his late forties.

The kitchen was tiled; perfectly tidy, spotlessly clean. the only thing that very much said peasant was the addiction to gaudy colours and artificial flowers. Castang had taken his hat off the moment Cécile opened the door. Noel's cap hung on the back; likewise his green képi that said he was The Law. Castang had no képi, so said that he too was the law, they were colleagues, he'd come on business.

119

"Sit down," said Noel – "call me Noel; everyone does."

"Thanks," said Castang sitting down. "Thank you, Madame, I've had coffee. It would be a good moment to do that shopping you were speaking of."

"Why?"

"Because I've the same questions for both of you." It was no moment to be devious. "You know it well, a witness hears what another says, he starts knowing things he hasn't maybe known before, his story's coloured by what he hears. Nothing to do with collusion. You do the same. Supposing I phoned you from the PJ asking you to pick up a couple of statements for me, you're a sworn law-officer, you know how it goes. I'm here myself, that's the only difference."

"Right. You get your dinner, woman, like the man says, and you can talk to him later." Arnaud got up and opened the glass-fronted cupboard, produced the two tiny glasses and the schnapps-bottle that are the formal expression of country hospitality. Castang disliked it at any time but, "Ce n'est pas de refus," he said in the consecrated phrase.

"Something to do with Monsieur Riderot, the wife said."

"She said right. I know him a bit. So the day he's upset and phones me, even if it's no sort of PJ job I do what I can to be friendly-like. His wife's disappeared. That storm was really bad, so he's got the idea fixed in his head she fell in the river. Job for the gendarmes if she had, and we've nothing really to show she did. They've enough on their plate with traffic. I report a missing woman and if they find one, great. But if they don't where am I? I know your missus does housekeeping for them; you oblige yourself the odd time; I come and ask you the background, natural and normal."

Arnaud nodded, tasted his drink. No denying that, and better; no need to deny it. Seldom perhaps is the truth as straightforward, but seldom too has Castang found the truth bad policy. You don't want people to tell you lies, tell none yourself. They will, of course; but fewer and perhaps less complicated.

"Can't see though, much I could tell you. Him I know well enough and he gives no trouble and who says better? Never knows what day it is, all right he knows that, he's sensible.

Messes in nobody's affairs, don't ask anyone to mess in his, fair enough; with him you know where you stand. The madam, my woman knows her better than me, and acourse if she were to play the hoitytoity the Cécile wouldn't go up there to work. It's not we have to crawl for the money. She's got the time, likes the occupation, I'm easy. You can ask her. Any time I've spoken Madam she's polite, got consideration; nice straight woman I call her. Fetch her up fodder for the horse, do the odd bit of gardening if things are quiet, no trouble. Keeps an eye on money, but no chicane. That's all I know."

"Never trouble with the village?" jerking his thumb towards the képi on the door.

"Not 'sfar's I know."

"And you would know."

"I reckon."

"Not much you wouldn't hear."

"Not round here."

"I reckon too," said Castang, "if the lady did go in the river you'd know it."

"In that storm? – no way. Could happen. Might go right downstream, and could hook on a snag. On the big bend there's old willows and stuff sawn off, there could be two foot good of water covering there now."

"We'll have to check that."

"Not very likely," with understandably small enthusiasm.

"But it could be. This far we've looked in the likely places and she's not there. She could have been on the bank and been swept over. And she could have jumped," with no transition, "and she could have been pushed."

He got nowhere with that. Noel had solid nerves. He poured himself a second glass and said stolidly that he was only a hick ranger but he knew enough about law not to go thinking nothing. Short of wondering whether he'd seen the question coming and rehearsed an unchallengeable answer, which was fruitless, Castang had to be content with an instruction to put on waders, get the help of a few boys if need be, and probe along those drowned willows, each a hedgehog of sawn and billhooked spikes.

"We'll have to see the mayor," said Noel, pouring himself a

third glass in anticipation of a horrible cold wet job.

Cécile came back with her shopping-bag. One thing Castang did notice was that Arnaud was in no hurry to go sort out the mayor, and invented rather crude pretexts for hanging about. You don't ask a countryman doesn't he trust his wife alone with you, then: it might not be too well received. Castang had to be a bit blunt, and say I don't want to go giving you orders mate, but if I have to remind you a PJ officer has the right to enrole the country constabulary if he sees fit . . . Noel put his képi on. The Mayor (who kept the local pub) had generally had three or four glasses of white wine by this time of the morning, and could be a sarky bugger . . . Castang saw that he would have to drink a few apéritifs before lunch in that pub, in the good cause . . .

Cécile sniffed rather, clearing away the glasses; an unsaid but marked hint that men shouldn't drink so much schnapps so early. It gave him an opening.

"Perhaps I could ask a cup of coffee of you." Her face cleared.

"I like to have one going all morning; I work that way." Hers was black and stewed but still drinkable.

"A cop," said Castang, "has to understand that nine-tenths of the time a man knows nothing, where a woman sees it all. We get nasty stories, women's stories, can't back out of them on that account. A woman sees another woman, knows all about her. What a man mostly doesn't ask and shouldn't know. She's got a period, it's no business of mine. But you see it on her face. You're not going to say, because women have solidarity towards each other. But there are moments when the cop has to know, you see. So we're confidential and that's why I sent your man away. You can say things you wouldn't, in front of him. And I want you to."

"I won't though."

"Try it this way. Say you have a daughter."

"I haven't. I've the two sons, and I lost one. Road accident. A lot of help the cops were, to me then."

"I'm sorry. I'd like to say I'd have tried to do better. I'm trying to do better now. Some people have daughters: it happens they get into trouble. They go, maybe, to some stinking back street angelmaker because they don't dare tell their mum: you agree, it happens. To me it's a criminal abortion and if the girl dies – it happens . . . I have to ask some rough questions at times, and you wouldn't want me to shirk that part of my job, saying tell the women to sort it out. Does that make me a bit clearer? I'm above board. Most police work, it works out in the long run as histoires de cul." This cliché, translatable as "Bottom stories", lessened the tension. Thinking about it, this honest and respectable housewife had to admit that sex was generally the key to troubles in the village, and she was only a country mouse but she supposed it was much the same even in the big city. Of course Paris, going by what one saw on the television: girls no more than fourteen and their breasts bare and then they're surprised when complications arrive . . .

"It's the same," said Castang bleakly.

Well; she'd do her best. If people didn't have dirty laundry, they wouldn't give it to us to wash. Madame Riderot? – she and her man were like most married couples. They quarrelled and they didn't: they slept together and they didn't.

"If Monsieur knows what I mean" . . . Words like periphrasis crossed Castang's mind. Roundabout obliquities; an antique puritanism. Was that altogether so bad? There was an even more antique quality called modesty. Used to the pretty well total, and mostly crude outspokenness of modern young women, he thought a bit of modesty wouldn't come amiss. Vera who set small store by fashion was highly modest, at times excessively, and he couldn't be sure it wasn't a fault on the right side. Saving arid souls like the Economics Squad, most policemen he knew complained that female immodesty was beginning to come in overdoses.

Facts: as he had guessed Cécile had worked for Marlene a number of years and the two women had a friendly relationship. A liking, a respect.

A biological kind of woman, highly physical: good at maternity and with small children, interested in people rather than things. Housekeeping bored her. Once the children grew up and that dismal menopause arrived on the horizon they did easily lose a sense of direction.

"Did she have a lover?"

"Look, I change the sheets but I don't keep her diary." Peasant euphemisms but also a peasant directness.

"Rely on your memory; say over this last fortnight. What has

123

been any small event that struck you? Any change in routine? For a start, who has been to the house?"

"To stay, you mean? Last week there was a chap Monsieur calls his editor. He's been before, he comes quite often. Don't know his name, Cyrille they call him. Left when was it? just the day before the tempest."

"From Paris?"

"No, London." Why hadn't Roger mentioned this? To get anywhere with Roger there were a number of firm factual questions one needed to put; getting a few clearcut answers instead of all the woolly haze.

"Can't remember anyone else. Young Gilbert was up there a few days last week; he might have –"

"Who's he?"

"My son, he works down the garage. Does a bit of plumbing or electricity extra like, to oblige from time to time – look, mister . . ."

"Don't worry; a bit of work on the black might be illegal but that doesn't interest or bother me at all. He was in the house?"

"Well you could ask him. . . the Peugeot garage on the main road."

"Any eyewitness to anything, you see . . . I forgot to ask your husband; was he up at the house much this last ten days or so?"

"Uh – no more than the usual. He isn't around the house much. Looks after the horse a bit." Was there a note of reticence there? or had his query been a bit over-casual? But no cop wants to start planing fine shavings off shades of meaning.

"And you yourself – after all you're certainly the best eye-witness I can imagine. Anything that would strike you now or struck you then as untoward or that jarred you a little bit."

"Can't say as I did." She had gone a degree or so chillier and quite a bit more wooden. Flattery will get you nowhere, mister! Better leave her for now.

"You've been a help, Madame, and I'm grateful. Don't want to hold you up any more for now." One can like a gossip: one can also feel another very out-of-date sensation; loyalty to an employer. There's something there. And that was what you came to find out.

The mayor had a brassy and aggressive manner, going well with, partially even a result of, the chemistry of cheap white wine which leaves a metallic flavour in the mouth; better not enquire what it does further down. Castang at home was strictly forbidden to drink it because he became quarrelsome. The mayor was an object-lesson in the truth of this.

He had no troops to spare, he said impatiently, on missing women who might not even be missing. Castang could sympathise, since the troops consisted of Noel and a man with a funny hat and a fledgling growth of patchy down on the face who looked like the village imbecile and very likely was. Even a PJ Commissaire has no orders to give a mayor, and precious few ways to twist his arm. Castang was greasily polite, and he agreed grumblingly at last to an afternoon's fishing along the Big Bend. Le Père Bache was added to the troops: being a pensioner he came cheap. Wouldn't be much use as work went, confided Noel over the glasses of white wine that concluded the agreement. You could call it laziness or you could call it rheumatism. However, nobody knows the river better.

Having a word quiet-like with "young Gilbert" was not as easy as all that. You can't buttonhole him at work, because the employer will appear and demand whether you're paying his wages, perhaps. Nor over a meal because the guiding principle of Cécile's life is always to have a good hot pot ready for the men and on the dot, and herself bustling round. And now that the tale would be spreading rapidly in the village, losing nothing in the telling, you would rather like to get the news in first.

So you act cop, arousing everyone's dislike and hostility, or you act the ignoramus whose car is behaving oddly, and pay for that. Castang didn't mind the one much, being well used to it, but thought the other might serve better.

"Got a stupid thing – short circuit I'd guess, distributor or something; ignition's dead. Borrow young Gil a quarter of an hour? – just down the road a piece."

"Why him?"

"Ach, I know his dad."

125

"Still got to charge you standard rate."

"Not to worry," said the idiot.

The boy was perhaps nineteen, with sullen good looks and an affronted air, who backed out an old rattletrap, drove in silence, not even glancing at him. More intelligent than he seems, thought Castang studying the profile, but not perhaps less vain.

"Battery all right?" opening the bonnet.

"There's nothing wrong with the car."

"What's the gag?"

"Right, it's a gag, tranquil. PJ cop – commissaire. But no need to question you in public start everybody looking at you. Like to put you in the shit. So by keeping it quiet I do you a favour. Okay?"

"Stolen car?"

"Mrs. Riderhood's missing, and she might be dead." The mouth opened, shut again. Surprise, alarm, curiosity, excitement – the lot maybe.

"Sorry about that. And so what?"

"You were up there just before the storm."

"Fixed a leaking tap, obliging a neighbour. My mother –"

"I know; she told me." Now that was alarm, or he had never seen fright.

"What she tell you?"

"Fix any more than the leaking tap?"

"There's always a few – what you getting at?"

"Mrs. Riderhood. Bit old. But nice-looking woman."

"You trying to say I was messing with her? – you crazy?"

"Just using my eyes and ears, and my loaf. Why d'you think I brought you out here? You tell me straight, and the whole village doesn't have to start yacking."

"Who told you this – him, the mister?"

"The name got bandied about, Monsieur Arnaud."

"Look, I can get all the girls I want, I don't have to go for married women."

"There's plenty say that, and find the other more fun. You like driving fast? Bit of risk, but for a good driver . . ."

"So help me I never –"

"Nobody's saying you killed her. But get me clear; something happened. Tell me in confidence, I'll keep it that way."

"I can't tell you. Leastway I'll tell you, nowt to do with me."

"Your dad? I understand, you wouldn't give your dad away, I wouldn't either if it were mine. I don't want a lot of gossip and I don't want trouble. I'd like to keep it in the family too. Help me on this, you'll be helping others, your mum for instance."

"You leave my mum out of this, she's . . ."

"What they don't know they can guess. A woman's like radar, picks things up that aren't seen or heard."

"You leave my mum alone, you hear me? Or I'll be after you. With a knife if necessary."

"Don't make threats, Monsieur Arnaud. Doesn't impress me and might turn me nasty."

"You are nasty."

"Every cop is nasty. That's what it's about, mate. I'd rather you fixed my car, and I said thanks and bought you a drink. I have to get this clear. One or the other was playing around with her and which?"

"The fellow who told you that, you'd better start looking closer at him. And that's it. I've fixed your car, you can pay for that. Not coming out of my pocket."

"I'm staying up at the house," said Castang. "You can come up and see me there."

A village constable is a lot of things, because these legal duties are rarely in demand. Roadmender, gravedigger, mason, waterworks, fire brigade . . . but all these jobs as well as shooting without a licence or tipping illicit rubbish are handled, in the most amiable way possible, in the pub; and there he found Noel.

Likewise, in a good cause, drinking rotgut white wine is like paying a hundred francs for a non-existent car repair. You can't put it on the police expense-note.

"My shout," said Castang, "what'll it be?" They brought their glasses to the table in the corner.

"That's fixed up for this afternoon. Can't do no more without gendarmerie, dragging or whatever."

"Finding her," said Castang, "is only half the problem. The

127

other half bothers me – how she fell in. If of course she did fall in."

"Wouldn't know nothing about that."

"I passed the time-of-day with your lad Gilbert. Battery was flat. Bright boy, good mechanic. Good looker too. Up at the house last week, he mentioned."

"May be. Ballcock or something bust, heard him say. Friendly boy. Likes to oblige."

"What I thought. See, Monsieur Arnaud, we're private. No snoopers. Off the record. I can keep my mouth shut, and I don't search to make trouble. Fabricating charges against anybody, that's not my style. But this business could turn out tricky and what worries me is getting to know where everybody stands."

"What you got on your mind you better spit out."

"If the lad fancied the lady – or the lady fancied the lad. You've experience; you can see it might make all the difference."

"That flat battery of yours . . ."

"Right; I didn't want to go questioning him in front of his mates. I'm not looking to do you any bad turn. But there comes a moment when these things go public. When that time comes, what has to give gives. Put yourself straight with me now and I'll see it's known in the right quarter – and I don't mean Mister-Mayor."

"That woman of mine been talking?"

"She didn't say a thing and don't blame her. Not-saying is also saying; right?"

"Monsieur Riderot put this in your mind? Because half the time he's pissed and the other half imagining things."

"Well I know it. But I still got to ask."

"Nothing like what you're thinking and that's the truth."

"How d'you know?"

"Never mind how I know: you can believe it."

"You mean it wasn't the lad, it was you?"

The brick colour suffused darkly.

"Easy," said Castang, "if your voice can't be heard your face can be seen. Don't be daft, man; I'm making it easy for you. In your job you've seen a lot of people telling lies. Little things, sometimes bigger ones. So've I. Let me handle this the

128

right way, and you won't regret it if it comes to a Proc and a Judge of instruction. Let them get something in their head and it's not easy to dislodge. While it's just a prelim enquiry is the time to tell it the way it was. Telling the judge, after, that you got screwed by the cops is what everyone tells and no one believes. You may be perfectly in the clear and who's to know? Unless you lay it out for me."

"What you got to go on, apart that drunk's opium dreams?"

"People don't just disappear. Not that kind. She had a baddish shock. As for the boy, he's not a fool. Saw or guessed more than he let on. Man, you know it, better start believing in it. There's no grounds for homicide charges. But if there's a suspicion of rape, a judge would think that a likely pivot for a homicide presumption. We don't find her we can't prove a thing? Just so. But a lot of chaps have spent an awful long time in jug waiting for PJ enquiries to disprove things . . ."

"There was a fellow up at the house, staying . . ."

"Indeed. That's a thing your wife did tell me. I haven't spoken to him yet . . ."

"Maybe she went after him."

"Maybe she built a nest in a tree and is living in it."

It was nothing and Arnaud had guessed as much. He was thinking, turning the thick glass between big scarred fingers. Shrewd, and has seen cops at work before. Whatever he had been drinking had had no effect upon him. He shook his head slowly with a sour grin.

"You been trying it on, Commissaire, to see if you could get me rattled, like. That's cop tactics and I don't particular hold it against you. Maybe you tried it on the boy too and he did get rattled. Which it isn't evidence. Intimidation, that is, and not good enough. No hard feelings, but don't go pushing because I won't be pushed. All right?"

"It's early days."

"You'd like a nice smooth sexy story, that'd look good in the paper. You aren't getting Bardot," laughing now, "to star in that. You do your job, and I'll do mine, and Salut Emile."

Roger had drunk most of the bottle of Rioja and gone down for another. He was not perhaps drunk, or not in a horrid way. He was excited and lyrical, and as long as he didn't go nasty . . . He had brought Vera up here to tell her something; he was seeking to confide in her, but talk about beating round the bush . . .

"You're a good friend, Vera. I'm glad you've come, I'm glad to have you. I rely upon you.

"I'm a book-lover. Love books and you begin to wonder whether you've ever really loved anything else. Books are so much better than people. Love books and you start thinking, Who needs friends? These never fail."

"They don't answer back perhaps. They tell you things, but they say nothing disagreeable. They don't hit you."

"They teach me," said Roger looking sly, "and I learn."

He reached out to the shelf nearest him, took a book from a row of others like it; French books of the old-fashioned sort, with paper covers, whose pages had to be cut by hand, with the traditional type-face, antique and beautiful. Roger was staring at it, handling it, forgetting to talk. Vera's painterly eye studied the book, looking for an exact definition. Those covers have the look and the unglossy, slightly irregular texture of a farm egg. A beautiful oatmeal colour between cream and brown. Roger startled her by echoing her thought.

"Like perfectly cooked tart-crust pastry." He's a writer, she thought, startled, and he's my brother.

"What is it?"

"Ach, it's Proust, stuff I read often, but can't take much at a time. 'Souvent et peu à la fois, comme disait le père Swann' . . . fantastic thing, the torments of the love affair with Odette; too long maybe, but never been better done: the extraordinary contrast immediately after, of the child's love affair with Gilberte – identical torment to that of the adult. And the terrible finality of that ending, how does it go, Swann saying 'I gave the best years of my life, suffered unutterable torture, for a woman I did not even really love – who was not even my style.'

"But it's the book itself, physically, I meant – a real book; they understood books then," handling it, with a totally sensual delight. "Fifteen volumes, each exactly the right shape, the right weight, fitting the hand like another hand; a living thing.

"And people go buying Pléiade editions! – awkward ugly thing like a lump of lead. This paper is so gentle to the touch. And pages hand cut, with a blunt letter-opener – there was no greater pleasure than having to wait to turn the page until you had cut it; the thrill of anticipation! Having to work by hand, with a tool – like a carpenter – that's the way a book should be read!" He was running his fingertips up and down the rough-cut page-edges, looking for a definition that would be sufficiently tactile.

"Rough and yet wonderfully soft, a powdery softness, like dry dead wood – but it's not dead. It's me that's dead."

"I've got to go down," said Vera, "and make some soup. You need something to eat." She made her way downstairs, limping a little from sitting on her leg, feeling strangely touched. Brushed? – as though by the dusty soft thickness of the book. He had been telling her something: what, exactly?

"There must be animals, somewhere, with skin like that," Roger was muttering.

Henri came back for dinner, hungry, saying the soup smelt good, which it did; finding a glass left in the bottle, smacking his lips and saying it was good, going to see if there was any more.

"Wind's gone right down, and 's not raining for a wonder. You want to go out, Roger, shake yourself up a bit, or your liver will give you hell. Like you to go with me as far as the river and see whether there's any sense to be made of that theory. All so improbable somehow. And by the way, la mère Cécile was saying you'd had someone to stay, who's Cyrille?"

"Cyril? – he's my editor. Old friend."

"In Paris?"

"No, in London. He was staying here too, I'd totally forgotten." Roger was now sober and looking, even, in good shape.

"He might be a good witness, to something or other. State of mind? Friends with Marlene too, was he at all, is he I should say?"

"They got on well enough," said Roger grinning for once less sour or sarcastically, "but better not construct any scenario like did she run after him. What Noel Arnaud calls 'A nancy kind of chap'. He was exclaiming exaggeratedly over some plant in the garden, in terms slightly to old Noel's disgust. Don't know if you've run across him, he's Cécile's husband. Village cantonnier."

"Yes indeed, and must have a word with you about that. But Cyril now, could we phone him or anything? Just to clear it up."

"Don't see why not. In fact nothing easier. He'll still be in his office, they're an hour behind us in London. Number's in the memo book there. D'you want me to go away? I mean, d'you want to talk Privately?" giving it a capital letter.

"Please yourself," said Castang, dialling.

A very English performance: the very fluty soprano (higher than that; a castrato?) brightly saying "Trying to connect you", the melodious, maybe mellifluous baritone of middle-aged English gentleman discomposed in pre-lunch quietude and thoroughly put out at the news, making the remarks suitable to gentlemanly fluster like "Bless my soul" and "How very dreadful". In common with most European people Castang was accustomed to say things like "Pederasts one and all": pressed to be less sweeping he might mumble "Easier to count the ones that are". It had taken Geoffrey Dawson to explain, in an hour of sheer fascination at their 'Stammtisch' in Munich, the niceties.

Well, these were now niceties: a civilised pederast in an office overlooking Bloomsbury Square is quick on the uptake; the line was beautifully clear; a rapport was established; there were chuckles; it was all very perspicacious.

Cyril had not seen Marlene, and she had said nothing to him while there. They liked each other; he would not have been surprised had she chosen him for confidences; possibly he flattered himself but she would feel safe, you know; but he was afraid he could shed no light that could serve for guidance. As for observance, and conceivably he flattered himself but he was a good observer, if not in the police sense, ha, she had certainly not been her normal self, in so far as there is any normal self but we might take a different view, don't you know my dear Commissaire, of what constitutes abnormal psychology. Hm, he wouldn't want to put a name to it for fear of being misleading, but broody

yes, and disjointed perhaps; let's say not altogether as consequent and coherent as he was accustomed to seeing her and let's
not place undue emphasis.

Interrogating a London publisher on the telephone half in
English and half in French was less difficult than he had
thought, and went on for twenty minutes and might have lasted
longer had not Cyril suddenly said, "Bless my soul, I'll be late
for luncheon."

Roger was sitting gloomy and sullen.

"He'll ring you this afternoon, before going home."

"I don't want to talk to him, I don't want to see him, I've
nothing to say to him."

"Possibly," said Castang raising eyebrows at the agitated
manner, "but I'm not the footman; I'm not passing on messages
like that."

"La Soupe," called Vera through the doorway.

A meal eaten largely in silence because of black depression
in which small talk did not flourish, and it was left to
Castang to patter.

"Odd that as a rule English has fifteen words for something
where French has only two or three, and opinions differ
whether this makes it a more interesting language, that's not at
issue," with his mouth full of bread. "The English have two
kinds of soup, thick and clear, and how many are there here,
each name with an exact definition according to the method
used, and a precise technical meaning?"

Just the sort of remark that normally interested Roger, who
paid no attention at all and sat slumped with his nose over
the bowl.

"Soup is a country thing. Proof, you can only put in country
bread, big thick slices; town bread doesn't taste right." He
looked to Vera for support but she only said, "Lydia, don't
slurp."

Late as it was in the year, the air was soft as milk. Why milk,
wondered Castang, and why is milk used for so many contemptuous expressions meaning soft and flabby; the French
'soupe-au-lait' and the English milksop, and what about the

American milquetoast? No, that is the chemistry of milk and bread together, odiously slimy.

If we deal in exact sciences we can look at the satellite photo of the weathermen, noticing that the odd patterns of cyclone and anticyclone are bringing us warm dry clear air from North Africa. The milkiness is caused by evaporation from the immense amount of water lying about on the ground. But does a cop deal with the physical sciences? If only he did! People think we do: we would like to think we do. They are of help occasionally, and this is why we have the Identité Judiciaire services with their cameras and reaction tests, and the laboratory with its highly sophisticated capacity for analysis. Or the Pathology service of the university hospital in the city. Given the merest scrap of human tissue . . . Professor Deutz, the distinguished specialist who was at its head, could do nothing for him. "No body, Castang, no findings. Habeas corpus." Where was Marlene?

The river, swollen still but beginning again to be manageable and look navigable (he hoped it was so) sailed by, glassy and majestic. Downstream there were barrages, weirs, power stations: filter devices of every sort that had choked with unimaginable quantities and varieties of débris. The gendarmerie had been working on this for more than a day now. There had been a lot of dead animals – and a human. Sex male, said the telex laconically.

A woman, with no papers at all and no luggage but a shopping basket, had been found in the filter of an English ferry terminal. English from her accent, claiming moreover to be English, able furthermore to give no very coherent account of herself. An interesting story no doubt, but not his own. Age, height and weight all wrong, said the PJ telex using Fausta's cool and dispassionate voice.

"By the Brook," said Castang, possibly with a vague recollection of Beethoven's pastoral symphony.

Roger was still standing there being null and looking dim, but becoming less obtuse since he said in an unpleasant tone, "The first movement is called 'Happy thoughts on arriving in the country'". But yeast was working in the inert dough, stimulating him to some human response. Perhaps they'd get somewhere now, and with God's help leap over this great wall.

"I am the man that marches on, and dares not turn his head,
For fear that there a frightful fiend doth close behind him
tread," staring dully at the water. Castang recognised this as
literature, but the thought was easy enough to follow.

"We're both paralysed by the same problem. If I were certain she was dead I'd be concentrated on the classic trilogy,
accident, suicide or homicide, and that would be that. A matter
of assigning responsibilities, where they belong. My task would
be at an end. Because the question of attenuated or diminished
responsibility belongs to a judge. I am specifically forbidden to
meddle with it.

"And being to my sorrow and undoing a human being; finding myself your friend, a guest in your house, summoned to
your help . . . of course I could have refused. Should have
refused. I thought about it. Richard – you don't know him, he's
my superior officer – thought about it, accepted it; willingly or
not is beside the point. It was a duty.

"I have no share, Roger, in guilt or innocence. Because
neither is an exact concept, neither is in law more than a legal
quibble, and I'm a law officer: that word 'Judiciaire' added to
'Police' is the fishbone in the throat.

"If she is dead, a conclusion forcing itself increasingly upon
our unwilling minds, you have a share in that death, even if she
died by accident. I think you know this; that is your foul
fiend, I think.

"I have a part in your suffering," looking into the blind misery of Roger's eyes.

"Go and walk, Roger, it'll do you good. Walk upstream,
because I have business downstream and I don't want you
obscuring my eyesight. And don't fall in the water." He turned
and made off, down towards the boathouse.

Castang got involved, unwittingly, a little earlier, in the death
of a woman shot by another woman at a blind hazardous meeting on the street. What part, what share, what guilt had Castang
in that death? Technically, none. He was meddlesome? He
interfered with a pattern? Crossing a road meddles with the pattern of that road and those using it. By the same token, on that
same occasion while crossing a road he was nearly run over. It

might not have been an accident, and what is accident? He was trying to cross in a stupid place and behaved stupidly, and a court would in judging the responsibility for that accident have taken as much into reckoning.

I have no guilt, thought Castang, but I have a part. Luckily, we are taught by philosophy to bear responsibility for ourselves. Not for others. And if we all obeyed that admirable precept – then there would be no call for policemen.

There is no point in asking what Roger did, caused, provoked or brought about. I don't think he knows himself. He is digging for it.

The boathouse and the banks told Castang no more than the last time he had looked. The shed was a solid structure, built out far enough on piles that even at low water it would be impossible to get round the riverward end. The landward end was firmly padlocked and nobody had interfered with it. Roger had produced the key when asked: the two boats were chained and showed no sign of anything in the least degree unusual.

If she had gone in off the bank all the policemen in France would have found no trace ten minutes later: wind and rain of that intensity could alter a whole landscape. And had. Even so he searched the whole bank again carefully, down to the end of the old quay. What had she been wearing? Roger could not recall. He could not recall anything whatever. He was sorry, he had drunk a great deal.

The end of the quay was marked by the stump of a mooring bollard broken off in some century-old piece of violence: scrub thereafter of willow and ground ivy and unappetising ground, black and sticky, boggy now where the height of the flood had invaded the scrawny growth, prolific and sickly and with no chance of surviving, like medieval children. There was no possible path here. He had to go back to the house, skirting the old ilex trees that marked the limit of Roger's squiredom.

They had a boat on a trailer, hooked to the Mercedes Unimog that was today's village donkey; a flat-bottomed thing like a large punt, descendant of the type of ferry that had brought voyagers and perhaps a horse, one at a time, across the water. They drove out past the village rubbish-tip: if they did not find her soon, reflected Castang gloomily, he'd have to get a mechanical digger and search those malodorous piles.

"When was that bulldozed last?"

"Month or more," said Noel, guessing what was in his mind. "Anything dumped there we'd soon see, because been hardly any tipped since. And just as I know how to look, I'd know better than to hide, in case you got ideas."

There was a clearing by the riverside at the head of the big bend, and here they picked up le père Bache, a wizened ghoul with reminiscences of his childhood when a poacher had fallen in during a flood, and been found some weeks later in a state he described with relish. Unless cut back branches of scrub willow grew out horizontally, and the river flotsam (there was a lot at the best of times) washed up by the current would hook on that, creating another merry little rubbish tip classified by the Prefecture as a public nuisance.

There was an outboard motor for the boat, handled by Noel with skill and judgment. It called for admiration; the current was strong and there were eddies and unexpected turbulences.

"Sandbank out there," pointing. "Shows at low water: couldn't tell now, less you knew."

"Lot of tricks in this old river," chuckled the old man. If these countrymen wanted to get rid of a body, thought Castang, they would know how.

"Fish?" he asked.

"Sure. Pike, eels, perch; better, if you know where to look." Decidedly ... A fellow like Noel Arnaud, who would and could go anywhere without attracting attention, who had everyone from the mayor on down in his pocket, who had a fourwheel drive truck ... what chance would a poor ignorant city cop like himself stand in that maze? Still, they wouldn't have been able to get the boat out, in the storm.

Noel steered them down to the bottom of the bend, and le père Bache brought them up, close in shore, using just enough throttle to hold them against the stream and foot by foot back up again while Noel and his dopey aide probed assiduously. Nothing. Two hours of hard work, and the mayor saying he'd send the bill for time and labour and material to the PJ, damn it, did he think they'd nothing else to do?

He'd have to get a team from the town with professional

equipment and skindivers, and that meant all the legal formalities he'd so far managed to avoid.

They gave him a leg up on to the quay, only a metre above water level. That boathouse was quite recent. Perhaps Roger's predecessor had built it. Piling went out quite a way. Simple wooden structure of rough-squared beams, whatever wood didn't rot under water; elm was it? Driven down into the bed by some simple traditional engineering technique. Braced at the angles with Y joints?

"How deep it go, there?"

"A good three; near four now. Used to bring loaded barges in under here."

"Just try under the staging there. I've got the keys, I'll open up the shed."

"She'd have washed clear," said Arnaud doubtfully.

"Not a chance," said the père Bache with expert dogmatism.

Nonetheless Castang was right. Marlene had after all not gone far.

Getting a still partially agile cop up the bank is one thing: a dead body another. He got back in the boat.

"I don't want any more damage: there's enough."

"Have to go back down the landing."

It was not 'all that bad'; she had not been in the water 'all that long'.

Noel Arnaud showed the same careful professional skill he had brought to the whole afternoon's work. Reliable, unagitated. Something better.

"La pobrecita," handling her with pity and dignity. You're a tricky complex character, thought Castang, but I don't believe you had anything to do with killing her. Nor tipping her in the drink afterwards.

The dopey chap showed his humanity, perfectly good if a bit dim, by helping stoutly before being sick over the gunwale. And le père Bache was delighted with a story that would light his declining days and lend relish to drinks for many a week.

"Who'd ha' thought that – jammed up against the pile that funny way. Must ha' slipped on that greasy wood looking was the boats properly moored when the storm come on. Knocked

138

her head on the bow of the sailer, like and gone straight under, got tangled that ol' mooring chain."

"It's feasible," said Noel. "Light's not too good in there, or it might have been round twilight when it came on bad. She used to sail that boat and knew how to handle it. She was clean-footed too. But anyone could slip. Pitch over like, into the dock."

True, true, true, thought Castang; it could happen. But if you came out just to look at the boats to make sure they were properly tied, in the rising wind and rain, wouldn't you be wearing a raincoat? He said nothing.

"We can't bring her home," said Noel.

"You must have a room in the Mairie, till she can be brought to the town. I'll phone for an ambulance."

The light was not good enough. Castang had done courses in criminal pathology at police school, had had his head stuffed with the sort of information one forgets happily the moment that the examination paper is completed. Over years of criminal-brigade practice one had kept a knowledge of a few rough-and-ready verifications. Petechial haemorrhage, for example, in asphyxia. But there are underwater creatures as well as flood currents to damage a body even less than forty-eight hours dead. Eyes and lips are the first to go . . . there was every imaginable kind of bruising.

"Flood wood," said Noel – still those surprisingly gentle hands – who could tell what come a-jolting and a-polting past, current running forty an hour and more."

"Get Cécile for me, Noel: we'll have to get her clothes off and keep them separate for the lab to look at."

"La pauvresse," said Cécile with the same sorrowing gentle-ness her husband had shown. She worked with silent com-petence. When finished she looked straight at him.

"Neither of my men had aught to do with this."

"I don't think so," said Castang, not asking why she should think so. He had made up his mind. He wanted Richard here.

He phoned from the secretary's office, upstairs.

"I think on the whole," picking words, "it would be valid – valuable – if you could take an hour or so out here, this evening

139

maybe." The lines had been repaired but Richard's voice was faint; there were squawks and buzzes: humidity doubtless in relays or whatever, if not still downright wet.

"Why are you talking Spanish?" irritatingly.

"Because I'm not anxious to take the world into my confidence!" shouted Castang in English.

"I'm sorry, I wasn't concentrating." Richard's voice came suddenly loud and clear. "Good, I'll see what I can do. In the interest of mopping up." The picture thus drawn of the Divisional Commissaire in an apron, equipped with floorcloth and bucket, was pleasing.

Vera had made a walk with the child 'down into the village' but was in the kitchen, bending the mind towards dinner.

"Roger not back?"

"Haven't seen him."

"There's another silly twit," obscurely, and with anxiety in the voice. "He better not do anything stupid. We found her . . . She was in the water."

"Ah."

"Pathology – I mean Professor Deutz – will likely tell us a good deal. And will it, I wonder, be enough?" The English, Castang was thinking; their system is better than ours. They have a specialist in criminal pathology, their 'Home Office Expert', and they don't hesitate to get him out of bed and bring him to look in situ at a dead body and the circumstances of its discovery. It might not make much difference here. But these things can hang on very small and trivial-seeming details. Castang, a careful and thorough taker of notes, who had written up his dossier at length in the secretary's office, was not at all sure it would be enough. Concentrated yes; conscientious yes. 'Beau, beau, beau et con à la fois' as Jacques Brel had it. The competent and experienced criminal-brigade Commissaire could also be a stupid cunt.

Use what help you can get, Castang thought.

"You sit down. We'll have a beer or something. And you tell me what you make of it." She had finished scraping her carrots, was meticulously peeling two onions. This did not make her eyes water – a job she did every day, and she had immunity.

"Typically Marlene, not to have a proper kitchen knife.

Make of it? I make little of little, and little at a time. 'Souvent mais peu à la fois, comme disait le père Swann.' "

"What has he to do with it?" blank and also irritable.

"Yes, I ramble. And take me as you find me," giving Lydia (who loved them) a raw carrot. "I know a certain amount about Marlene. We were to some extent friends. She didn't go pouring out. And I'm not a heart-to-heart kind of woman at all.

"As for Roger, he's been reading too much Proust. There's someone who can say very acute truths, who can light up the most banal tiny detail of social behaviour with a paragraph of marvellously accurate observation and deep understanding, and who could talk perfect piffle. 'A woman is made only for love . . . A woman will do anything for love . . . Any woman can in the end be conquered . . .' There are more women in the world than Odette . . . Is it the Duchess who says 'I make it, often, but I never never talk about it'? Marlene didn't go gassing on about love. Very secret, very proud person."

"For whatever reason, do you think she could have got into a compromising position with other men?" Thumbnail sketch of the two Arnauds, and Castang could well imagine that either (and both were far from being stupid lumpen) were capable of making even a thoroughly balanced woman yield to fantasies.

"You don't get into compromising positions unless you want to. Hang around at the foot of a haystack looking coy, stands to reason you'll be pushed into it."

"She was out and about in the garden, in the stable – on the river in summer. Without it being intentional –' "

"She was the kind of woman who doesn't even change her skirt without locking the door and drawing the curtains. I ought to know; I'm that way myself. No point in arguing. I tell you she didn't."

"Adultery is no longer exclusively a bourgeois pastime."

"No but it's a bourgeois mentality. You meet a lot of women. Some stink of sex a mile off. Nothing better to offer."

"Some, sometimes. Beware of generalisations."

"You asked me. You don't have to ask me. Go right ahead and search the hayloft for evidence."

"All right, let's confine ourselves to Roger."

"Ah . . . I've spent the day with Roger. Hints enough get

dropped to fill a casebook. Are they real? Invented? Does he even know himself? With a writer you can never be sure; at least I can't."

"This is just my trouble. Roger is full of Coqcigrues – oh it's one of Richard's words. Intellectual French way of saying bullshit. I mean, do you see Roger out there on the riverbank, in the pouring rain, pushing her in the water?"

"No, it sounds like something out of *Wuthering Heights*. He's found out that really she's his illegitimate sister and he's been committing incest all his life."

"He doesn't have to plan theatrical scenes: he gets into them without thinking. But however much whisky he'd drunk he'd say it was getting far too wet and he was going home."

"I can't believe in it," he said. "She was the right kind of wife for a loony like Roger. I mean strong character, not at all intellectual, totally loyal. Rock to cling to, no, however hard the wind blows?"

"I'm not sure," said Vera, hesitant, "she said to me she was fed up with being a decorative object and I think she refused to sleep with him any more, which really would be asking for trouble."

"How do you know?"

"He's been on that divan in the studio for months."

"But this stuff about the big bed being so empty that I keep on waking up? . . ."

"A mask. One hides pain, nicht, and humiliation?"

"Christ!" said Castang in consternation. "This opens up a lot of very dodgy reasoning. Well – it's to be presumed that he'd have no great difficulty in finding someone else to sleep with."

"Who d'you suggest? Me? I'm not sure it's all that easy. And can't you hear him saying – 'Mistresses dear boy; so much trouble. Such a nuisance and in the long run such a bore'. And not really his style."

"I suppose. Slave of his routines and little habits. Too lazy really."

"And basically a very moral person."

"No proper evidence for any of this," Castang, dissatisfied.

"I can tell you this much. He drank a good deal this morning and suddenly he said 'I used to be a good writer. And now like

Theseus after the death of Hippolytus, the god no longer speaks to me!' "

"Attitudinising," said Castang. "What does it mean?"

"Phaedra, dear, Phaedra, didn't you do Racine at school?"

"I can't claim to have taken a close interest."

"She was Theseus's wife. Hippolytus was his son by a previous wife. She wanted Hippolytus to make love to her; he refused, rightly shocked. In revenge she accused him of raping her. Theseus equally shocked invoked a death curse upon his son, and found out the truth too late."

"You've got me hopelessly muddled. Marlene is no Phèdre."

"No, but I've been thinking all day," said Vera. "She didn't have any lover, I'm convinced of that. He might find it necessary to invent one. And to drown his own rage and grief, to drown her in the flood."

"God!" said Castang, holding his head. "Where is that animal anyway? Hope he hasn't drowned himself in any flood; or maybe I hope he has: save us all a lot of trouble!"

"What's that, then?" The noise of a car on the gravel outside.

It was not, however, Roger. There was a short bossy ring at the doorbell, very 'Police!', and before Castang could even get there the door had opened and Richard walked in.

He surveyed the company briefly with his hands in his pockets and then said, "I'm hungry."

"Oh dear," Vera beginning immediately and unnecessarily to worry. "I bought bourguignonne from the butcher but it seemed so ghastly, all fresh and pink and wet, that I turned it into hamburger. Never mind, there's plenty. Or would you rather go out to the pub?"

"Dearest Vera," said Richard who loved her greatly. "I'd rather eat your food than the pub's even if it is hamburger. Do get me a drink Henri, I'm fainting. Talking about food reminds me of a preposterous advertisement that's been appearing recently. Reopening of a palace after redecoration. All sorts of wonders promised. Specimen menu given, chosen off the carte." Richard put on his soprano voice, indicative of extremes of sexual inversion.

"Pétales de Saint-Jacques, my dears. Délices de sole something. And Mignons of beef of many colours. Now what does this call to mind? – thank you, Henri, that's nice."

"I won't spoil your pleasure in an aphorism you've probably had all day to prepare."

"Country mouse comes to town, to dine off a smirk, a snigger, and a wee small squeak."

"I see exactly."

"And this," theatrically, "is why I'd rather eat Vera's hamburger."

"It won't take long," said the lady, humble and serious.

"Now, Castang, give me the briefest possible résumé of your case as you see it."

"Gets madder by the minute," said Castang gloomily. "I think there's a good chance of breaking it suddenly, and I don't think I'm going to be very good at that – too much wood and a lot too many trees – and I think the fresh eye from outside."

"Mm. Mum. Sha," said Richard.

"If not suddenly busted is the sort that can hang about for months highly inconclusive. Three witnesses, call them suspects if that way inclined, likely to drive a judge of instruction raving bonkers. A circumstantial psychological pot of –"

"Yes," said Richard. "I'd like to have you back at work."

Castang tried not to explain anything: Richard loathed explanations.

"Well, where are these three clowns?"

"One's out in the rain, and it's time he came back. The other two in the village, five minutes with the car: do you want them here or in the mairie?"

"Ready," said Vera in the doorway, "but should we wait for Roger?"

"No. I can't eat at table with a suspect; that's what's blocked you. Give me my dinner in the servants' hall and let me think over what you've told me. When you've eaten get me the village Lotharios. Here; I don't want any mayors mucking me about. If by then the Artist has not turned up have him picked up by the cops, I'm not having any more nonsense. Garde à vue, back in town; shake the feathers out of his head."

"Come on then or it'll go cold. Here," said Castang, taking

the Luger pistol out of his raincoat pocket where it had been forgotten, "this might help. And on the subject of raincoats if she went out to the boathouse in a storm why wasn't she wearing one?"

They had just finished dinner. Vera had that moment said "Good, I'll just put Lydia to bed." Castang had lit a post-prandial cigarette. And Richard, looking for a suitable interrogation-room had picked on 'the conservatory'. The outer door opened and Roger appeared. Hilarious, not to say euphoric.

"Sorry to be late, Vera. I made rather a longer walk than I'd intended, and stopped at the pub for a pick-me-up, and time slipped away somehow." Was it because he hadn't heard the news? Or because he had . . .

He stopped dead on seeing Richard.

"Dear me, this house gets more like the Gare Saint-Lazare every minute; who's this?"

"Divisional Commissaire, Regional Service of Police Judiciaire," in accents of the most extreme politeness. "The queries, Monsieur Riderhood, into the disappearance of your wife take of necessity a new frame of reference, that of a judicial enquiry. To make use of your house is nowise to abuse your good will; it is natural." The quiet voice, like new powder snow, was light, dry and cold; held an authority no one would question: it much impressed Roger and it much impressed Castang. Well! Who thought (or perhaps said) that Richard had gone a bit overripe and maybe sentimentalised in his old age? Excuse or apology is, to use a favourite Richard-word, otiose . . .

"Have your dinner," said Richard kindly, as to a small child, "and have the goodness to wait here until I call you. Perhaps Madame Castang will bear you company with her knitting. Do not drink."

Richard stalked away into the 'conservatory', turned in the doorway and said. "Find me the witnesses, Castang; leave one in the car. In mine you will find a tape-recorder." And shut the door.

It had been Marlene's pride and joy, and would please Judith Richard, a mighty gardener. The outside walls of the southwest corner had been replaced by glass, the wooden floor tiled: there was a vine, two orange-trees in tubs wintering indoors, and some flowering plants not hardy enough for this climate. There was an old Persian rug on the floor and some cane chairs. On an autumn night it was sinister, with the dark prowling in from outside and the plants throwing strange shadows on the darkened glass.

Noel Arnaud felt uneasy here; hemmed-in and somehow diminished. Accustomed to being shouted at by mayors or whoever, and paying no attention, he was also disconcerted by Richard's satiny manner (which Castang called fulsome).

"Your full name if you please, date of birth, address and profession. The voice level up a little bit if you would; you are being recorded.

"You have been evasive, Monsieur Arnaud, you have prevaricated. There are certain questions you have not answered to the satisfaction of Monsieur Castang. Some indeed you have refused. You will now please make a statement both full and frank.

"You are aware that this is a preliminary enquiry and that you are not upon oath. You are also aware that further questions will be put to you in the office of the Judge of Instruction, and that inconsistency in your replies may form the base for examination by counsel – and another judge; the President of the Assize Court . . . Please do not mutter.

"Do you often go out in the evenings, Monsieur Arnaud? . . .

"Monsieur Riderhood is accustomed to doing much of his work in the early mornings. He goes early to bed. Madame was often rather later. There are people, my friend, who develop the maximum of their energies and attention in the evenings . . . Quite so. I too keep daylight hours. I am aware; so are you. You would oblige me by abandoning this pretence at stupidity.

"Just go into a little more detail, would you? . . .

"We come now to the evening of the storm. The storm had been blowing all day with increasing violence."

Richard sat quite immobile and without smoking in the cane chair. The standard lamp behind him threw an unreal pool of yellowish light; a tree to his right stood stiff and hieratic in exotic shadow. One could be in India, thought Castang. Or Malaysia. One would not be a bit surprised to see, of a sudden, a cobra. A big one would be about five feet long. About the height of Richard sitting down. They rear up sitting on their fast muscular tails and stay there immobile: perhaps they sway a little from side to side. Do they have their hoods spread? Booh, getting frightened with imagination.

"Madame Arnaud has a very natural – highly laudable – anxiety to show loyalty to her husband. In rather blunt, everyday words, not to give you away . . . I am aware, monsieur, that a wife does not bear witness against her husband. I congratulate you. There is no question of being 'against'. Such testimony is technically termed a *recoupage*. A cross-bearing, would we say? A verification, monsieur, we may define as a test of veracity. Veracity is a polite term for not lying . . .

"Madame Arnaud would be much embarrassed. I am not anxious to enter upon this terrain . . . She is in a peculiar position, is she not? She worked together closely with Madame Riderhood, for a number of years. These two ladies formed an esteem for one another. We would not be amiss in calling this a friendship, and even an affection. Nor am I mistaken in believing that there were confidences between them.

"You do not weary me, monsieur. I have all the time in the world. The tape will run for up to six hours. And I have spares, in the car. I am not convinced, mon cher Arnaud, that you have altogether deserved this loyalty . . .

"We are among men, here. There are subjects which among men can be discussed with understanding. Even a certain sympathy. We have all experience of these situations, knowledge of these emotions.

"I wish to point out that upon the jury of an assize court women are to be found . . . And the judges; not quite the same old male indulgence; not quite so quick to accept the old arguments. And may I say? – neither am I. 'Oh, she was asking for it – and even if she wasn't well, she was a consenting party: just another mal baisée who didn't get enough from her own man.' No, monsieur. I do not listen to those stories."

When is the cobra going to strike? When the music stops. Noel Arnaud is piping away there, sweating and the whites of his eyes showing. He is aware that he isn't magnetising anyone.

"What was she doing, hey, down there by the boathouse?"

When he led Noel away there were no bruises showing on the big hard face but Castang thought him trudging heavily. Flat-footed. Like a boxer who has been bodypunched for eleven rounds. Looks all right still to the unprofessional eye, but is ripe. Richard said nothing and lit a cigar.

When the boy Gilbert came in and sat down with an easy looseness, the sullen swagger that catches the eye of the girls, Richard went on saying nothing, and went on smoking his cigar. It takes a minute or two for a boy of this age to realise that he is not among the girls.

A display of technical brilliance, this time. Richard very rarely interrogated anyone, in the office or out of it. It had been years since Castang had seen him do anything much but put a few supplementary words to some recalcitrant or plain dimwit person who had already been exhaustively yacked at by the criminal brigade, or perhaps the financial squad – or perhaps most often the violence squad, termed prudishly Search and Investigation but called simply the bandits. A few words drifting like the cigar smoke, sidelong, edgeways.

And here was the orchestra. In recent years one had forgotten that this mild and silvery gentleman – in his sixties after all – had been a PJ cop for a long while. Forgotten more than Castang knew, he now thought. The boy got the orchestration thrown at him: from the pianissimo opening to a querulous and irritable series of interruptions and interjections, culminating abruptly in a towering rage. Gentlemanly? Using coarse expressions in thieves' kitchen argot I didn't know he knew . . .

"Don't come it with me, laddy, I can slot you into jug with such a complicated dossier you'll be there four years before the thing ever gets to court, and by then you'll wish you'd never been born so don't try the Black-Widow act with me." Castang had quite forgotten the Black Widow, a classic from what –at least twenty years back – who had poisoned he forgot how many husbands, as everybody knew perfectly well; but had combined obstinacy, tenacity and peasant cunning with so much talent for legal chicanery that the whole court had practically dropped dead from sheer exhaustion: what arsenic could not accomplish cerebral congestion did.

"All right, Castang, take them home. You might ask Vera would she have the extreme kindness to make me a cup of coffee and I'm ready for Mr. Riderhood whenever he is – and you are," generously. Noel hadn't waited to be driven home. He'd walked. With what thoughts? And would he be telling them to Cécile? He didn't look too good: not good at all . . .

And the boy? A boy's pride will always insist on taking as much punishment as a man, and he gets that much more badly hurt. A police officer will not habitually use a word like 'saddening', for it is part of his profession to see that boys like this become saddened, and the quicker the better. Castang in the rôle of ringside judge felt a moment's sympathy with the amateur, now crying quietly in a corner after a nasty moment when he had lost his heart and lungs there on the floor in front of him.

Mr. Riderhood now – that is a professional.

"I am sorry," said Richard courteously, stirring his coffee, "to keep you up so late."

"I'm not all that keen on it either," with a pleasant smile.

"Nor is it to have to question you, upon a matter so personal, in your own house, an agreeable job."

"Ah. My house. The Owls' House, and the Playhouse, and the House of Commons, and Come onna-my-house, and our House at Eton, and our Town House in Holland Park, and Charterhouse, and the Last Homely House. I miss them all. Nostalgia."

"I remember asking you not to drink," finishing his coffee. "You will bear it in mind that I said so, and I want it on the record. Your wife fell in the river, from which her body was recovered this afternoon in Mr. Castang's presence. The fact is not in dispute."

"I've never denied it; or tried to hide it. It was my fault."

"I'm not interested, Mr. Riderhood."

"Then what are you doing here?"

"There are three ways of finding oneself in the river. Falling, jumping, and pushing. Since one does not walk in. It is not a bath."

"Accident suicide and homicide, why can't you say so?"

"Because you deal in words, and abstractions. I deal in facts,

149

and the concrete. People fall, Mr. Riderhood. It does not happen naturally. It is contrary to natural laws. This fact, and this fact alone, interests the police."

"Are you telling me you don't believe in the law of gravity?"

"There are other, more important laws. You will understand. Your mind is good and, once cleared of this fog of alcohol, you will begin to reason. Words like accident, suicide – these are emotional words, and imprecise. She fell, regardless of survival. That is an essential law. It is built up, in the adult, through experience. Children fall. Not "dryly" as often as people try to lead us to believe. But they do fall, not having yet learned prudence and a sense of balance.

"If an adult falls, Mr. Riderhood, an agency is at work. An agency that may be physiological, conceivably psychological, but quite simple. For example, vertigo. A malfunction of the inner ear. For example, alcohol, inducing a sense of euphoria and subseqent recklessness, such as I observe in yourself.

"The psychological factors, such as despair leading to a suspension of prudence, a suicidal impulse, or romantic notions called a death wish – these are observable, traceable, and are found also to depend upon an agency. This agency interests the police officer. The rest is cant.

"Your wife fell. An agency was at work. This agency brought her to the bank of a river in spate, in darkness, violent wind and heavy rain. To isolate, identify, define that agency is my task. To explain it, not in the least. Are you still too drunk to understand what I am saying?"

"No," said Roger. "I might be drunk but I'm quite lucid, thank you."

"The agency that has brought you to that point is myself. If I had wished I could have worked upon you to produce confusion, fear, irritability, violence."

"If I allowed you to do so."

"I can do so; you may rely upon it. I have done so twice, this evening. Talk of legality or justice is cant. A mechanism, producing effects that serve as a test. An imprecise test, serving no more than possibilities. Experience can sometimes guide one to a probability.

"The probability here was that the agency I am looking for was to be found in yourself. Entirely so? That is not certain. In repeating so stupidly 'My fault' you confirm to some extent that you assume responsibility in the mechanisms leading to your wife's death, but you confuse and emotionalise the issue, which is futile. Are you ready to go on?"

"Why don't I just sign a confession or whatever it is you want?"

"Tell him, Castang."

"Anybody can sign a confession and frequently does. Easy to say next day, 'Oh I just said that for the sake of a bit of peace and now I've changed my mind.' Short cuts are evasions. Take responsibility for what you do."

"You kiss my arse," said Roger.

"There's a certain resemblance between you two," Richard said. "You're both trying to be judge and witness at the same time. You're both blocked, and you have to get yourselves unblocked.

"He's a witness, Mr. Riderhood. A friend of yours, who has been a number of times in your house, who knew you both and liked you. He testifies to the effect that you were a singularly united and harmonious couple, perhaps because of your acceptance, a generous and open acceptance, that each of you was singularly dependent upon the other. Forming an objective opinion, you agree?"

"How can I form an objective opinion?"

"Yes you can, you're a writer."

"And what are you?" furiously. "A doctor? Doctor Scheissgrüss the head shrink?"

"No," said Richard smiling. "I'm a picture dealer. Perhaps an editor. Somebody with no creative powers but who sympathises, who tries to understand. And who has, to be sure, a professional interest."

"That's less stupid," admitted Roger. "I can accept that. All right, I can accept the other remark too."

"What worries one hereabouts is that you were sleeping apart." Roger threw a startled, reproachful look at Castang.

"Did something traumatic take place, to bring that about? You used force on her? Raped her maybe?"

151

"Force!" with indignation. "She was twice as strong as me!" The tiny note of comedy helped to break the tension.

"Somebody else raped her maybe," offered Richard, lighting a cigar.

"You've had the two Arnauds in – you ask them!"

"They both did. Or both tried. Or both at least very kindly made the offer. I don't of course necessarily have to believe them. It would be nice to have some independent testimony."

"She told me."

"In those words?"

"Something about I was lousy in bed and she could do better."

"Come, you're a writer; you must know that's been said some time by every woman to every man. Still; you believed it? Just a little? You thought perhaps of testing it? Lay a little trap? Exact some suitable little vengeance?"

"What are you getting at?" asked Roger. Genuinely curious to know.

"As a writer, you ought to know how to be honest with yourself. And I'm Scheissgrüss enough for this – that in every man, mark my words, every man – there is a sadist streak. Just as there is a streak of narcissism."

"I'll agree to that."

"Upon a painful humiliation – to turn the tables in some manner?"

"You're guessing."

"Yes I'm guessing, but I think it close to the truth. To take an example from classical mythology, Candaules or was it Gyges arranges for the captain of the guard to see his wife naked."

"That would have been difficult," quite earnestly. "You didn't know Marlene." Vera's very words!

"The general idea," said Richard, "I think."

Roger was silent.

"Patterns . . . I have, as you remark, examined the two Arnauds. They are both in a state of much confusion. They too are hurt in their vanity, their maleness. Vaguely aware that a trap had been set for them, too. And complicated by the fact that they're father and son, so that a jealous rivalry existed. And both liked your wife – a nice woman, in their words. And both devoted to Madame Arnaud, Cécile as you call her. Another nice woman. To you – only the cleaning woman. But your wife's friend. A dirty trick to play her too, wasn't it?"

Silence.

"And they both liked you, too . . . They still don't really know what happened. Well well. We'll take them down to headquarters and work on them a little and it will all come out bit by bit. It means the Procureur de la République, Mr. Riderhood, and a criminal instruction. And the Press. You don't play a very shining rôle in all this, do you?"

Silence.

"So we shall have to know, shan't we, what it was that happened down at the boathouse. I haven't seen it yet. We might go down together for a look. Castang tells me there's a lot of summer stuff stored down there. Picnic things. Air mattresses. Camping gas. Even on a night near the beginning of winter one could arrange to be warm and comfortable. And then a storm. Quite an emotional affair, a storm. Heightens the excitement. A favourite mechanism for fiction writers."

"That's all you're doing," sulkily, "writing fiction."

"As you did. That is the basic mechanism, the agency we have been looking for. That is all I need. The rest is decoration and can be left to the judge of instruction.

"I have no powers of creation, Mr Riderhood: if I had I would not be a cop. In my life as a human being I have learned things. I have frequented enough artists to know that they make a scenario for a story, or a picture, or a piece of music. They arrange that personages, lines – whatever the medium – should follow a certain composition. And at some moment, during the work, a thing happens that none of us understand. Least of all the artist. The thing takes on a life of its own and begins to deviate from the pattern. With unforeseen results. The artist tries to be aware of this, to keep control of it. Submit to it, follow it but keep a grip upon it. That, as I imagine, is the hard part. And with other human beings – you aren't the director of a play, you cannot say Stop: I'm not happy with that scene, just run through it again.

"To manipulate other human beings, Mr. Riderhood; it isn't in the penal code but it is among the gravest of crimes."

"I want a drink."

"Not while I'm looking at you," said Richard getting up. He walked through to the living room. "Vera dear, could you find us something nice to drink? Some of Mr. Riderhood's delicious whisky? – if there's any left!" He came back and offered Roger a cigar, who took it.

People who accepted one of Richard's cigars, blackish Brazilian things looking rather like liquorice, regretted it at once; after one puff and a disgusted look, mostly searched for a surreptitious means of throwing it away. Roger accepted a light from Castang, blew a long jet of smoke, looked at the cigar and said. "This is rather good." Castang marvelled. He could say nothing, because they were on a rocking stone, such as is sometimes found as a caprice of natural history balanced upon another. If two or three people try to stand upon it and rock in unison – further and further – will there come a moment when the balance is broken? One does much the same with two cars that have collided, and locked fenders together. By standing on the springs and rocking harder – harder – one can sometimes jump them apart.

It was Vera who, unconsciously, provided the 'déclic', the trigger mechanism. As Richard called it the agency . . . She came in hobbling slightly from having sat still too long, carrying a tray with glasses and the aged malt hoojah that both Roger and Castang liked too much (Richard wasn't above it either; knew better at least than to put water in it). She handed everybody a glass, saying. "No, no, I'm not having any, I'm going to have a tisane," and gave everyone a smile. Smile of trust, both gentle and brilliant. Roger took the glass. Vera went out and shut the door. Roger took a small sip, closed his eyes, nodded twice and said. "It won't be necessary, to go down to the boathouse."

"Vera had worked out something very much like that. I didn't lean on it hard because to be honest I thought it too far-fetched."

"Not very long ago, Castang – where were you that you don't know about this? that's right, of course, you were in Germany

154

making an ass of yourself – the financial squad brought in a schoolmaster. Sixty-two, height of his profession in a respectable smalltown way. Ordre de Mérite, Palmes Académiques, full of honours. Six children grown up, no problems anywhere; an impeccable gentleman. And he started gambling, and to gamble he borrowed, and people were happy to lend. In three years he made away with three million, including seven hundred thousand from one widow who gave him the run of her safe-deposit. Now what d'you make of that?"

"Look closely at the wife."

"Which of course is what we did – another impeccable type, pillar of the parish . . . but what's the object lesson?"

"I don't know, except that anybody, anywhere, is capable of anything whatsoever."

"And one will never guess; until one looks."

"Are there loose ends? The raincoat?"

"Arnaud took it with him to hide it. Which? – it's of no importance and I don't want to know."

"You want them all taken in? That I should call the wagon?"

"No. Let me think. When you were in Germany, you got blocked. A woman died. Nothing to do with you but you had a part in it – there was a phrase that struck you. You got locked in. Being a witness, you tried to judge, you tried to be a bit of a cop, and you made a balls of all three. You were the trigger, a bit, that precipitated a catastrophe. In so far as I ever understood your highly incoherent account. Am I correct?"

"You are, yes, thank you, and fuck you too."

"Something very similar happened to Marlene. She got a foolish idea as Vera tells me that the rôle she played in that marriage, that household and that career, plainly a very important – vital – one, was in some way not good enough, that as a woman she deserved better. She started persecuting her man, and he over-reacted very badly, feeling threatened in the deep inside. She had a foolish idea, and he had a wicked one. The tempest precipitated it.

"She had a part in her own death, a suicidal share. She did much to bring it about. The law would not say so, but you might."

"I would, yes." It was not only in Germany that such things could happen . . .

"And how much share is homicide? Since her death was precipitated by the violence of others."

"Certainly." Most road accidents followed the same pattern. On the face, there is no homicidal intent. There is the definition of homicide by imprudence. It isn't sufficient. Every traffic-detail cop recognises a criminal irresponsibility, but where is the doctrine of an unconscious will to homicide? Get picked up with the smoking pistol and the prosecutor will claim intent. Twelve years, members of the jury. Be found grinning foolishly, at the wheel of your flying bomb, and even the alcohol in your bloodstream can get seen as mitigating circumstances. Please the court, my wife cooked a lousy dinner and kept nagging me.

"And how much is pure accident?" went on Richard. "Quite likely she only went to the boathouse to see that floodwater didn't get at those rugs and stuff. Stupid Riderhood gets it in his head that she's creeping off for a midnight court with Arnaud: does it even matter which? – both notable studs in their fashion.

"Even Cécile, good and kind, who knew her well, liked her. Use the word, loved her. And on that very account finding her own marriage threatened."

"I wondered," said Castang. "But where the hell would one find a scrap of evidence?"

"I wouldn't even try. Maybe nobody pushed her, in any physical sense. If you once admit any other sense, they all pushed her. If they had a will to her death what part had they, what share? Poor girl." Richard, who had never met her, had perhaps understood her better than anyone.

So who had been in the boathouse? Marlene, and . . . four ghosts, Vera might have put it. Men are perhaps better at physics. And women at metaphysics.

"You'd call her stupid?" asked Castang.

"Not terribly bright, as you tell me, and what is being bright to boast of?" asked Richard dryly. "Riderhood's bright! Neurotic like most of us, and that means psychotic under pressure. Ah, well, cail him for me . . .

156

"Sit down – sit down, fool, I tell you. Listen to me.

"By your account, on your admission, I can charge you formally with homicide; bring you in, lock you up. End of my duties: I've no further responsibility, a nice clear conscience. From then on it is the examining magistrate who instructs, who decides. So says the law. A lengthy process. It would be many many months.

"Just as with Arnaud. I could probably charge him with at least attempted rape.

"Possibly, the court's decision after deliberation would be a non-lieu, a nolle prosequi. It is by no means certain.

"After I have written my name at the foot of an official form, a year and perhaps much longer follows, of misery, suffering, and confinement. That is certain as death. I sign: the law grinds.

"In the Middle Ages, Riderhood, where our law comes from, there were a good few picturesque varieties of death by torture. Commit a misdemeanour and you could look forward to an appalling end. It was taken for granted. And between then and today there was another important difference. Mercy also existed. You might be pulled apart by four horses and you might be let free with a laugh. Because it was a saint's day or because the king felt sorry for his own sins.

"Today's law is impersonal, and it doesn't let you go. I like to try to bear that in mind.

"So I'll pronounce my own non-lieu."

Roger cried his lungs out: spat his heart. Very much like the young Arnaud, an hour or two before. No bad thing, that tears should be shed for Marlene. Cécile's turn would come, to cry.

Vera, also, thought Castang.

"Get a glass of water, Castang . . . Drink it slowly. Castang here could tell you a story of how he became involved in a woman's death. It happens. You have guilt as well as part, but what difference does it make, or ought?

"As a cop, I have a part. A death involves me. This one I refuse. I reject.

"There are three other people involved, in this village. I'll handle that. And you have your part to play. I want you out of

157

here. Sell the house or let it or dynamite it. Go live anywhere you like, it need be no concern of mine. Castang will destroy those tapes. But fuck off – understood?"

"And now I'm about to leave myself; there's work waiting for me at the office. Since I'm leaving you with a mess," to Castang, "you can take the rest of the day off; who's to know?"

"You don't think he'll go jumping in the river?" said Castang in undertone.

"No," said Richard. "Too much imagination. Tell him to go stay for a change with his pederast pal. Say goodbye to Vera for me."

"Asleep. What about the Arnaud family?"

"What about them? Nothing about them. You say nothing, I'm sure they never will. Got to live with it; you'd be surprised how easy they'll find that after a little while."

Before leaving Castang strolled down to look at the river. The flood level had sunk some fifty centimetres already, leaving a lot of mud, shiny in the winter sunshine. The river rolled full, glassy, tranquil. The water no longer brown and muddy looked quite clean. Nice pastoral landscape. Very quiet, very gentle: by the brook . . .

Let's see, in the sixtieth symphony of old Beebee you had first the happy thoughts on arriving in the country; and then by the brook. Then you had the tempest; just so. And then – no, first you had the Revelry of Drunken Peasants. We've had That! and then the storm; got it right now.

And when the storm is finished and the sky clears and the wind falls we get a very pretty rocking melody, a berceuse. Ti – daa – da, ti – daa – da.

It reconciles. We have to try and leave it at that.

Part Three

'I have killed Ourselves'

The telephone kept ringing and Castang kept not answering. It was not making a disturbance; more a mouselike squeak in the kitchen next door but it disturbed Vera, who had to exercise her self-control. Like most wives she had much: she did not fidget but a small frown appeared. He was meticulous and she was conscientious. These two qualities can bring about disharmony and even lead to discord. She worried lest the telephone should have urgencies to announce. If, said Castang, people have any thing of importance to say they will ring again later. When I am working, and listening to music is work, I will not run after bells; I am not the footman.

There is also the automatic replier, nasty invention to discon cert the caller by bidding him state his business quick before getting cut off. This only increases slavery because of 'Bloggs here: call me back.' Who is Bloggs? Why the hell should we call him back? Now or ever?

The music was Carlos Kleiber's 'Tristan', and he had given it to Vera as a Christmas present, resisting the temptation to give her a new lavatory brush in pearly iridescent pink plastic. He had nearly resisted this temptation too, having no love for Wagner, but she desired it with insane longing, so he bought it because he loved her. Carlos could make even the Star- Spangled Banner appear as though the world heard it for the very first time, and the orchestra is that of Dresden . . .

"Outrageous," said Castang after one hearing. "East Germans. Communists. Stalinists. They aren't allowed to do anything at all but weight-lifting, or maybe a bit of waterpolo. The President of the United States must be told at once: he'll put a stop to this." The magic went on. Decidedly Carlos is the Head Zauberer.

The phone rang again at half past ten, and was again disregarded. The strength of this magic is such that the Pentagon, and the Palace of the Elysée, and Number Ten Downing Street, have all sunk deep beneath the wave; lower than Lyonesse.

At one minute to twelve Castang answered the phone. It was still by a fraction the twenty-eighth of December and the feast of the Holy Innocents.

"Geoffrey Dawson," said a voice. "From Dorset. Perhaps you recall."

"In Dawset. Well. Fancy that. Happy New Year."

"Where have you been all night then?"

"Sitting on the lavatory," answered Castang.

"Oy. If you want me to drop dead or anything, just say the word."

"Not in the least. I was attempting an ill-judged pleasantry."

"I do understand. The Trève des Confiseurs." Phrase for the pause between Christmas and the New Year when the French refuse to do anything but overeat. "What would that be – the Pastrycooks' Truce? Can you bear it for just one minute and then I'll take the nasty castor-oil bottle away?"

"No no, I'm fine, just I was far far away and only this second got back . . . Do stop apologising, Geoffrey, but is this just an offer of your left-over pudding? – I'm terribly sleepy."

"Only that I wanted to give a word of warning in your ear, that in the office in the morning will be a telex, and do look at it carefully for once because it's serious."

"Has it anything to do with Tintagel?" frivolously. There was a dead silence and then Geoffrey's voice said much astonished,

"Now how did you guess that?"

"I'm a Head Magician," said Castang. "Okay, I'll be back when this is untangled and don't ring off, Vera wants a word."

Having gone late to bed he was not extremely early next morning. Curtains of mist parted at the office, disclosing Richard reading a telex form. "Caesar, beware of Brutus; take heed of

160

Cassius; come not near Casca; have an eye to Cinna; mark well somebody or other."

"What," asked Richard with resignation, "is all this?"

"I don't know. I can make a guess. Geoffrey Dawson was on the phone last night. Have I told you about Geoffrey Dawson?"

"Attempt brevity and lucidity at the same time, would you?"

"He's a criminal brigade cop from Dorset whom I met in Munich and he's very nice as well as horribly bright and I take him very seriously and he rang me up at home to say there was a boring official telex but would I please read it carefully and that's all."

"Do so now." Handing it across.

"A double suicide of two French children in his district and he doesn't feel happy about it and would like me to come and look."

"Just to be friendly?"

"No, they belong here. Damn. He's not the sort to be frightened with false fire."

"Doesn't matter if he is because the answer's no. Any more of these little trips and I might as well admit you to Special Leave, like one of these Prefects that is suddenly found to be surplus to establishment." Castang however was doing what he had been told; reading the telex carefully.

"Last summer," he said, "you might remember. Suicide of a pair of children. Not such children either; in their late twenties. Chose a romantic setting, ruins of a clifftop castle over there in the Cornwall country – Tintagel. A Tristan-and-Iseult performance."

"Nonsense," said Richard at once prosaic and accurate. "Tristan died of a wound. She arrived too late, found him dead; flopped down on top of him and died of chagrin. Your mind is stuffed as usual with superstition."

"Yes," humbly. All Carlos Kleiber's fault . . .

"I do remember though, because of the odd grammar. Left a note saying 'I have killed ourselves'. Perhaps typical of today's university graduates to be illiterate. You'd have had a zero for that in elementary-school, a generation ago."

161

"That's the one," suppressing the thought that it was typical of Richard to say that something was of no interest and immediately become interested.

"And this is another? In Dorset? Tiens. Whereabouts?" Richard was the last person to have snobbish pretences towards anglophilia (like an imbecile Parisian bourgeois) but had a perverse attachment to Dorset, where he had spent a memorable holiday.

"A cliff or hill on the coastline called Golden Cap."

"Tiens. I know it well."

"Good, that makes it all the more cosy."

"What's peculiar about this one?" oblivious to sarcasms.

"Nothing perhaps, except that Geoffrey Dawson finds it rather too much of a carbon copy of the other."

"One always finds that phenomenon. A spot sets off a rash."

"More than six months after? And in the middle of winter?"

"Well," said Richard pretending to busy himself with papers, "find out more about it."

"And it does no harm," said Castang mildly, "to show ourselves smart and co-operative towards an English police force." Quite; a French bureaucracy showing as a rule so emphatic a determination to be nothing of the sort. Geoffrey Dawson had managed things tactfully. An official telex to the Regional Service of Police Judiciaire would on its own arouse little enthusiasm.

He had not much to go on: a young man and a young woman both born, and apparently domiciled hereabouts. One would have that verified by dogsbody.

Dogsbody, after an interval in which he busied himself with official duties, appeared with the word that the information given was accurate, as far as it went, but out of date. Here were addresses of the families to which these persons belonged, but neither had lived there for some time. Neither household, judging by impressions received, was much interested. But dogsbody had made enquiries unofficial, as though from a friend anxious to trace a person lost sight of. A commonplace, but one easily interpreted as someone to whom money is owed.

162

I'll have to tell them, thought Castang. Bringing news of a death is never a pleasant task, and leaving it as routine to underlings a piece of barbarous insensitivity, to which police forces are all too addicted.

Work was under control: the Pastrycooks' Truce has produced no untoward happenings such as bombs, ransom demands or dotties running amok with firearms: let us be grateful. He had himself been moderate in overeating, but could do with some fresh air.

Fresh air was as usual in short supply in the city, where it was foggy and windless, a condition accentuating bad smells, with a temperature exactly on freezing point. Luckily one of his addresses wasn't in the city at all, but in a village quite a way into the hills and there the air would be fresh. And there was a car with snow tyres – a small but nimble Renault: he knew this because he'd had it seen to. Such things were his job. Last winter half the criminal brigade had skidded off the road and fallen in a ditch full of wet snow, because it had not been seen to.

> "We die because we never knew
> These simple little rules and few"

unconsciously reproducing a Cautionary Tale. Barbiturate and alcohol, said the telex, succinct.

The hill road climbed in a mild but steady gradient up a twisty valley, one of the numerous tributary streams feeding the river which had overflowed so catastrophically a week or so back. The water was still coming down these mountain becks with a lot of force, yellowish-white and noisy, but no longer torrential. Since the exceptionally heavy rains there had been a still period lasting over the Christmas holiday and now once past the five-hundred metre level there was a sprinkle of snow on the uplands: there'd been no real fall yet. Everything uncompromisingly winter, though. The temperature fell a degree with every hundred metres climbed, and the fog was freezing. Rims of dirty slush crusted at the limits of the wiper blades before the warmth in the car melted them. But off the road was a clean, lovely grey and silver landscape: rime on stone and grassblade and bare branch; rime on the red-tiled roofs except for the warmed patch where the chimneys broke through, woodsmoke mounting in a straight line before mingling with the mist and hanging in the atmosphere, giving the haze a horizon-blue tint which Castang sniffed at with pleasure – that was something like! after the exhaust gases and diesel fumes of the city.

The villagers were still and silent, wrapped in the self-containment of winter. During the floods they had sat dry and a little sardonic, watching the water jumping and pounding in its rocky bed, pouring in sheets down the tarred road. They came out in capes and hoods, poking with sticks to clear the culverts of débris before they choked, urging the water on downward. Floods did not worry them! One felt a certain detached sympathy for the people of the plains whose houses flooded to above the door lintels – but they're a stupid lot, the plains' folk.

Now it was their turn. In January the combes and narrow dales of the hill country would fill with up to two metres of snow. The spine of these principal valleys could be kept clear by bulldozer and shovel piling loose stuff to the eaves, but the tiny sideroads – the fine bones of the fish, as it were – they could not be kept clear; filled with snow and so they stayed, with no more than a foot-track of a sleigh's width packed down, sprinkled near the houses with ash to keep it from getting too slidy. Even in April there could still be deep drifts in the shadowed combes.

But they didn't complain. Their self-containment was not the un-neighbourly selfishness of cities but the grim solidarity of mountain folk against the foreigner; experienced, stocked to the roof with necessities, and profoundly contemptuous of the government; so feeble-minded in emergency, who wrung their hands over fallen power lines and whose helicopter was always grounded because of poor visibility. These people who knew how to help themselves would help one another. For the summer residents with weekend cottages they had a good natured contempt: for the deserted from their own ranks they showed intolerance, even hatred.

So Castang found. He found the house, parked the car, adopted the look of an insurance-man, knocked, had his credentials carefully checked, was admitted politely but with small enthusiasm, got sat in the kitchen and had his business asked fairly blunt. There was no use in dressing it up.

"It concerns your son Daniel." The faces could not be said to become suspicious or hostile or stony, being already all three.

He waited a moment. Cops always do, for a remark is often now blurted out and afterwards seen as telling or significant, of the "Not again!" sort.

"The news isn't good, I'm afraid. I have to bring you word that his death has been reported to us." Young policemen try to find variations on this abominable phrase: a notion of diminishing its brutality through euphemism and cliché: a pleonasm since every euphemism is a cliché. If the dreadful "Accept my sympathies" be true it is unnecessary.

Nothing happened. Man and wife glanced at one another before bringing their look back first to him, then to the table. No change in expression. The usual reaction is disbelief, cue for the next phrase.

"Well, we'll have to verify this identity." Castang said it anyhow because it is necessary. "Daniel Cardenal, twenty-five years of age, date of birth seventeen of the eleventh, place of birth here. One metre seventy-eight, build slim, features regular, face described as long and narrow. I have no photograph as yet. Hair dark, fine, straight. No distinguishing marks or visible scars. Can you confirm that?" Any attempt at delicacy of phrasing will have the opposite effect to that intended.

"Yes." One stony monosyllable.

"The appearances of this death are suicide. The circumstances were peaceful and without suffering. As far as is known from an overdose of barbiturate – you understand? – sleeping pills."

"Pills!" An intonation of disgust and contempt, but he had to finish.

"In the company of a young woman, roughly the same age, one sixty-five, build medium, hair dark-brown, worn long, named as Anne-Sophie Bontemps, an address in the city here."

"Is she dead too?" The question came from the woman. The answer would be some comfort to her?

"Yes: together." No indication. "Does her name or description mean anything to you?"

165

"No."

"This happened two days ago in England." And both facts, he thought, were interesting. But not, it would seem, to the parents.

He got them to talk, at last, but the facts were as few and as bleak as the phrases.

'Bookish', the boy. Intelligent. 'Delicate'; fine-boned, no muscles, thin fragile arms and hands. Given to colds; always a scarf round the throat – Castang made a note. No use around the house, couldn't even chop kindling without a cock-up. Obvious, hunh, never be any use in the woodcutting trade. Nothing much else around here. Not the hands for a mechanic, right? Always a good place to be had for a good reliable book-keeper though, right? Not though if you can't even add up a column of figures straight. These calculators do it for you, but you gotto be able too, no?

They'd played fair. Schoolmaster said the boy was bright; go to the lycée. All right, and once back home you sit down okay? and do that homework thorough. That went all right, but come to this baccalaureat thing, it's no good without you have the math, and if you don't, well, you gotto become a teacher. Nothing wrong with that, that's necessary and honourable. So he went to the university, and that costs money, mister; lodgings and board and coming home weekends, and we paid, every penny, never say we were close-fisted, and that's where the trouble starts, you got no authority and control any more, your own son starts treating you like a hick, that university's nothing but layabouts and taking drugs . . .

Did he take drugs?

How do we know? We know nothing. We've never known anything. We're just the hicks. We find out a year late. Is he studying for a teacher? Is he hell: psychology, he says he's doing. What's that, and what good is it?

Castang had sympathy with the outlook, but did not make it known.

Start not coming home weekends – not that he ever brought anything, save a load of dirty washing – it's the writing on the wall: y'can see all the rest. Ashamed of his own home. I've got my pride, right? If he doesn't want to, I'm not the one to force

166

'm. Now our Christine, that's his younger sister, there's a girl to be proud of, and work! Even in the forest, I'm telling you, man . . .

Note. See Christine.

The criminal brigade ran it through the mill for him, no problem whatever: an hour's work. Two years reading psychology at the Faculty. Good marks, dropped out inexplicably: oh well, so many of them do. Military service exemption. Borderline case: no, no tuberculosis or anything organically unsound but yes, a history of upper respiratory-tract infections. Not really turned down, you know. IQ high, but psycho tests not very satisfactory, and taken in conjunction with the physical there was a feeling of a subject likely to be more trouble than he was worth.

Castang bleak, monosyllabic. Any work record?

Well yes, a trace at one of these places that do temps. You know, supply the interim, and you want a few people for a few days to do billsticking, or house-to-house canvassing: you know . . . He knew.

And then a job, temporary at first, off and on helping out: storekeeper stuff, place with a huge inventory, do-it-yourself materials and tools. He was good, they'd nothing but praise, excellent marks there, and one day they'd offered to take him on permanently. He'd accepted, and worked very well, nigh on a year, and could have worked up, and they'd been ready to give help, you know, housing, a bit of a raise maybe, put him in charge of paint, or ironmongery – and then one fine day he just disappeared, and never been seen since. You know how they are. Just when you think they're reliable . . .

You know; you know. No, Castang didn't know.

Christine, the solid, plain, reliable girl. The whale for work. Never the last to arrive and never the first to knock off. Count on her for anything. Hardy. Never ill. Always smiling, never any of this crap of I've the curse or I'm in a bad mood.

Surprising himself? – not really – Castang liked Christine too. She'd make some lucky fellow a very good wife. And she'd loved her brother. They'd been close as children, and protected each other. He was difficult, she'd grant you that. Nervy-like, secretive, funny ways. But true, loving, loyal. She had a warm

167

heart, she thought nothing of it, wore it on her face, so what? He had one too but kept quiet about it.

Not once did Christine say "you know" and he developed an affection for her. She'd lost sight. Not her fault. When did she have time to dress up and go down the city? And if she did, would she have been welcome among 'the students'?

"I'm a tactless cow, mister, and I didn't want to embarrass him with some big plouc Bet out the backwoods."

"Anne-Sophie? No, never heard of. I never knew his friends. He wasn't a type to stay in the bog with 'zfeet stuck. Go to Paris, more like. He was looking for his thing, Mister, and I hope he found it." And now at last she could have a really good cry.

He had enough for the present, he decided. Since he had been presented with this handsome pair of binoculars there was no sense in looking through only one eyepiece. The address on Anne-Sophie's identity card was close by: bang in the centre of the town in fact. The address had a strangely familiar ring; why? Some enquiry in the past?

Any of the young inspectors could have told him. Number Fifteen, Quai de Génève was an address shared by twenty or thirty businesses of great pith and moment on the first two or three floors: on the five or six above that lived executives with immense salaries. Oh it's That, he thought gazing at the massive building with two river frontages and a palatial décor. 1867. High water mark of the third Napoleon.

Numerous entrances, very large, opened vistas of parti-coloured marble and gilded stucco within, where the Businesses sat, but the doorway to private apartments was much more obscure (it took a good five minutes to cover the two street façades of this appalling structure). A small lobby was made smaller by tremendous drapes of dark blue velvet: it was like the entrance to a very grand bordel. There was a little pulpit in carved mahogany, and here sat a solid person in a dark blue uniform like that of a cop, with the insignia of one of the private security services.

"Have you lost your way, sir? The entrance is just along the street."

"No, I'm calling on a private individual."

168

"Who would that be, sir?"

"Monsieur Bontemps."

"I have to announce you, sir. You wouldn't mind showing me some identification? . . . I beg your pardon, Commissaire, I didn't recognise you." He got up politely, displaying a nicely polished black Sam Browne. On his left hip was a matching leather pacifier sixty centimetres long: on his right an open holster in which sat a blued steel (matching the décor) .357 revolver with a black checked butt. Perhaps his penis is very very tiny, thought Castang, shuffling into a small lift with a wrought-iron grille, lined with the dark blue velvet and three splendid looking-glasses two centimetres thick judging by the bevelled edges.

The lift sailed slowly; his thoughts continued to wander. There was a small town in the Middle West of the United States where the Chief of Police believed in shooting first and asking after. All his men carried .357 magnums and obeyed instructions faithfully. Well, said the mayor with just a scrap of unease, there's no denying it; our crime rate's down.

An oval brass shield let into a carved mahogany pilaster bore the name 'William Bontemps'. Castang admired the Anglophile spelling, belonging to the epoch and a pretty touch. And William opened the door and let him in. The flat was immense. Same gilded stucco, but here the velvet was dark crimson: William's smoking jacket matched this. There were a lot of immense rooms, but he was brought to a small octagonal confessional (one of the oriental-turban turrets, like those on the Brighton Pavilion, that decorated the roofscape). This was austere, with chaste bookcases and grand high-fidelity in dark teak. Castang sat. Explained at some length. Got given a smallish whisky in a large cut crystal tumbler with much unwanted ice. Explained some more.

William showed no more emotion than had the peasants out in the hills: the difference was that he was a Director of Marketing, and had been to the school of Business Administration.

"Yes," said William. "Let me explain." He had taken command.

"She did everything you can think of, including the most disastrous, to show her revulsion. Well-meant but foolish indignation. My way of life; I won't bore you with it, it's a commonplace. One waits for them to grow out of it. Sometimes they don't. Not drugs, or not as far as I know. Far worse than that. Married an African. Not much I could do: she had unfortunately some money in her own right inherited from an aunt of mine. And once she came of age . . .

"She had a child by this black. He's a fellow of parts; I was surprised that I got on quite well with him. The university here, a good degree in commerce. Job here, nice little flat – I did what I could. Socially, of course, it was . . . What my wife put up with – however. But a black, as I dare say you know, remains always a black. One fine day he skips, leaving a note. I've been offered a good job back home in the Côte d'Ivoire or whatever, we remain good friends and all that, I've taken the child – since it was a son, of course – my regards to all and Goodbye. You are perhaps unaware that it is impossible for justice to recover a child from Africa. It's regarded as belonging to the family . . . Well, from that moment you can date it. Anne-Sophie was irrecoverable. I've had to face this. I'm facing it now. I've no instruction to give you. Have her brought back. I'd like to have her decently buried, for my wife's sake."

"Will you have the boy brought back too?"

"Why?"

"I could, I suppose, say that his parents are poor and could not afford it. It looks as though she loved him. They died together. Perhaps they deserve to be buried together. It's for you to decide."

"I'll think about it."

"Nothing further then. A few points of detail. She continued to give this address."

"She was oddly attached to this flat. It had always been her home. How much attachment there remained to ourselves is a matter I cannot speculate upon. I am allowed to indulge a hope." Castang did not wish to press this wounded man.

"You spoke of a largish sum of money. Would you know what she did with it?"

"No. I might, I imagine, find out, through the bank. If there is any left. I suppose, that in the circumstances, her natural heir, would be myself . . . Probably there's nothing."

"You wouldn't care to speculate?" without sarcasm.

"Boats conceivably. Always mad about boats. The stage in adolescence when most girls go horse mad, she took to boats. Had her given sailing lessons, in La Rochelle. I recall . . . I prefer not to."

"You won't mind if I follow that up? Might explain this English connection, in some part. How much money was there?"

"Several hundred thousand francs."

"One last thing then – have you a photograph I could copy?"

William got up abruptly and left the room. Came back with a rococo silver frame.

"That's all I have," undoing the clips at the back. "You'll take care of that. I'll get you some tissue paper. You see; it's all I have."

In the office one should be reasonably free from incursion and interruption. A policeman's job can only be done by being open to all and sundry. There's a lot of sundry. But the job is seeing that wheels go round smoothly: shutting oneself up and saying, "I'm thinking" is not a helpful attitude.

Castang had hardly unwrapped the tissue paper before Lucciani strolled in whistling, dumped a lot of paper on the desk, glanced at the photo, said "Juicy piece" and went on out. One would say "barged" because of an offensive and oafish manner, but it is inapplicable as Lucciani is light on his feet (Davignon who is no bigger nor heavier walks like two men carrying a ladder) and has moreover an in-toed mincing walk sniggered at – and imitated – by other inspectors, and the adjective generally used is 'fairy'.

Why feel annoyance? The girl "had the right to a bit of privacy" as though Lucciani was leering under her skirt! It's a photo. She is dead. And nobody who is even remotely police business enjoys privacy. We are the great invaders of same. The chronic brutalisation consequent upon this is among the worst handicaps inherent in this trade. A kind of moral silicosis gains a progressive footing in our lungs.

Pushing Lucciani's nasty papers to one side Castang adjusted things to get a good light. The cabinet-size photograph

171

had been made, printed, worked on by a high-class professional. Monochrome; the shading really delicate, the outlines really fine. Alive; but he'd had a good subject, and done it no more than justice.

A girl of about eighteen, the face still soft, childish meaning sensitivity, meaning innocence, because all the adult bones and features were there and fully developed. Castang's daughter was still a 'tiny one': here was the ripened treasure and still within its budding grove; had not forgotten how to play. A rarity, now that children are forced into a false and vicious maturity long before they are ready for it. Like the tiny azaleas sold to the public at the new year – the shops full of them right now. In full pathetic bloom, a ribbon round the pot. They bloom for thirty days, and die of exhaustion.

The forehead was low and rectangular, with two straight fierce eyebrows, a thin straight nose springing high between them and the eyes set wide, with an open directness, ready to meet anything. There were plenty of imperfect features. The jaw was too square and would be hard once it lost the immature softness. If she had lived long enough the chin would have gone heavy. The ears were flat and featureless. The nose was really too sharp. A beautifully outlined mouth, tender, exquisite, yet upper lip a little too short.

Boldness, generosity, resolution. A vivid quickness. Not perhaps very much intelligence, but enough.

"You pass this address on your way home," he told Maryvonne. "Drop it in for me. There's a security man with a big pistol!"

"Is that all he's got?" He reached for his telephone.

"Inspector Dawson please, tell him Commissaire Castang."

"Castaing, right, will you hold the line?" The English pronunciation was also the commonplace French spelling: he was used to being 'Castaing' everywhere.

"Hal-ló," with a jaunty accent on the ultimate.

"Geoffrey, I've done some police work on these people and got quite interested. Nothing silly like intuitions or curiosities. But I thought I'd catch you quick and give you no respite."

"Réspite, old boy."

"Why?"

"I don't know. One says despite, but one also says réspite. In spite of this Brit dottiness and to answer your question no, I never have curiosities or intuitions, they're the Bangkok influenza, but I must confess to feeling fidgeted. There's a good English word for you."

"We don't have it in France but I think I understand: would we say énervé?"

"That's a thing you all are permanently."

"Tell me, have you come across a boat at all in your travels?"

"Yes I have and I'm not quite sure what to make of it."

"This fidgets you?"

"*One* of the things that fidgets me. Can you connect this at all? Boat's registered in Saint Malo. It would save me probably laborious enquiries among a lot of Breton cops who probably insist on talking Breton. Brets enjoy being tiresome to Brits: it's all on account of fish, lobsters and things. Relations are a bit strained just now."

"Good, if I can get away I will, but I need a strong motive. Could this be put as diplomatic representations at all? Is your case for enquiry strong enough?"

"I might be able to make it so. Would be a big help if you could. I'll try and create a panic among Consuls. You could stay with us, that would be very nice and you could pad your expense account."

"Excellent idea, and do what you can: what I need is a fuse lit."

Geoffrey Dawson must have lit the fuse with great promptness because that very afternoon Richard summoned him.

"Castang, I've had a bit of fusspotting from the souschef in Paris about that English thing, and ten minutes after there's the Royaume Uni embassy, one of these terrible men that speak far better French than we do: I've been much perturbed. This is a damned nuisance. That awful man of yours in the Dorset CID. has some bee in his bonnet about contraband, and you know how the English are about dogs and parrots."

"Quarantine."

"Unless we do something they'll begin creating incidents,

173

leaking nasty quarter-columns in *The Times*, banning chicken imports, their usual performance. Obliging me thus to eat my own words, splashing ketchup about, what is ketchup?"

"One of those colonial things no? Like pyjamas?"

"You'll have to go; there's nobody else I can spare." The implication, doubtless not involuntary, that Castang could readily be spared was just Richard being énervé.

"Now what about la Bonne Année?" asked Vera. Not being nasty; just enquiring. Castang had never heard the classic definition "being sick on the pavement in Glasgow" but it would have appealed to him. "You were going to let off fireworks for Lydia."

"So I am." And did. The whole city resounded with small arms' fire. On their way home, slightly stimulated, from departmental drinks they met the fire brigade, considerably stimulated, who stopped the car in the middle of the street by surrounding it with menacing waved arms, dragged Vera out and passed her from oilskin to oilskin with lavish hugs and wet kisses: over-affectionate Newfoundland dogs.

"You don't mind, do you, Missis?" Their officer, still resolute to put out fires if the occasion arose. "The boys have their traditions."

"Bonne Année," said Castang, waiting patiently for his turn. Both the police and the firemen are disciplined bodies. The rest of the New Year passed unprofessionally enough. By the following day he was sufficiently recovered to arrange his affairs and have a word with Mr. Dawson.

"The chef was énervé at being jiggled by diplomats but it's all right now."

"I'm more than somewhat enervated myself. Buoy up the sinking feeling with Bovril. Make for Weymouth when you're able to walk and I'll meet you there."

Castang took a train to Paris, passed an hour with friends, tottered as far as the Montparnasse station, woke much refreshed in Rennes, and had breakfast in Saint Malo, amid vivifying sea breezes. Harbour masters and such folk provided some information, unwillingly: more came, on receipt of drinks, from Old Sea Dogs. There are plenty of these around.

It is a small town, a mediaeval walled fortress perched on a rocky promontory, with a small harbour tucked in behind and surrounded by dismal suburbs. Here they are resolutely modern and there is talk of containers and refrigeration facilities: nothing for him there. Within the fortress 'intra muros' small boys wearing red caps pretend to be corsairs and folklore prevails: privateers sailing out armed to the teeth, under letters of marque, bloodthirstily prepared to skin the tourist of his last farthing. In early January they may appear somnolent but this is an illusion, as Castang discovered while buying a seaman's jersey. He had failed to make sufficient provision for woollies, under the widely-shared delusion that the climate of maritime Brittany is mild.

There is however another aspect to Saint Malo. The fish industry is much depressed, and the concomitant small-shipbuilding trade suffers likewise: there are no longer 'terra nueva' boats and captains-courageous plying across to the Grand Banks to bring salt cod back to Europe. Nobody would eat it if they did. No picturesque wooden schooners, no schnapps-sodden Fécampois skippers: even cabin boys flung overboard because they were such a nuisance are a thing of the past. Nothing now but one or two Russian style factory ships that turn monsters of the deep into frozen fingers. As for small ships there is a tendency to buy them in Japan.

The ports of the Brittany and Vendée coasts were perplexed about this for a longish while, but they have been resourceful. They have turned to building and sailing pleasure craft, with a lot of skilfully arranged publicity based on ocean racing in every imaginable variation: transatlantic solitaries, round-the-world doubles and the Rum Route. This has made for a booming industry, heavily sponsored by commerce, which lacks humour: racing boats aren't called 'Spinnaker Sunrise' but baptised 'Dogbiscuit IV' instead. After his chat with harbourmasters it was this world that Castang sought to enter. Things in January are fairly slack so that there was plenty of it about in pubs.

A sea dog explained. "As with everything else there are fashions and the fashion industry works like hell dreaming up new designs, with results that lead to a few resounding fiascos, as when an over-sophisticated brand-new prau capsized – right here in the bay at the launch of the last big race – bleeding thing decided to become a submarine before it had as much as crossed the start line.

"However, the big deal these last years has all been multi-hulls. Trimarans, catamarans, dinky-toys or a hundred metres long, you name it. They don't want a boat that sails, you see. Interested in nothing but hydrofoils that will do a hundred miles an hour with a following wind and enter the stratosphere the moment you try to tack. The only thing that still spells boat is it's wind-powered. A Formula One Renault, replacing the motor by a big tall mast that snaps off every half-hour or so, but that adds to the fun.

"Now follow me closely: there are still a few real sailors like Malinowsky that preferred to sail with a real boat, up to just recently.

"But sponsors want to win, they're not interested in sailing. Come up with a manta ray built of titanium and tissuepaper, a moondocker costing millions, they cough up. A monocoque, that's right, a single hull, you can't give them away. So you can get a good one cheap, that's your answer."

"What about girls?" asked Castang.

"Sure there are girls, some making a big name already. Women everywhere. Some of them real girls too. Lots of lesbians in leather suits with little whips, bound to be, but sailors there too." Castang only lost interest when little diagrams of multi-geared deck-winches started to appear.

It would still cost a packet. Everything cost a packet. But we had been talking in terms of several hundred thousand francs, and even William wasn't quite sure how many made several. There were plenty of races where a good monocoque that can beat against the wind – there's a Tour de France where crews from all the different ports compete as teams . . . There was still genuine ocean racing – the English did it . . . look at the Fastnet or whatever. Need a proper hull there, real spars, real blocks and cordage instead of this weight-reduced nonsense, all streamlined but jams if you look at it. Anne-Sophie had found such a boat, bought it. What was it she proposed to do with it?

176

"Not knowing, can't say. With a crew, race it. With two – even alone, a clever one like that, ketch-built – cruise it; she'll go anywhere. Round the world? – no problem. A real boat, the right size and shape, will live in any sea, even if pooped." Started to go technical again, so Castang paid for the drinks and buggered off.

And twenty-four hours later was disembarking from – sorry, getting off the train – in Weymouth, and an hour after that Geoffrey Dawson was saying. "Oh, I rather fancy the guernsey; that's very chic."

"I thought it was a jersey."

"Use your wits, man; they are two Channel Islands; take your pick which one has your emotional preference. If one's rich that is, like you. Mine's Navy, submarine issue, about twenty years back. Army Surplus Stores, ten bob." Castang's mind reeling; have to buy a multi-geared deck-winch before I get dismasted.

"Now you are weary and travel-stained, so we'll just have a nice cup of tea and then we'll go home and you get unwound and I'll lay it all out for you: there's nothing to do here." English police tea, vulgar and restorative, a brew leaving bright orange stains inside the cup and his stomach, like a stream flowing out of an iron mine. Real tealeaves floating about and a sticky deposit of sugar at the bottom; disgusting and delicious. The inside of the car, like the inside of the police-station, had a powerful English smell, spellbinding, incantatory, foreign . . .

"Lip of Turk and Tartar's teeth," said Geoffrey, who always knew what one was talking about; a blessed person. "Instead of opening the window they stick a plastic box on the wall with Air Fresh inside it. Too lazy to clean the lavatory but throw in half a tin of Harpic. Don't use soap, use deodorant. Cigarettes will give you cancer, but what will chemical lavender do to your lungs? The English think that France smells of coffee and Gauloise cigarettes."

"Whereas it's really Rhône-Poulenc." He was very tired. He was also over-stimulated. Impressions were flying past him, and by him, and at him rather, at far too high a speed.

A suburb? He had always thought the word pejorative. This seemed very grand and uh, leafy; golfcoursey. And was this

177

what the English called a semi-detached? As though it were a dirty word. Playing it down again. Subtle, not to say machiavellian of them. Thing about Brits, said Richard, to remember, is they're perfidious. Not necessarily in a bad sense.

Was Geoffrey perfidious? He hardly knew him at all.

The very Englishness of things: children with those little round funny caps that would keep off neither sun nor rain. "Tribal badges," said Geoffrey casually. Did he play cricket?

"It always bored me out of my mind. Now stop being so suspicious."

Pavements, with trees, with grass; wide enough to ride bicycles on. In Castang's quarter there weren't any pavements at all! He was rapidly getting complexes. Dazzled, that's what he was.

A house full of sunshine and flowers. How bare and grim his own seemed to him. A wife. Wonderful smile, a pink sweater, and the famous English rose-petal looks.

"Her name's Emily. Occasionally Emmeline."

"But never never Em," she said in her high soft English voice.

"Sit down, Henri: how about some coffee then, Em?"

"Oh you!"

Cretonne armchairs of a funny shape, to be seen only in expensive Paris shops. Gate-legged table, ditto. Very cosy? – wrong word. Very splendid? – likewise.

"Very comfy," he managed at last. Geoffrey's eyes shiny with amusement. Not with mockery, save self-mockery – too nice a person. Expert, certainly, in that English art (for which there is no French translation) vulgarly known as taking-the-piss out of the pompous.

"Ha!" said Geoffrey. "You don't know, yet. Flies in the ointment – tiens, there's no more disgusting expression than that. I'm very frowned upon indeed; looked upon by the neighbours as thoroughly unsound. Lawyers," in a hideous and sinister whisper. "Prim. And the woman's name is Primrose," falling down laughing.

"Nonsense," said Emily with a coffee-pot, "she's very nice."

Wide grey skirt. Legs thickish but not hockey-playing.

178

Peculiar shoes, nice once you got accustomed to them. Enormous electric plugs fit for a high-tension line of three hundred and eighty thousand volts. "A mania," Geoffrey explained. "Quite certain that all those horrid Continentals electrocute themselves, very Victorian."

"He's only frowned upon," interjected Emily – "sorry, my French is quite High School and thus primitive – because he will walk about with nothing on." She didn't!

"To business – no, you were going to have the nice bath, first."

"Give me the rundown, or is it the breakdown, and I can think about that in the nice bath," suggested Castang.

"Good, you're aware, there was this suicide, so-called. To me it smells to high heaven. Nobody agrees with me. The Chief Superintendent, who is an old woman – saving Emily's honour, an old cunt – thinks I'm out of my mind and says so a great deal, blunt and forceful and so forth. I frightened him enough to get all that diplomatic pooha done because the one thing that terrorises him is Trouble in Whitehall; Questions asked in the House, Home Secretary in a paddy, a Minister saying Who, What, Sack that Bastard. And on the other hand an obsession, shared by all around here, about standing-up-to-the-French. By skilful play upon both fears and vanities I persuaded him to have the inquest adjourned for further-enquiries. A fortnight, so we haven't much time; if I get a flea in my ear meaning reprimands." Castang as usual with Geoffrey Dawson learning colloquialisms in a hurry but not very clear yet.

"To business," he said.

"Right, there's this hill, about thirty kilometres off: well would you go up there in a howling gale on Christmas morning to commit suicide: would you, Em?"

"I can't imagine committing suicide at all but as I'm for ever being told, I've no imagination whatever."

"Describe this hill."

"Sorry. It's a headland, roughly 619 feet high, happens to be the highest point on the south coast, there's a fine view in clear weather over the whole width of Lyme Bay, and none whatever in the middle of the night. You can get within a mile by car, or walk along the coast path, and there's a moderately steep but

179

easy climb. Some pretty stuff called greensand slid over on top of the chalk: this shows up in sunlight and that's why it's called Golden Cap."

"Arguments in favour of suicide."

"Christmas for a start, everyone tucked up drunk and haha over pudding and you miserable, pass that."

"Technical."

"Lying peacefully, what is called embraced, full to the brim with barbiturate. Thermos that had contained cocktail of coffee, whisky, pills."

"Arguments against."

"All so *staged*. No car, how did they get all that way? Why go all that way? The place has no significance. Carbon copy of the Tintagel thing, it's claimed; the Tristan'n'Iseult thing. Well those things do have carbon copies as you know, but not six months after in the middle of winter. And there's nothing romantic there: it's just a hill. There are little nookies among the gorsebushes, suitable it might be thought for a kiss-up on a fine summer evening, save the place is alive with tourists. If you insist on killing yourself there's fifty places just as good closer by."

"Closer by what?"

"Living on a boat moored in Poole Harbour. Quite a big cruising sailer but no houseboat, wouldn't be comfortable."

"I know about the boat."

"Good, because that will shed light. I've nothing evidential but to my mind it's stinking fish."

"Have you any arguments for homicide?"

"None," admitted Geoffrey, alarmingly cheerful.

"Found how soon?"

"That afternoon. People wouldn't go up there much in winter, I should think, but the English will do anything. Some geezer with his dog walking off an overdose of pudding was all that was needed."

Castang went for a bath; initial euphoria was leading to depression. This was all beginning to sound like the Tale of Roger Riderhood (which that over-imaginative gentleman said sounded like Beatrix Potter: and the moral of that is, Do not break into other people's vegetable gardens.)

180

He had asked Richard afterwards, perhaps imprudently.

"If you could have proved it on one or another; would you still have let them go free?"

"No. Leave that to the court. Avoid falling into sentimental liberalism. You ought to know that they all have such pathetic stories when caught."

Vera had said the same.

"The alcoholic pa and the cruel step-ma are platitudes. You're still responsible for what you do. Peter Rabbit's father got caught and put in a pie by Mr. McGregor. And serve him right."

Castang told his troubles to Geoffrey Dawson.

"I don't like these tales which could be homicide and you can't prove it."

"No. First catch your hare, as Mrs. Beeton did or did not say." What hare? All these English literary allusions were too much for him so he kept quiet. Beatrix Potter again, doubtless.

"The one thing I've got hold of is that the boat is a strong argument against suicide," telling Geoffrey about William Bontemps and Anne-Sophie's defunct auntie. "They've only had it a few months."

"This boat interested me from the start," said Geoffrey. "I started enquiring among the yacht people. It's got quite well known because all autumn they've been working it along the coasts, here and on the French side. In all weathers, as though they were practising for something bigger."

"You mean like in the spring we'll set sail for the Marquesas, like Jacques Brel?"

"That's it, it's feasible. It belongs in the suicide scenario. You have two romantic idealists, brought up as you say on Brel poems, and for some reason it goes sour, and on Christmas morning they go off together to a high point from which there's a good view of the sea and the stars and put an end to it. This is my chief's view, and that of all the sensible people. The homicide theory is ridiculous. Do you bring people up a hill and at the top you say 'Just drink this, will you?' Alternatively, do you drug them somewhere else and then carry them up a pretty steep scrambling climb – these two limp and heavy burdens?

181

'Don't be so damned obtuse, Dawson'." Castang realised that Geoffrey had asked him to come in the hope of moral support for a highly unpopular notion.

"Well, what *have* you got in support of homicide? – since plainly you've something besides funny feelings."

"I've an old lady," said Geoffrey, reluctant, "but I'm not going to put her into evidence until you've worked it out for yourself and decide whether I'm loony."

Castang prepared for police work. They were sitting in the living room, with drinks. Emily was cooking the lunch next door, with clankings and good smells of roast mutton while the men 'lolled about on the sofa boozing'.

"Was it a clear night?"

"It was. Dry, windy, not very cold." Facts, like the voice, came out crisp. "Pertinent times, between midnight and four. Temperature up there about plus two. Soil dryish, hardish. No help from footprints – in the morning it turned mild, cloudy, and there was a heavy shower between ten and eleven."

"It would be possible, to carry people up?"

"Technically yes. Two strongish men, taking their time. More likely that they walked up."

"How d'you get barbiturates into people?"

"That thermos is plausible, no? 'Chilly up here, let's have a shot'. I had the dregs analysed. Strong coffee, plenty of whisky. Might taste a bit funny but not so's you'd notice in the dark and the cold. Don't need that much barbit if the alcohol level's high enough. Which it was."

"Police doc any good?"

"Fair. Competent for a thing like that."

"What harbours are there along here, apart from Weymouth?" asked Castang.

"I think that's a good question. For a cruising yacht with an onshore wind there's no good harbourage all along Lyme Bay. One or two fishing boats off Bridport and nothing else till you get round Portland."

"Have you a motive at all for homicide?"

"Yes. Tenuous, hypothetical. Go on thinking the way you are."

"Is contraband what we're thinking of?"

"I'm not a maritime expert," said Dawson pouring more beer. "We have a working relation with the coastguard and the Customs people. I haven't let on to any specific CID interest in their doings, so my information is sketchy. Historically there's always been a good deal of contraband along here, precisely because of the long stretch of coast and the absence of harbourage."

"I don't know much about boats. Dodging along coastlines would teach you a lot about navigation in shallow tidal water: not much I'd imagine to do with ocean cruising. Except learning to be handy about the deck."

"It occurred to me. Why all this interest in a place like Poole when you could have got to Vigo, or the Azores?"

"Is there much contraband, or is it folklore?"

"Of course there is. The risks are pretty high, the rewards are high too. In some cases I'd say you'd have quite a solid motive."

"Detail a bit."

"Drugs of course. There's always boatloads of amateurs ready for a try, up from Tangier or wherever. You catch a few off Brest; we catch a few off Falmouth or Plymouth. More get through. So many damn small boats. Then there are the funnies; Pakistani brothers in law, or dogs and cats dodging the extremely stiff quarantine. That can be lucrative because the penalty is high. I'm not keen on illegal immigrants because the boat is the wrong type. Drink and cigars, there's a steady nice grocery racket. We could disregard that maybe, since everyone does it more or less. The business is there but it's a fragmented tuppence ha'penny trade. 'Four and twenty ponies, Trotting in the dark' – up the Marshwood Vale: no, forget that. Under the main heading of drugs, including a lot of funny pharmaceutical products; it's as a rule light, portable, concealable."

"The weak point with all these operations is the distribution."

"Correct and that's what I've been trying to concentrate on, but I haven't got far, with all this Bonne Année lark. If we can put a finger on contraband it could lead us to homicide. And vice-versa. Which would do me quite a bit of good. You know, Henri, Christmas can be a good season for suicide, agreed. And isn't it rather well chosen for homicide too? Like it is for breaking banks. Long weekend, with nobody paying notice."

"Tell me about your old lady."

"I'll do better than that, I'll show her to you."

"I want a drink," said Emily, arriving much pinker than she had been, and slightly dishevelled. "I'm rather an English cook but the mutton is real Dorset. Contraband!"

"It doesn't make any sense otherwise," said Geoffrey belching as a result of roast mutton (it had been very good) and getting into a small car. "Look at Devon, all indented like the Breton coast, chockfull of lovely deep safe harbours and intricate fascinating estuaries, all stuffed with boat people. Why come to Dorset where there's nothing? If you were excited about birds or fossils it would be a different tale, but an ocean-going sailingboat . . . I made up my mind there must be something – or someone – hereabouts exercising magnetism. Now look, you'll have to put up with the other old woman first: the Chief Superintendent."

This turned out to be a bony person, sitting at a desk, with large chalky hands, dry and overwashed like a doctor's, occupying much of the desk top, and an obnoxious spaniel with its lead tied to the desk leg and francophobe sentiments. The Chief Superintendent was very polite, and so was Castang. There were a number of mild remarks about "our friend Dawson's little eccentricities" and Geoffrey managed to tread on the dog's large outstretched paw. Castang got a general impression that he himself was looked upon as harmless as long as he stuck to birds and fossils, and would be treated hospitably, in the interest of neighbourliness. All he had to do was smell of drink, wear a beret, and carry a long loaf under his arm: there were those inescapable condescending jokes about Maigret, hor-hor.

"Ridiculous old fascist," said Geoffrey outside. "Didn't mean to tread on his dog, beastly smelly thing: I was a bit pissed, I suppose."

"He's all right." Castang thought that the head of the CID did have a notion sometimes that Mr. Dawson was too bright for his job, but was well-disposed on the whole towards an intelligent, conscientious and hardworking officer.

"I suppose so. To do him justice, as reactionaries go around here he's quite liberal. Comes from Yorkshire. 'Danes are all right but the French are awful'."

"So we are awful."

"*Some* of you are awful. So are some of us. Good, here we are." A sea front. In fact an Esplanade. Palm trees: Castang had to have it explained about the Gulf Stream. Not like Nice though. The palm trees were wrapped in polythene and the wind turned his nose blue and made his eyes water: Geoffrey was used to it. Nor was the domestic architecture like Nice. Small, compact, simple houses which he found very beautiful. Where baroque at all the curves were plain barrel: others were flat and straight of front, with the generous height and harmony of window, nicest contribution of the Georgian and Regency periods. Castang gazed, delighted with this plainness. French houses of the period have the same beauty of proportion but are taller, with steeply pitched roofs. The observer accustomed to a French skyscape is always struck by how tiny the houses are, how low the churches, in England.

"*Not* like Munich," said Geoffrey.

"No."

"I should like to write a learned book," straight-faced, "with a title like *The Sociological Correlation of Architecture and Crime*."

The comic note was struck by a building monstrous, and ludicrous, in any surroundings but the more so in these. Hotels do not reflect national characteristics, perhaps being cosmopolitan by definition. The principal styles, as Stock-exchange Classic, Scottish Baronial, or Hollywood Spanish, are to be found in all countries. This one, a good example of Railway Gothic, was perfectly familiar to Castang: it could have been picked straight off the front at any French seaside resort. There was an unhappy moment between, say, 1940 and the mid sixties, when these monuments to the age of Plenty of Servants fell upon evil times. The dissolute soldiery billeted therein amused itself with vandalism, and post-war economics did not know what to do with them. Strenuous efforts to turn them into Civil Service departments met with limited success.

185

Another generation of nouveaux riches has arrived to give them a new lease of life and there they are after over a hundred years, triumphant elephants with castles on top and electronic accountancy in the bowels.

The racism round here is of a special sort. You can't of course have a notice-board saying No blacks, No communists, No niggers, No policemen, No – the list is too long, that's all, and where do you stop? Instead you have, the more distinct for being unwritten, No poor.

There is still a church parade, but there is no longer a sergeant to shout "Fall out the Roman Catholics and the Jews". Take a closer look at my pectoral cross there, lad, and you'll see that Meyer Lansky is my investment adviser.

There was a mid-afternoon silence, curtained and carpeted, in the hall. A few widows were drinking tea; the Japanese weren't back yet from the smilingly courteous circuit of Management. Castang was interested to see Geoffrey Dawson on his home ground.

There was a haughty Mussolini with not much hair and striped trousers in the Reception Area. Mr. Dawson pattered across and gave him the candid blue gaze. From his trouser pocket Geoffrey drew a paper handkerchief, unwrapped this carefully and with deliberation blew his nose. He looked around him and in a friendly tone said, "Is there a wastepaper basket?" Castang wondered whether Geoffrey possessed any of those odd masonic signs he had heard about, like a public-school accent. As far as he could tell, no accent at all.

"Miss Martindale, please. Mr. Dawson." The dignitary looked at him, at Castang; meaningfully: drew the telephone towards him, stared at the ceiling, which depicted Britannia and Neptune having an apéritif in between ruling the waves. Tapped with a pen, said, "A Mr. Dawson. And another gentleman . . ." Hernandez the bandit and an unshaved bodyguard. Pointed the pen at the lift and said "First."

"I prefer stairs," said Geoffrey going the other way. They reached a landing with palms and mirrors, both large, before he added, "in a book there's a Prime Minister called the Right Honourable Walter Outrage. That's him. The book is called *Vile Bodies* – that's us." They walked along a huge passage. A

186

middle aged woman in a skirt-and-jacket, with a fattish, placid face, was standing in the opening of one of the vast doors. She took a good look at them, said, "Correct, the detective inspector," over her shoulder and stood aside to let them pass.

It was the drawing-room of a suite, with the usual Empire furniture upholstered in striped satin, crimson and offwhite, and plenty of it. The double french window to the balcony, looking out to sea, was closed. At an angle to this, getting the last of the daylight to read by, reposed a stout old lady on an Empire day-bed; not at all like Madame Récamier. Sturdy black walking shoes below grey cotton stockings were planted on the day-bed: an ample dress in some woolly jersey material was draped over the knees which were drawn comfortably up, so that she could perch her book against them. Beside her on an occasional table stood a powerful, wide-angle and very expensive Zeiss binocular. When they came in she swung her feet down and stood, in a muscular, active fashion. On a low table between them was the débris of a lavish hotel tea: toast and scones and things. Two greedy old girls· no wonder they were fat.

"I know you," in a clear carrying voice, to Dawson. "More boring interrogations and wearisome periphrases? I suppose I have to put up with that. And who's this, another pleeccman?"

"A colleague from France, concerned for obvious reasons and for whose help I am grateful."

"Never thought to live to see the day I'd have French fuzz under my feet."

"Mr. Castang who speaks excellent English will know how to appreciate these sentiments."

"Madame." Castang bowed.

"I'm not married."

"It's a title of courtesy," said Castang, and Geoffrey Dawson's lack of expression underlined "palpable hit". She didn't miss it: there wasn't much she would miss. "I have only to say that I am an onlooker."

"Stay that way," determined to have the last word.

"I haven't brought my sergeant since I saw no need for interrogations," began Geoffrey conversationally. "We'd also be glad to do without periphrases. You gave me to understand that you held some title in this boat. In the light of information received the point of legal ownership needs clearing up."

The old lady – one wondered how old she really was – had taken post behind an empire bureau and was making no pretence of having no head for business.

"I have interests. They are numerous and varied. I no longer hunt but I like to watch horses and I back my fancies. I no longer sail but I know a good boat. One can buy a piece of a boat as of a horse. Of this young woman I know nothing. She had papers of ownership; she was agreeable to selling me a one third interest. If the boat continues to do well, which remains to be seen, I might make other plans. Her death naturally I regret: as a matter of business I deplore it. Who inherits?"

"Her father as far as we know, with whom Mr. Castang can put you in touch."

"I might be willing to buy him out and I might not. You can refer the matter to my solicitor."

"I am empowered," said Castang who had to pick his words carefully, "to represent his interest."

"In any doubt," said Dawson, "a telephone call resolves the matter but all we need at the moment is to recover personal effects and to see that the boat is properly looked after."

"The boat stays where it is and you need be in no doubt that care will be taken."

"That's in no doubt, Miss Martindale. We want access, and if need be we'll apply for a court order. Nobody challenges your interest but it's plain the decision belongs to Monsieur –"

"Bontemps. He's a banker," said Castang. "I see no problem."

"Dorothy. Get Jenkins on the phone and tell him to arrange with Inspector Dawson for a suitable moment to visit the boat – in his presence, that is understood – to tidy up whatever personal property that girl and boy left behind them."

"Yes," said the secretary, or companion, or whatever she was. She seemed to be a woman of few words.

"Tell him I want an inventory made."

"Yes."

"That clears it up then, Miss Martindale. Barring unforeseen snags formalities remain with the Coroner's Court."

"You'll keep me informed," said the autocrat. The plump woman came back from phoning in the next room.

"Mr. Jenkins, at the solicitor's office, can find time for you at the end of the afternoon. So if you'll clear that with him . . . He'll be in to see you before dinner," to the ogre.

"Have to play along with this solicitor person," Geoffrey was saying. "You see it, Henri; hereabouts a detective-inspector is a clerk in the eyes of these notables; a barely tolerated nuisance. She has a double pull, that of being one of themselves in the eyes of the county, meaning County, and being exceedingly rich, so well in with that select band into the bargain. Was very high-handed when I went off to look over the boat. Lives up in the countryside with stables and horses and stuff, but spends quite a lot of time here, keeps that suite on permanently. Besides that female dogsbody she has male ones. The news of those deaths wasn't out five minutes before she had one rowing off, slapping padlocks all over the boat."

"France is full of them. When they're shopkeepers the phrase is 'âpre au gain': with the higher bourgeoisie one simply speaks of 'le sens des affaires'."

"You bet," said Geoffrey.

Mr. Jenkins was a horsefaced personage, long and lawyerly, living amidst much mahogany in a Georgian house in the town, whose social standing might have been lowered a century ago by the brass plate outside; it was definitely not the case now. Polite with the police, meaning Mr. Dawson: a chilly courtesy, neatly graded, was accorded Castang.

"We'll do a little telephoning." Castang suggested. "Oh you can reverse the charge. At home we're an hour ahead but we'll find Monsieur Bontemps in his office still." There was a little chat, with Mr. Jenkins listening on an extension to the rapid French with a frown of concentration and a long shaved lip.

"Put him on," said William. "Monsieur Jenkin?" in English. "I send you written confirmation, O.K.? but you accept Monsieur le Commissaire as my representative. 'E as legal training and is officer of the court. Any little question of maritime or international law, 'e knows ow to deal with; you can take my word for that, okay? Inventory I agree, on 'is counter-signature. Loose items like navigational instruments, like cameras or binoculars that's personal property, all right? O.K.? That's fine then." Not to be behindhand with the sens des affaires. Castang,

189

who had forgotten all he had ever known about maritime or international law, concealed the fact: his social standing had improved.

"Didn't know you chaps had such impressive titles," said Mr. Jenkins pleasantly. "Let's get out to the harbour then. I'll take my clerk for the written work – follow your car shall we?" He was conversational and quite friendly on the boat. "Now you have this excellent system of putting things under seals, literally. That still goes on, does it?"

Mildness, firmness: Castang found little to quarrel with.

"All right, Hardcastle, the definition's quite simple: matter of common sense. Items like uh, cordage or uh, anchors and lifebelts and so on plainly go with the boat, as distinct from portable objects of decorative purpose. Or of utility when in a hm, shorebound sense as opposed to a marine sense; would you agree to that Monsieur Castang? A few are bound to be both but we take them as they come shall we?" In this way Castang had deplorably little opportunity to look properly at the boat; he liked boats. But he felt he could rely upon Geoffrey's eyesight, and invisible antennae. Copwise, one was enough. His own attention had to be given to being lawyerly – within this cosy English context. Mr. Jenkins was – he'd have to ask Geoffrey once they were again alone.

"Spry," said 'the police gentleman' (Mr. Hardcastle's expression). "And so were you spry. And so," comfortably, "was I."

"So," they were safely back in harbour, drinking Emily's tea; different from police tea; more . . . more – Ladylike? suggested Geoffrey, "have we any conclusions and if so do they differ?"

"The possibility," thought Castang out loud, "that the boy made it a sort of revenge suicide? That the girl was twisting him maybe? Like another fellow? You refuse all that?"

"Typical French idea. 'Nous étions deux amis et Fanette l'aimait'. I don't think it fits the set up."

"No? All the romantic stuff – Tristan and Iseult on a hilltop drinking a potion?"

"I'll be quite honest and say I don't find anything romantic about it at all. That English people might think such behaviour

190

plausible from a French couple – I'd accept that," said Geoffrey.

"I don't know what to make of your old lady Martindale. She worked quite openly and above board. Solicitor and all. Jenkins, by the way very correct, gave me back the boat's papers; all quite in order – Inscription Maritime, certificates, all duly stamped, signed, sealed, witnessed. A bit odd perhaps that the girl should have been ready to surrender a part, but she might have been short of ready money, or steady finance more like. The old dear offered some sponsorship in return for a part ownership, maybe. Putting a boat in racing trim costs as much as training a racehorse. I can't see any conceivable grounds for killing anyone. Nothing in the boat struck you? – I got no chance to look at it."

"Normal loving couple," said Geoffrey, thoughts seeming far off. "Forward cabin made up for two; clothes and gear lying around."

"There was no note left? Suiciding couples mostly leave reams of explanation – when French that is, and from an articulate educated milieu."

"It's one of the things that worries me. When you leave your precious boat, which is all you've got in the world . . ."

"If you've any sense you don't try to fake a suicide note," said Castang, "it would never ring true. But it's an open question."

"Giving due weight to the imponderables, as old mother Armstrong puts it." This was the Chief Superintendent.

"I thought imponderable meant you couldn't weigh it."

"That's French logic," said Geoffrey crossly. "Everybody tells me I haven't a leg to stand on. All I know is that I'm Miss Clavel, waking in the middle of the night and saying Something here is not Quite Right."

"Then it isn't," with firmness, "but to get any further we need leverage and where are we to look for it?"

"I asked Miss Agatha Martindale a classic question," said Geoffrey. "I said when you heard about the suicide, were you surprised? And she answered Young Man, I'm never surprised at anything. Which isn't an answer. You aren't just in business together. A young couple crewing the boat . . . Maternal isn't a

191

word I'd use about Aggie. And business people keep human relations out of the deal. It still sticks in my craw. Which is somewhere here near my larynx and my pharynx," pointing at his throat.

"You got nowhere with restaurants on Christmas night?" asked Castang.

"Good, Henri, but Armstrong wouldn't give me the scope, and on or off the coast, between Poole and Lyme there are a good few. I got the coroner to suggest that anyone who saw them in a pub or wherever would be a valuable witness to state-of-mind. People here will generally come forward in a case like that. Nobody has. They may have eaten on the boat."

"A French couple on Christmas night, eating corned beef out of a tin?" disbelievingly. "Not very likely! And where was Aggie?"

"I had a quiet word with a head waiter in that hotel. Aggie was away on the night in question, they rather thought in London."

"Stomach contents, at the autopsy."

"Yes of course, in France a pathologist would get interested in the grub and probably reconstruct the whole damn menu. Here not a bit, and they just say a Heavy Meal: toad-in-the-hole for all they care. Ham, they said when pushed. Might be corroborative in the long run, but we need some pretty strong pointer first."

"I'm in this damn foreign country, Geoffrey; in your hands. Wax, am I? Putty? Where do we go?"

"If you'll agree, I rather think we go to Plush. Which is a village. Some small way up the road there. Friend Aggie has a house there."

"Pflusch," musing, "is a good German word for a horrible fuckup."

"Exactly," said Geoffrey. "A place to approach with much prudence."

"You see," pushing the car along a Dorset country road with a good deal of up and down in it, and a lot of blind bends between high overgrown hedges, "this wouldn't do at all," said Castang, "for the French driver who is both highly suicidal, and highly homicidal, at the wheel of a car. "There must be a socialist or two, even in Pflusch."

192

"Are you a socialist, Geoffrey?"

"I'm not any kind of ist, I'm a bit like George Orwell; it's discouraging when all the socialists are so bloody awful."

"Is this farming country?" He liked the look of it, but night was falling too rapidly to make much of the infinite variety.

"Cows, sheep, depends on whereabouts. Modern, skilful, mechanised and on the whole pretty prosperous. We'll stop in the pub for you to get your bearings. Have to be the right pub, to distinguish the locals from weekending amateurs dressed up in funny clothes; television producers. Both have funny accents."

And indeed they had difficulty in avoiding the Brass Rubbers' Arms full of hunting prints and warming pans and Victorian watercolours of churchyards, and the type of furniture that is sold in France as super-English, in favour of a tiny, squalid and dimly-lit hole where incest and alcoholism could flourish unselfconsciously; much more to Geoffrey's taste. Guinness for brainwork, but Devenish for Detection.

"Can't understand a word anybody says," complained Castang.

"Difficult," agreeing. "'f I speak English every ear flaps, if we talk French we're stinking tourists; could we talk German I wonder – not that different from Dorset.

"Lookit, ordinary people round here are the same as anywhere, about politics think everywhich way, vote according, be bloody-minded and don't vote at all, if you don't feel like it. Just like in Bayern, Franz-Josef save us from the Prussians. Prussians here is Whitehall, by extension London, and arbitrarily, anywhere else at all.

"But the notables, Aggie's crowd. Hunt Balls and an inherited-income; you'd call that thoroughly Gaullist. Funny word to use in England but liberal doesn't have the same meaning here it does in Europe or America: if I were to tap a farmer here on the back and say You know something, mate, you're Ultra-Liberal, he'd probably knock me down. Whereas in California . . ."

"Or Clermont-Ferrand," interjected Castang.

"Correct. We're very strong on nationalism and take lots of umbrage over our sovereignty, and our independence has to be very Strong and backed up with lots of arms, and what else have I forgotten?"

"Security, dear boy. Build lots of prisons and shovel in delinquents as fast as you lay hands on them . . ." but Geoffrey Dawson was staring at the wall with his mouth open.

"Arms," he said to himself; mumbling through closed lips, moving it around, a professional taster with a mouthful of wine. He spat it out. "A traffic, in arms? Now I wonder."

Castang's face must have been expressing something more than scepticism because Dawson looked suddenly irritable.

"Just because these people are French we don't have to look at them with rigid minds. Be flexible, for Chrissake."

"Sounds like an idea of Roger Riderhood's," sarcastically, in his turn irritated.

Dawson got up abruptly. Brought his glass over to the bar. Struck up an animated conversation by some joke that made the locals laugh. Castang sat there in the corner being irritated. What had he come for? This was an English enquiry. His contribution could have been expressed in a telex message, and should have been left that way. There was nothing for him, here.

He would have proceeded logically to the brilliant conclusion that east was east and west was west and never the twain should meet, but for realising just in time how ridiculous he was.

I had a part, in the death of that woman, in Munich.

And by the brook, in Marlene's death? Everyone had a part. That was just the point. It was as though everyone who knew her, had known her, were forced into the roles of a play of sorts, that led inevitably to her death.

But here? I have no part. But if Geoffrey is right some person – plural almost certainly – have an active share, in the deaths of two young people. I cannot disregard this.

And it behoves me, I think, here in England, to have some humility. On both sides of the Channel there is all too much of a noisy braggart mentality, a noisy display of offended vanities, frenzied waving of tricolours and union-jacks (surely the world's most hideous flags?)

Castang picked up his glass, brought it over to the bar.

"Another of the same, please." Geoffrey was telling a probably obscene story about 'two young men in a Jaguar' which was amusing the company.

194

Roger is human. The Arnauds are human. These people are human. And the bourgeoisie? And France? Always technically in front: always humanly behind. A lesson Richard said he'd had to learn – coincidentally not too far from hereabouts.

"Forgive me, Henri, I took rather a time."

"It was good for me. To be patient a little."

"I've learned quite a lot. The little one in the corner who looks like a groom" – this description had frequently been applied to Castang himself – "does odd jobs for Aggie from time to time. She doesn't keep what you'd call a staff nowadays. House is quite a way outside. Village women help out. But she has a full time fellow. Houseman, butler, I don't know what you'd call him. And I think we'd quite like to have a word in the ear of this worthy soul. Agree? He keeps house while she's away. Has a Rover car. Sounds as though he did quite well for himself in her employ, would you say?"

"Lead on, Macbeth."

"No," said Geoffrey grinning, "it has to rhyme with Damned be he who first cries Hold, Enough."

This English countryside, full of crooked ways and high hedges, was hard to follow in the dark, but the house showed up plainly once they found the gate and went up a long drive between paddock and woodland. A smallish Georgian house, plain and compact, classically ordered with a large window on either side of a severe porch. But all closed, shuttered, silent: nobody at home. They prowled about.

"What's so nice about these houses is you can tell at a glance what's inside. Front drawing room, back drawing room: t'other side dining room and study behind. Central hallway leads straight back to the kitchen. Four bedrooms, two bathrooms, what looks to me like a self-contained flat at the back over the kitchen. Just like Jane Austen, beautifully clear. Folding doors to the back drawing room, keep the grand piano there." At the back a paved stable yard. Horses on one side, carriages on the other. They peeked through chinks with the torch. No Rover car. "Strange, that there's nobody. Pushover for burglars – or maybe not! However . . . we do have a fallback position, and that's the doctor in the next village, whom local gossip tells us is a bit of a drunk and a friend of Aggie's." This was also a little Georgian house, but in a block between two others: freshly pointed brick, smart black and white paint, shiny brass. Geoffrey rang the bell and adopted a new manner, filled with charm and altogether engaging. The door was opened by a middle-aged gentleman in a handsome small-check suit, showed off by a largish spread of waistcoat, a weatherbeaten face with high colour and grey eyebrows, plenty of teeth with yellowed ivory and some very good goldsmith work. Geoffrey explained, at length and plaintive. The doctor was very affable. Village doctors often are.

"Dear-dear. Well, come in out of the draught, and we'll see what can be done for you." The dining-room-and-study side of things here would be the waiting room and consulting room. The hall was very nice, thought Castang. Grandfather clock, pretty faded carpet.

"Awf'ly good of you."

"Nonsense, man, gracious me, what would you think of our hospitality – friends of Aggie's?"

"I hope I might so call myself" – merry laughter – "Dorset CID actually. Dawson. No, not my sergeant" – more merry laughs; even in horsy clothes Castang had not quite the right look – "friend of mine from France." When in doubt Castang was also a believer in telling the truth.

"Well now I myself always say I've nothing whatever against the French." (Some of my own best friends are Jews.) "Little glass of sherry?" proposed the doctor, to prove it.

"With pleasure," in an off-duty way.

"You aren't going to tell me we've any crimes hereabouts?" returning with a little tray and three glasses of very good wine.

"I should hope not indeed. Oh, very nice. No no, really it was her young man I'm in pursuit of. Splendid stuff this."

"Tommy Ross? Nice young chap. Fits in well. Been driving too fast again, has he?"

"Has he? Oh well, amnesty in that direction. Unprofessional pursuit I should have said. Of no real moment. Young chap who gave his name as a reference – I'd be quite glad of your opinion as to character."

"Tommy's a good chap. No, no, I insist. Mother's milk, couldn't harm you." Castang could see easily enough that it

196

was a pretext for having three himself. Not at all uncommon. Hardworking, old-fashioned medical men. Above all, One of Us. Between us, there's no harm in slight indiscretions, and there's always the hope of picking up a nugget of news. CID indeed! "Tommy? – reliable I'd say from personal – but that's of no value to you. But as you probably know, Aggie Martindale's a careful lady, and pretty shrewd. Employing someone in a position of trust – she knows her onions! If she gives him good marks . . ."

"If she didn't, as you remark, she'd hardly . . . But if you do too," generously, "then I think we could put faith, don't you?"

The doctor found himself conveying social niceties.

"Well, he's like one's paid deck-hand of course, all on a footing of equality at sea: shorewards one likes them to keep a civil tongue in their heads."

"Ah yes," Geoffrey welcoming the opportunity, "I've been hearing about Miss Martindale's new boat. Tommy going to sail it for her, is he?"

"Well, there was this wretched pair of French youngsters – dear dear, been tactless again –" making faces of apology towards Castang, "dare say you heard about that."

"Vaguely."

"Sailing stuff – John Masefield, lonely sky and all that, after the Army I felt I'd had enough. Abroad, I told myself, I've been abroad. Stick now to dear old Dorset." It was time to get rid of him. Whatever else – garrulous . . .

"Curious," said Geoffrey, driving home, "curious that Tommy Ross should be away from home when Aggie always insists – oops," finding a truck almost under his nose. English country roads, thought Castang; we're as far as could be from the striding distances and those ruler-straight Napoleonic stretches. As well there aren't too many French drivers hereabout . . . He felt a bit sleepy. If the truth be known, a bit stupid. Couldn't in all honesty say he was paying the closest attention to Geoffrey's intermittent mutterings – as much soliloquy as anything.

"One could always search that boat for caches . . . get the Customs people on that . . . chief objections about arms – apart

197

from who wants them – bulky surely, heavy; hard to conceal . . . fishboat a better bet you'd think: West Bay or even Seatown. There's Weymouth of course . . . mm, the Doctor. Wonder whether that old piss-artist knows anything worth knowing. You'd say he'd be competent enough t'look after foxhound puppies. Bind up their sore paw or whatever . . . Master Tommy. Know just about enough to want to know more, concerning the personage. A beige Rover car. Long dark hair. Surprising Aggie hasn't told him Get-y'r-Air-Cut, what's this then, the Ugandan Navy? . . ."

Castang woke up suddenly.

They were nearly home, no? A roundabout: main road and quite a bit of traffic and Geoffrey waiting in disciplined English fashion for a gap.

"Hoy," said Castang suddenly, loudly. A beige car – a Rover that, no? – turned off the roundabout on to the road they were leaving. The extremely bright lighting both helped and hindered. A sharply-etched glimpse of features, and the colour values quite distorted. Dark straight features. Known as saturnine. Hair long, that was for sure.

Geoffrey had been watching the traffic but reacted smartly, nipping out under the nose of a pacific trundler who scowled blackly at him. Bad bit of driving that – egoist. French, probably.

Nothing for it but to scour round the circle, leaning hard on the outside wheels. The Rover was well ahead by this time but Geoffrey unperturbed.

"Now if that is Master Tommy," accelerating, "then it's a good chance to lean on him a little. Excuse me Sir but you seem to have a defective rear light. Like to catch him quick, because I've no mind to go trundling all the way back there: I'd rather like my supper." He accelerated more. And at the next bend there was a view of the Rover's sedate English buttocks, proceeding without undue haste.

"I don't have any winkers or sirens," said Geoffrey, feeling in an inside pocket, producing a folder with a plastic window on the inside, "first chance I get I'll pull up alongside him and you flash that under his nose. And if it isn't him at all we clamp our teeth and bow politely – officious bastards . . . Worth taking the chance – here we go!'' Castang rolled the window down and held the warrant card flat on his palm.

As they pulled level the saturnine features glanced sideways, with a quick passage from irritation to surprise; and as his eye caught the card, to something else again. The face tightened up into lines along the jaw. He saw nothing else because Geoffrey swerved violently, avoiding the ditch on that side by no great margin. They had been doing a sober sort of speed, up to now.

The driver had thrown his gearbox back into third and pushed the accelerator hard: the Rover's powerful motor did the rest.

"Now why 'd he do that?" asked Geoffrey between his teeth, gripping the wheel with both hands. He kept his mouth shut thereafter. It was no longer a time for muttering, for intellectual speculation. Castang no longer felt sleepy.

On a French road the Rover would have had no trouble at all in losing them inside three minutes, possessing everything that was needed. Here things were different.

Tommy Ross, since he had now become at least a probability, was not a very good driver: he changed down too late and braked too hard. No better in fact than Castang, who had no sensitive feelings towards cars and was not more than barely competent when in charge of one. He detested anything like a car chase (they should be reserved for television serials) and felt profoundly unhappy with anyone but Orthez driving. He was now slightly astonished at rather enjoying this. Geoffrey, giving the lie to the slim-bespectacled-intellectual look, was nearly as good as Orthez . . .

And the car was helping him; a sturdy thing, sitting firm on a wide solid wheelbase. Cornering better than the bigger heavier thing up front. Well geared, and the much smaller motor at no great disadvantage. The sensitive hands and feet of a good driver did the rest.

And it was enervating, weakening the driver in front; that he could not get away from them. His nervous snap glances in the mirror above him were not helping: he was using too much road and taking bends badly. Sometimes Geoffrey got close; sometimes, when the power counted, he was less close, but never less than a hundred metres and making that up. Sooner or later the Rover would have to stop and they'd have him. Unless they ran out of juice: when had Geoffrey tanked? Ross now knew that there were cops after him; two professionals knowing how to take even a violent fugitive in a pincer. The knowledge was doing his nerves no good. He's cooked, thought Castang.

But there is the unforeseen. The Dorset landscape, so wonderfully varied, provides good examples.

They made a sharpish long left-hand curve down into a steep valley, with another right-hand bend beyond climbing out of it: a big S in two dimensions together. Right at the bottom of the valley and hidden till one was right on top of it – a broad-arsed crawling mass of red-painted farm machinery. The arse was not just broad. It bristled with blades, teeth, harrowing huge claws. Coming down the bend at the far side, the lights of a car could be seen. The narrow road serpentined between tall hedges.

Geoffrey braked hard, dry-skidded, went on doing so, correcting each time with the lock, slithering at the limit from side to side, never quite losing control, regaining progressively as he got down into second. The motor howled, the tyres screeched and spat gravel. The car stopped. Two good metres from the claws.

Ross had done something totally insane; suicide and homicide in one: rammed his car straight at the gap, oncoming car or no. The oncomer, given the choice between a head-on crash with a fast car and the slower but nastier meeting with modern agriculture, behaved very sensibly and took to the bushes. He had been prudent twice already, braking for the hill and again for the monster, and now he was rewarded by meeting an elastic mass of hazels and bramble which broke the resistance of a young ash tree; it split his front end in half but left him unhurt, still sitting there when the three running men reached him. Neither gesticulation nor vociferation; no blood on his face, only immense surprise.

"Police," said Dawson. "No time to stop. Contact CID in the morning," dragging Castang by the sleeve.

"What's the use? Miles away by now."

"Not convinced of that," flinging the car up the hill, "I've a notion we might surprise him."

"Whatever he had on his mind he'll have time to ditch it."

Mixed metaphor, but clear to them both. Why should Mr. Ross be so frightened at being stopped by the police? A bad conscience? Or something in his possession?

The hill was only a ridge between two valleys and Geoffrey was already down. He slowed the car, searching, went Ho, and turned sharply into what looked to be a rutted farm track. Rubbish was piled; bricks, corrugated iron, the carcase of an old car. "Oh dear Jesus," said Castang, pious. In front of them was a river. The rivers of Dorset are neither broad nor deep. Some are chalk streams, clear or cloudy as the case may be. Quite fordable to a highwayman on a horse; to four-and-twenty ponies; the Volkswagen Company might make faces though. Castang's piety was owed to steep-looking, clayey-looking, slidy-looking banks at the far side and more than a suspicion of mud at the bottom.

"Hup then, Susan," ejaculated Geoffrey as the wheels slid. Castang had no impulse to get out and push, having ruined in bad causes, too many trousers which the police department then refused to pay for.

One wheel bit and the car went sideways. They both closed their eyes and perhaps Geoffrey uttered one more incantation; it straightened up and pulled.

"Well well, good old Michelin." There were more ruts and they had got back into them. Other people did it! "Yes," admitted Geoffrey. "But in a Land Rover . . . Stole five good minutes there," reaching a road again. Castang made a noise that was neither French nor English but expressed large admiration. "And with any luck he slowed down, once he lost us." The windscreen was still covered in dirty water but Geoffrey, besides the skill to use just the right amount of acceleration, had the foresight to put the blades on high speed before hitting the ford. I must remember to tell Orthez, thought Castang. It's black as pitch and if there are any drunken peasants in Dorset given to bicycling home from the pub without lights then it's them and us both: there's said to be a God that protects drunks and maybe there's one too for cops . . . Exists; I've Met Him, Castang felt. He could feel sudden and inhabitual pain in the upper left arm, which between the shoulder and the elbow was mostly built of plastic.

He recognised nothing before the open space, the stone bays

and pillars of a formal gate, the gravelled driveway ending in a circular loop round turf and a large fine hydrangea bush. There was no other car there.

Geoffrey cut the lights and the motor and said, "Quiet – listen." There was no sound at all in the Dorset night but that of hot metal beginning to cool. A breath of wind in treetops where rooks were asleep. And then, unmistakable, the note of a car motor. But there was nothing to be seen.

"Of course. The back," whipping round the corner of the house, running to reach the stable yard. They gained time: Ross had to get out to open the gate at the bottom. The headlights of the Rover were shining straight in their eyes and they dodged apart to avoid the glare. Not before the man saw them.

Once again he wasted no time. He was out of the car already and slipped in behind it, opening the boot. There was altogether something too nervous and panicky about his movements fumbling there: Castang didn't like it; circled further outwards, his feet not very easy on the greasy cobblestones.

Geoffrey didn't like it either: he stood stock still and said in the slow patient tone of the English official, "Come now, Mr. Ross, be sensible."

There was reflection from the headlights off the white plasterwork of the back of the house. It gave quite a lot of light, but of a tricky sort. The man stood still, but his arms moved. Castang still didn't like it.

A cop in France must by law give two verbal warnings. "Halt!" he must call. "Police!" And if disregarded he must again call, "Halt, or I fire!" The 'bandit brigade' can sometimes be fairly perfunctory about all this. Better in the long run, Castang had decided a good while ago, to have no gun at all. Too often Johnny at the-other-end decided to anticipate matters. Naturally, if Johnny goes bang, you go bang with no further ado. You're in a state of legitimate-self-defence. If it isn't too late by then. Either way, you'd rather be somewhere else. There are too few options.

"Do not attempt to obstruct an officer, Ross," said Mr. Dawson's quiet voice. He began walking.

Geoffrey should have waited longer, to defuse the more panicky kind of reaction. Castang wouldn't have budged, would

202

have got down, as low and as far out of light as possible; and sure as eggses no approach yet awhile. He was damn *sure* the bugger had a gun.

An English officer, and small blame to him, does not have this sort of experience. And his undramatic manner (trained that way) has generally served very well indeed. But even in England there are too many people who are not very bright and look at too much American television.

Quite a big gun and it went off big. Cobbles, and walls of the stable buildings on two sides, and the higher house wall on the third. Makes the noise much bigger. Quite a muzzle-flash. Nine millimetres at the least.

There is a phrase. Bowled over as though shot. And when bowled over like that – you *are* shot. Poor Geoffrey.

There is likewise a phrase that Castang had not heard, that became something of a catchword in the summer of 1940 and which went "Right – in the final, now". And now he was in the final.

Geoffrey lay on those fucking cobblestones. Castang had no gun. He wouldn't have been allowed to carry one in England anyhow. Hadn't even one at home. This is my lot, he thought. But maybe it isn't my lot. This fellow won't be very used to guns. First, he can miss me. Even from close up. It is the thing about pistols: they do miss, a great deal, even from very close up. Only on television do they shoot your death-dealing umbrella out of your fingers.

Second, it's quite likely the fellow is more frightened than I am. Highly shaky, and now shakier still. Discovering that guns can hit people is a considerable shock to the amateur. One pro, without gun, in reality equals one amateur with gun. You stinking murdering amateur, thought Castang, taking very small steps forward.

"French cunt," said a harsh unpleasant voice. He was glad that it was an unpleasant voice. "I know who you are. Dawson's French pal. Rather fuck than fight, huh?" Very very small steps. And do not say a word. There is also the technique of a flow of chat kept up. In English Castang had no flow of chat. It is also important not to stop some kind of movement, because if you do it is so very hard to start again.

Quite close now, Castang could see the gun. Largish, an automatic of some sort. His left arm and shoulder were very painful: the nerves have memories of their own. A man had held a gun on him. He had been very frightened indeed. Among numerous good reasons for this had been a bigger gun even than this one, and with a magnum charge. It had knocked his upper arm to pieces then, and was castrating him now. Was it a pleasant smile he had on his face or a rictus? He was trying to give it no expression at all but the face kept going stiff.

The fellow could certainly see the fear all over him, and was enjoying that.

A lot of talk nowadays about karate, arising from a vague notion that Japanese are modern. Police cadets got taught tough chesty attitudes and a confident aggressiveness. In the days when Castang went to school there wasn't any of this. The Physical Training Instructor put them through the antiquated techniques of boxe à la française which came, oddly, to the same thing. 'La savate' – ungentlemanly. Castang was quite a promising pupil. Savate – a humble, clumsy peasant's shoe.

Ross was expecting the left arm. It is good for spoons, cigarettes, perhaps an aerosol can. A sort of lunge with the right arm foxed him just enough for a goodish shot with the left instep. The gun skittered on the cobbles, without even going off in that spiteful way automatics have. Ross reeled a little on the cobbles and Castang got a soft target there with the knee. You shouldn't frig with guns and you shouldn't shoot my friends.

And you shouldn't tease me. I am not really French (come to that who is?) being what Vera calls an Aquitanian Bastard, but you got me there afraid of being frightened. Whatever I believe in, violence still gets the upper hand. I got hold of the gun.

The scenario was now plain. One had to tie this Lump up, if need be tapping him with the gun to keep him quiet. Got no string. Well, there had been horses here, perhaps there would be harness. Reins and things; being tough one could cut some with one's knife. Had the gun anyhow. Czech CZ, nine millimetre; efficient gun.

The scenario went all wrong, as they do of course. Cut and start again. There were no banana skins, no cowshit, but Castang managed to slip and stun his bad arm. Mr. Ross's crutch wasn't in great shape either, but it had left him manoevrable enough to jump about. He ran, even. He ran for Geoffrey's car parked at the side of the house. Castang, sitting up and wishing he wasn't paralysed, suddenly noticed that Geoffrey wasn't dead. He too was sitting up, with his mouth open. Neither of them was in shape for running. Ross got into the car, and there was a frightful moment of realisation that Geoffrey had left the key in the ignition.

Sitting, Castang pointed the gun. The motor roared.

"No!" howled Geoffrey. "My good new Michelins!" No time for laughing about this. Instead of Ross getting knotted up there he'd got them both knotted.

The priorities were easily established. Even if this infernal Ross was now a-gallop through the Dorset night on board Geoffrey's car that was a matter for the CID and Mr. Castang could not care less; how badly was Inspector Dawson hurt?

Another pair of trousers ruined! A lot of blood. The bone all right as far as he could tell. A nasty wound, but not really horrible. Calf of the right leg. The pull of those guns is very light. Ross had shot too soon and too hurriedly. Castang had a silk scarf. Cracked but still a good one. So is the cause.

"Oops. Try to hop, as far as the car." The big damned Rover was at least easier to get into than the Volkswagen! But one-arm supporting one-leg is productive of much heaving and puffing.

Geoffrey once installed, Castang had an idea. What was it that had made young Tommy so scared of being stopped by the police? What was it that he hadn't had time to ditch, on arrival? The boot of the Rover was not locked.

Amidst junk and wrapped loosely in an old blanket were two heavy boxes of weatherproofed cardboard, strong and greasy looking. The weight for the size told Castang what was inside, even without the stencilling saying Czechoslovakia and a lot of code numbers. More of those pistols, nicely packed in greasy paper, eight or ten. And ammunition for same, in some quantity.

"Arms," said Castang starting the motor and swinging the Rover round. "You were right." Mr. Dawson was in a good deal of pain but could call up a satisfied grin.

"The wound is clean, no bullet left in; I think the foxhoundpuppy man will fix you up." He had locked the luggage compartment. The village street was quiet and empty. Perhaps Tommy Ross had more friends around the place but not to worry. The original gun, with his prints on it, sat in Castang's pocket. The CID would find that bullet somewhere in the stable yard.

"Feels wider than a church door," grumbled Geoffrey. "Never been shot before. Valuable experience. Just as soon it had stayed yours. Nice though, having someone who knows what it's all about. Woo . . . don't hurry me."

"God bless my soul," said the doctor. "That's a gunshot wound! Haven't seen one since I was in the Army! Bless my soul . . . Gone through. Not too bad. But we must get you to hospital. Dear-dear. Terrorists!"

"No hospital," said Geoffrey. "Fix it up."

"My dear boy!" A tutster. This sort of elderly practitioner who talks about tummy is still a familiar figure in the countryside. Says little prick for a local anaesthetic. "These muscle tissues are quite mangled, you know."

"Straighten it out. Don't want hospital – lots of gossip. Henri – don't let that fucker get away with my car!"

"What's the number? . . . Use your phone, doctor? Emergency."

"CID," said a police voice. What was the name of the (other) "old woman"?

"Superintendent Armstrong please, urgent, I'm calling for Mr. Dawson."

"I'll put you through to his home."

"Mr. Castang. Yes, that's right. Look, Dawson's been shot." And Mr. Armstrong was exactly like Divisional Commissaire Richard to talk to. He simply said, "Badly?" Castang did his best to be lucid in English and was told, "That's all right. You can leave it to me."

"Tommy Ross a terrorist!" said the tutster, binding up the leg.

Geoffrey sat up on the examination couch, rolled down the leg of the broken trousers, said, "Henri, give me one of your little cigars, will you . . . Bound to be painful, when the anaesthetic wears off. Got a couple of Disprin or something better?"

206

"I'll find some tablets but you mustn't . . . you really should . . ."

"Let's not be afraid of a small technical irregularity, Doctor." He had turned back into Inspector Dawson; it was disconcerting.

"I'd like you to answer me a few questions. Unofficial. I rely upon your professional discretion. But not too much of it. You take my meaning? You know a good deal about this local countryside, doctor. Are you or have you been aware of arms dealing here in the neighbourhood?"

"Good heavens. Uh. Among the local farmers, one, one winks the eye a bit, I mean there's a certain latitude – one, one wouldn't like to say whether all the firearms certificates are quite . . ."

"I'm not talking about a few shotgun cartridges. I'm talking about modern, automatic, military style weapons. There are some outside in the car, which Castang can show you."

"No. No. Of course not."

"Have you knowledge of anything – group or organisation – that could be thought of as a militia?"

"Well. There's the County Yeomanry. No longer on the reserve myself of course – some time since I went into camp, ha ha."

"I don't really want an evasive answer, doctor."

"Now, now, now, what would you mean by a militia? Extraordinary word."

"So you can't offer any explanation to me of why Tommy Ross would be smuggling arms?"

"None. None."

"Or where they come from. Or where they're intended to go to."

"Good heavens, Dawson, you can't ask me questions like that. I make allowances for your injury. That's shock, and . . . But really, really. Nobody has ever suggested that I would fail in my duty by neglecting to report any knowledge of any criminal activity to the duly constituted authority."

"And suppose it were not a criminal activity. Or not regarded as such. Or regarded as only technically such. Like certain kinds of pills – not just to be bought over the counter but freely enough prescribed. Mm?"

Doctor got stiff and haughty.

"I really couldn't say. The question is improper, I'll go so far as to say indecent."

"That's nice and comfy now, with much thanks to you. I'll hitch-hike as far as the car, Henri."

"Quite luxurious this," settled in the Rover. "We'll go back to headquarters now."

"We'll do no such thing," said Castang. "Beddybyes for you, mate, with a loving Em." And on the (careful) drive back to Dorchester Geoffrey appeared to be sleeping, but for a sudden question:

"Where do these arms come from?" It was probably a rhetorical question but Castang answered it.

"I'll make a guess about that. Not a very informed guess. There's been quite a bit going over the Austrian border in recent times, and some very respectable gentlemen in Vienna with gunsmith businesses have been clapped in the Austrian jails."

"Nobody, the king said, could call me a fussy man, but I do like a little bit of butter to my bread." Feverish? In any case, the source of this very English remark remained obscure.

Emily wasn't a fussy woman. Castang got an impression that she did look upon him with something of a beady eye. You let the man out with a French cop, this frightful individual he had somehow picked up (drunk no doubt) in Germany, and what happens? He comes home with a gunshot wound. Men are like small children and must never be let out without a nanny. This was the halt leading the lame: c'est le cas de le dire . . .

And the children have lost their car! And picked up another that doesn't belong to them! Really!

If we weren't both hurt we'd both have caught a richly-deserved smack, thought Castang sneaking guiltily away.

Chief Superintendent Armstrong was seated behind his desk and a row of telephones, and smiled rather grimly upon him. There was also a tall dark man with long legs sticking out, and the sleepy sort of look it is as well to beware of.

"I think you've done very well," said Armstrong. He had told his story, as best he could. "And you've got this gun; splendid. One up on the Met, wouldn't you say, Peters?"

"Definitely, sir."

"I'm so sorry, this is Sergeant Peters, and while our friend Dawson's laid up he'll try and be of some help to you. They work habitually together." The tall man had got very quickly to his feet, and with great politeness said, "Very pleased, sir. I'll do my best."

"Try and be of help," is definitely a phrase, thought Castang. I am now assisting their enquiries. It was a foregone conclusion that the Dorset CID wouldn't let me out without a nanny.

"As for this tedious young man," went on Armstrong, monument of calm, "we'll have him by the heels, you may rest assured. We're watching that hotel in Weymouth but the odds are we were too late there – his employers will be anxious to get rid of him, not wishful to be compromised. It is likely that they'd want him out of the country."

A telephone rang. Armstrong listened awhile and merely said, "Good" before putting it down.

"Found the car. Poole Harbour. Your guess about the boat was a good one, Monsieur Castang." He put his hand on another telephone, bethought himself and said, "Look after the Commissaire, Peters."

"Like some tea?" in the outer office. "Get nowhere without, here."

"Very much ... What was the thing about Met?" Peters scratched his jaw and grinned.

"We're very provincial down here. Makes us snobbish you might call it. Dare say you have something the same. We enjoy saying that the Met – that's London – is a monument to incompetence and the moment they all got given guns they started shooting one another." Grin.

"And what's 'nobody, the king said, could call me a fussy man'?"

"Oh dear." Grin. "That'll be Mr. Dawson? A child's rhyme. I'm afraid there's no explaining the English. I'd better say by the way that 'well done' isn't faint praise at all in the Old Man's mouth: it's the best he's got. He's never said it to me."

Castang was thinking – a sergeant sounds nothing much and is in fact a lot. Same rank really as one of our inspectors. Orthez, say.

"What are we waiting for?" he enquired cautiously.

"Well, it's not a thing we'd be able to do ordinarily, but shooting one of our chaps is cheek, wouldn't you agree, and the old man doesn't look it but is very niggled indeed. So he ushered us politely out so he could scream down the phone to the Royal Navy in Portland and will they very kindly take the finger out of the bum long enough to give him a helicopter with a searchlight and surface radar, out there in the Channel; get a fix on the boyfriend."

Castang drank powerful orange tea, in great content. Nice, how little there is to choose between Strongbow there and Mr. Richard.

When the phone went next the voice was sharp – and brief – enough for Castang to hear.

"Boat waiting for you on Custom House Quay."

"C'm on," said Peters.

"But d'you allow me?" asked Castang humbly.

"Believe me, sir, we need you. Got to watch the doings with this boat carefully, and you're the owner's legal representative. You give the orders." Tactful of you, that!

Smallest sort of boat the navy has: sixty-foot launch. Coastguard, air-sea rescue, fishery protection – he did not really know much about the subject. Fast. Didn't seem to be armed but they've probably a rocket or two hidden away somewhere. A lot of antennae. Surface radar, sonar, he dared say a few other secretive surveillance things. An Ensign, or was it a Sub-Lieutenant, who was politely talkative for a few minutes, and some crewmen who were politely taciturn.

"Ocean racer's I understand. Fast, and tide's with him. Not a lot of wind, what there is west nor'west. Head straight out most likely past Studland and Anvil: idea of making it the shortest way across, aim for Cherbourg and hope to dodge inside Alderney where it's quiet. Further out, tide's dead down-channel five knots, how good a sailor is he, how good a navigator, just how fast is he? – chopper had to get his sums right in a hurry computing away up there. Overshot him in fact. Chap can't have had that much of a start – two and a half hours be about right? Bee-line for us to St. Albans and a fresh fix there. Should get 'm before he makes the frontier," grinning naughtily at Castang, "all those tankers and shit, on the rail heading up the Seine

210

estuary; have to ask La Royale for permission and they're rather touchy! Get a black mark at home for that. Some rivalry, y'understand me sir, emulation or what's it called, being punctilious about our escort duties. Hope you won't feel sick!" Castang hoped so too.

"No such thing as navy rum nowadays," muttered Sergeant Peters.

Bloody cold out here! Fending off the cold, hoping to fend off being sick (inshore against the tide makes us pitch a wee bit) Castang made some desultory conversation.

"What make you of this arms business?" Sergeant Peters took his slightly-funny English without effort; it wouldn't be that much funnier than native Dorset.

"Speaking for myself – just for me – I don't think it surprising. The recession has made people that bit more disgruntled. So's the outside world; every little thing one grievance the more, d'you know. Taking it personally. Thought up expressly to pester us. Pushing us about, they thought. Couple of loony Argentine generals set them stamping potty. Never thought I'd be alive to see the Boer War. Said to myself, you better keep your mouth shut, they'll be handing you white feathers.

"This could be another hysterical shriek of the same sort. Arm the Met, they shouted. Something like four thousand chaps in the Met, most of whom don't know which way to put their boots on. Give them guns, is it? You know all about that."

"We give them three weeks training with tests, on little pieces of paper."

"That's right. 'Stead of ten weeks squarebashing, somewhere really horrible. Look for police on the cheap, and cheap is what you get. So old ladies start their own militia . . ."

"Pick 'm up on the radar any minute," said the Midshipman. "Been told to follow your instructions, sir."

"I haven't any," said Castang. "We'll have to watch that he doesn't do anything silly like jumping overboard, and we do have to be careful about damage." He wished they would say something nautical. 'Stand by to go about'. 'Square your main yard, Mr. Jackson'. 'Lay out any mutineers with a belaying pin' . . . Instead, the radar operator pointed to a squiggle and said,

"Ketch-rigged boat, about eleven metre."

The orders were sadly prosaic. "Slow. Lights. Fenders. Pudding!" This last did excite him for an instant – plum duff even if no rum? – but turned out to be a net filled with bits of old cork and lucky it wasn't expanded polyurethane. The one thing remotely Nelsonian was "Boarding party ready", and even they had no cutlasses. A big glare of light was the only weapon used. "Jump." Two sailors with nothing more lethal than rubber boots. The wretched Ross might be half paralysed, but Castang was most impressed by the gentleness used. The midshipman brought his clumsy craft alongside like a barge in a lock. There is no sea, but approaching a sailing boat doing fifteen-eighteen knots without scratching – faut le faire!

"Easy. Easy! Make fast." He was learning English too. "Lovely boat," said the officer. Modern navies are so stuffed with electronics experts that nobody is left able to recognise a pair of sculls. The officer laughed. "Out of Brixham those two boys – know a lobster pot when they see it."

Nobody twisted Ross's arm or kicked his shins. They took him below and gave him tea. "Stretch out then, lad," said Peters putting handcuffs on, careful not to hurt. Castang did not want to see Ross. He stayed watching the sailors take the sails off the yacht and fix a tow-rope in a cunning way that included a shock absorber.

"Mustn't brutalise," said the officer. What might he be – twenty-three? No relation to Mad Max.

Violence is today's Black Death, rolling inexorably over Europe. Yes, said Geoffrey Dawson, and I might remind you that the Black Death arrived in England through Weymouth.

Are there villages still where Force is held in lower esteem than gardeners? A few, said Geoffrey. But for how long?

A sailing boat came in from France, with a French boy and a girl, carrying the plague. What happened then?

We have to distinguish, between some piffling little conspiracy suitable for what Geoffrey called the Pirates of Penzance, and the real thing. Is this an amiable sort of dottiness, or the real plague-struck madness?

I have seen the real madness: Europe for the past ten years has been overrun by it. The ideologies appear loony, whether extreme left wing or extreme right (so incoherent that it is not easy to distinguish which is which) but all coherent in their extreme of hatred, brutality and violence.

Sometimes manipulated: it has been an eye-opener to be reminded that criminals against humanity from the National Socialist time were protected, employed (and well paid) not only by the American and Russian services. By the French too, the English too – and doubtless all the others.

Manipulation – by whom? for use against whom? – is often so blurred, masked and faked that the police officer no longer cares. The characters in this world are all stock figures of romantic – or anti-romantic – fiction. Invented by Roger Riderhood. Dick Hannay or George Smiley: all the same pot of piss.

Miss Agatha Martindale is a Boer War relic: nostalgic for the old days, when servants knew their place and police came to the tradesmen's entrance. If they got uppity, lay into them with a riding crop. But whatever her ideologies (idiot word) they are of no importance. She's Mad Max.

It was too late at night to go knocking up poor Emily. Sergeant Peters, a man thoughtful for others, offered a kip on his own living room sofa. Castang accepted, gratefully.

Peters' wife, delightful woman, in no way behind Emily in her notions of hospitality (the French don't even let the French into their houses), provided an enormous breakfast, bathroom, pink soap, wizard electric razor: result, New Man.

"Armstrong thinks," said the Sergeant with his mouth full of toast, "that he has only to cook Ross awhile, turn him Queen's Evidence, have the lot like baked beans. Can't see it myself. Ross is just an errand boy to my mind. This old lady's house-man . . . that mean he commits murders when she gives him a phone call? . . . Wonder how Mr. Dawson is, this fine morning. Be glad to get his car back."

But this morning they took a police car with Peters driving.

Geoffrey's leg was stiff and sore, but his brains well dusted off. It was sunny this morning, a pale but warm mild January sunshine that went well with the palm trees on the Weymouth esplanade. But Mr. Dawson saw no point in coming-the-heavy at Aggie.

"She'll slap our faces and dare us to do anything about it. What have we on her anyhow? Ross? A servant. 'What do I know or care what he does in his spare time?' Did she commit any murders? Did she even instigate or encourage same? Highly dubious. Did she even have knowledge before or after? – dubious and very difficult to put beyond doubt. No, there's a missing planet somewhere. Attractions point to it even if we can't see it." It was a 'Richard' metaphor. Castang recalled thinking the same thing last night, on the goddam deck of the goddam HMS *Dainty*. Peters had said the same thing this morning: they were in harmony. "We let Armstrong pig with arms smuggling and I wish him joy of Aggie. Who committed murders, huh?"

"Does the arms smuggling lead to the murders?" asked Castang.

"I don't know: I lay in bed trying to reconstruct; fat lot of good that does. These French children buy a boat, probably in perfect innocence, bring it over here; likewise short of evidence to the contrary. Aggie – hypothesis – gets a bright idea. Boat would do nicely for arms. Not much, or much at a time, but they aren't proposing artillery. The box of pistols would be a try-out; if that goes smooth we'll bring a few assault rifles next time. Say the French agree: steady source of income, what? And exciting. But what went wrong? Why bop them? Did they get cold feet, threaten to blow the gaff? – God, talking in clichés means I'm thinking in them. It seems so unlikely and yet I'm convinced we're on the right lines."

Chief Superintendent Armstrong had also said – at some length – that he didn't much care for murders without any motive and neither did the Director of Prosecutions.

"Still," said Geoffrey, cheering up suddenly, "there's a weak link there too which I intend to rattle and that's that loose-mouthed ass of a Wentworth-Brewster. Ring him up would you, Pete, and say I'm coming up for loving care."

Sergeant Peters on the telephone was fearfully bland but immovable: Doctor could be heard to be reluctant, but couldn't wriggle out of treating a Patient. Geoffrey was grinning before it was finished.

"Now let him stew for a bit."

Indeed the doctor, amid a lot of fuss about antibodies, antibiotics and antitetanus, was bursting with curiosity he could not restrain.

"Must have been some misunderstanding surely, about Tommy Ross?"

"Hardly. I was laid up of course, missed all the fun. You'll have to ask the Commissaire here. Ow!"

"There's a degree of inflammation," said the medical man, "and we won't get that down until you promise to keep quiet. All this agitation's doing you no good."

"I do promise," humbly. "Tell him, Castang."

"Serious business, contraband in arms," said Castang with solemnity. "Mr Ross attempted to evade justice. He got arrested by the Royal Navy. He tried to get away to France in Miss Martindale's boat. It is interesting. We've a question about that we'd rather like to put to you."

"I'm afraid I can't allow any questions on our soil from any French official, however highly placed."

"With respect sir," said Peters with unction, "there you haven't a leg to stand on, legally. The commissaire here enquires into arms traffic passing through French territory. Associated with CID enquiries here."

"But let Sergeant Peters put the question, by all means," grinning because now the fellow couldn't get out of it.

"What worries us, you see sir, is whereabouts round here these arms were getting to. We place great reliance in your knowledge of the neighbourhood."

"Damn it, Sergeant, I've no evidence to offer you."

"It's a grave matter, sir, that Mr. Dawson was wounded. He might have been killed."

"But good grief, ask Ross."

"Ross is only a servant," said Geoffrey. "A catspaw."

"But man – nothing but hearsay."

"It is also possible," said Castang, funereal, "that two people have been murdered in connection with this affair."

The doctor turned away, busying himself with clinking metal objects, fussing with them. The lid of the steriliser shut with a snap.

"Miss Martindale is Ross's employer after all."

"A lady, sir? In connection with contraband in weapons?"

"You're not serious, about two murders." It is inconceive-able that the French would ever be serious about anything. "Well, I can't help you." There was a silence, while the three men looked at him. "The only person whose name might come to mind; who I suppose might barely be able to throw light on your problem . . . Borrowed Ross one time, I recall, giving a party . . . Tommy Ross is a very good cook, they say. I suppose there's no harm in asking; and that's Sevenhampton. Not that I think for a moment . . ."

"Give me an arm would you, Pete? And pass me my stick," said Mr. Dawson.

"Drive us to the pub, Pete. I want bread and cheese and pickled onions. Mm, what goes well with stale Cornish pasties?"

"Champagne, think you?"

"You crackers? What'll you have, Pete?"

"A French drink would go well. Pastis? The champagne will be Bulmer's Woodpecker."

"Pete, could you sort of gather about Mr. Sevenhampton, think you?" Geoffrey had caught some of Castang's English phrasing.

"Your sergeant is one in a million," said Castang.

"Without quite going that far, recalling moreover that all CID officers are run by their sergeants who are, of course, far brighter than they are – Peters is very good indeed. Damn, I've dropped my stick. Oh, the bollocking I got from Em, for letting myself get shot. Cheers."

"Cheers."

"Lives about seven miles off." Peters took a swig of pastis.

"Military gent?"

"Has been. Nowadays more of a sporting gent. In the busi-ness – this'll interest you, Mr. Castang – of wintersport equip-ment; frequent visits to Alps-and-things I'm told."

"It does indeed. Be that France, Switzerland or Austria."

"And a daredevil chap. Bobsleigh. When there's no snow, hang gliders and suchlike." The three men looked at one another.

216

"Get your seven-league boots on," said Dawson.

A wintry day, with a sharp wind blowing. No sun, but an open day with a high silvery sky of subtle colouring. Under this the landscape was most marvellously varied in colour as in contour, so that Castang felt frustrations that Vera was not there to explore it, to concentrate with all her being upon a palette. Greys that were pearl, that were lavender; greens all the way from blue to yellow and all the browns from yellow to red. Blues of every tobacco he had ever smoked. After years of black and white she was beginning to advance, timid and humble, towards colour. Terribly beautiful, she would say, and far far too difficult. Frustrating.

He felt much the same. Stuck by himself in the back of an English police car. The CID inspector and sergeant there in the front had no need of him; they didn't even really want him: were being polite, that was all.

But he had a part in these deaths. To be sure, the obvious, crude, nationalist part: a French cop 'helps' in the enquiry into the deaths of two citizens of the Republic. But they too had wanted to board a boat and float away; unsatisfied by the narrow rigidities of France.

He too, after years and years and years of blacks, whites and judicial greys, was beginning to discover colours. The tones and tints and hues of light and shadow.

A part in these deaths. Were they just crude and crapulous murders?

The car hit a rise, bumped, scrunched on a drive whose potholes had been smoothed with gravel.

"Fine house," said Geoffrey, struggling out.

"Must have money," said Peters. "Wouldn't you say?"

It was indeed a fine house, commanding the valley.

"Wonderful view," they said, one after the other. It was, indeed, a wonderful view. How splendid, to be rich, to be Successful. They were all probably thinking that the police are seldom successful and never rich. Castang thought about Richard's house, which had been a lot less grand than this but had had a sightly view, and which a police officer who had wanted to be rich had burned down.

These thoughts did him no good and he went back to colours.

A maid opened the door, listened, didn't understand much, would call Madam. The hall was nice. Much bigger than the doctor's. Room for three grandfather clocks.

Madam came; youngish, pretty, pullovered and trousered, all rather svelte. Listened, understood more – perhaps too much? Very dubious, but kept an uncracked exterior. Said quite politely that Esquire was outside somewhere, she'd try to find him and she'd put them in the office if they didn't mind.

The office was a large white room, furnished as an office and decorated with a lot of wintersport equipment that stood about or hung on walls. Whatever country with Alpine interests it came from – and there are five – it had all be rechristened. Glued on, stitched on, transferred on to every single piece were prominent Union Jacks.

"Patriotic chap," said Peters.

"Wouldn't you say," said Geoffrey.

Mr. Sevenhampton was rapid: he would always be rapid. Tall, strongly built, bursting with energy. Handsome too, and exquisitely dressed in the best sorts of west-of-England materials.

"CID hey?" in a strong aggressive voice that knows, and doesn't care.

"Inspector Dawson. Sergeant Peters –"

"And who's the little chap at the back, a shorthand specialist?"

"Commissaire Castang of the French State Police."

Sevenhampton looked, taking his time; decided to say nothing: Castang did likewise.

"What's wrong with your leg?" turning back to Geoffrey. Mr. Dawson decided to lose no further time.

"Be in tomorrow's paper, no doubt. In *The Times* a small paragraph, but pithy. In the local perhaps more. One of your damned arms shot me in the leg. To save prevarication, I should tell you that we've got Tommy Ross."

Sevenhampton did not bother with prevarication. Nor even what Wodehouse called stout denial. He looked at them with contempt.

"You people haven't the patriotism of a flea. And about as much guts as a piece of wet seaweed." He strode to the office

218

desk, sat and reached for a scarlet telephone. "*Times* indeed! Local paper indeed. I'm going to call my solicitor and see that the place rings with the craven-hearted gutlessness of you people. Pack of fucking socialists no doubt," including Castang generously. "Publicity!" he snorted. "I'll see you get plenty."

"Better not phone," advised Dawson, "before you know just where you stand."

"Oh, I've no doubt you'll find a magistrate somewhere as gutless as yourself to sit there on his pompous backside and tell me I'm a naughty boy. Sit quiet and be trodden on by Icelanders; trodden on by the Frogs coming over to pinch lobsters; trodden on by sodding paperpushers from Brussel-Sprout-Land. Even inside your own country the useless police won't back you up. Mealy-mouthed. Who shot you – Tommy Ross?"

"It is so alleged," gaily. Geoffrey was enjoying this by the look of him.

"He's an ass. Should do a better job if you do it at all."

"No doubt," keeping his sense of humour, for which Castang admired him.

Thumping the table brazenly. "People have the right to bear arms. And in Switzerland they do. Hitler didn't dare invade them! They know enough to keep the wogs out, too."

"And on occasion they get arrested by the police – just like anywhere else."

"Oh shut your frog mouth!"

One is accustomed to this, of course, but he valued Geoffrey's laughing.

"You have plenty on your ground, Henri, and you see we have them here too."

"A boastful Brit," said Peters. "With our big lip we farted through India."

"Frolicked, Pete, surely."

"Kicking niggers out the way. I always did say we should have bombed Buenos Aires to teach the wogs a lesson."

The man straightened his back and gripped the corners of the table, staring at them.

"Traitors!"

Castang's mind had been freewheeling during the crosstalk.

The cops doing their comic turn is something he indulged in as a rule. Was it something to do with frogs? Dawson and Peters (Bones and Sambo) moaning that they'd gone through every damned restaurant in Dorset doing Christmas dinners without finding where Daniel and Anne-Sophie had eaten that evening. "Why couldn't they nosh in the Sea Cow Bistrot like all the rest of us?"

They'd eaten here! He'd borrowed Tommy Ross to cook the dinner!

"We are interested to know how you spent the night of Christmas Eve."

And it brought him up short. They could all see it.

"I'm looking after my legal rights," he said at last.

Geoffrey was on to it, quick as knife.

"We'll respect legal rights. Human rights, too. You can answer the Commissaire's question. No? We will suggest to you that you had a little dinner-party here. Inviting perhaps Miss Martindale? And her associate in the new yacht venture; with her companion? To celebrate perhaps the first successful trip. No? Well, it's only a hypothesis. We'll see what Mr. Ross has to say on the matter."

The talk of eating had given Castang another dotty try-out.

"Would the gentleman perhaps lend us a photo of himself? Might try showing that round the pubs in Saint Malo." Barmen or waitresses never recognise anybody but he might not know that. And it had to be him, who had made the original link, looking out for a suitable boat.

"Nothing to say?" asked Dawson mildly. "Then you can phone your lawyer. Tell him I'm taking you into custody on a charge of illegal contraband in prohibited weapons, and also on suspicion of concern in the murder of Anne-Sophie Bontemps and Daniel Cardenal on the night before Christmas. You are under no obligation to say anything whatever, and you may tell him that I have respected the customary caution, that anything you do choose to say shall be noted, and may be offered in evidence before a court of justice."

"You can get stuffed, One-Leg, and note that."

The room full of gloves and skisticks, helmets and shiny

bright-painted metal; the Games Room; was suddenly filled with physical violence. Sergeant Peters was standing up, with it swirling around him, though the man had not moved.

"Make your call," Peters said.

"Well," said One-Leg, comfortable-like, to One-Arm, "two down, and one to go."

"And that one the worst. I didn't feel too happy there for a moment – all these policemen who have fallen off bobsleighs."

"Oh that was all right. Pete used to play a little rugby. They sacked him because the referee was for ever blowing his whistle. Elbows there you in the line-out! True though, he can't very well scrum down against Agatha. Brain-power needed there!

"Strictly speaking," tapping his front teeth with the rim of his coffee cup, "that should be left to Armstrong, to come the heavy with the full weight of officialdom. He went on though going Poo Poo for such a length of time that I'd really rather love sticking my elbow in his eye in the line-out. Just a wee bit. Also he thinks I'm in bed."

"Where you ought to be," said Emily, trying not to be cross but sounding, no denying, like nanny. "You're all flushed, your temperature is probably round a hundred and two and you look like nothing on earth. And Henri nearly as bad. I'm responsible for him to his wife."

True: Castang's arm was hurting like sin. But the job was not done.

"We'll shovel down a few of the Wentworth-Brewster pills. And some aspirins to help."

"On top of a lot of alcohol, indeed. You'll do no such thing; the mixture's mortal."

"As though we needed telling, dearest Em. There indeed is the rub. They'd been drinking a lot all evening, and a heavy dose of barbiturate – I've the figures here somewhere; no, they're in the office – turned out lethal. Was it meant to turn out lethal? What was the point of drugging them in the first place, if it wasn't meant to? It was. Q.E.D. But it does have to be demonstrated that they knew that. Tricky, in court."

"And what was the point of dragging them up that hill? Did they walk, or were they carried? Technically feasible, I sup-

221

pose, since both Sevenhampton and Ross are strong athletic characters and the first at least in excellent physical condition, but it means a lot of work and would be ridiculed in court."

"I think they walked," said Geoffrey, "and I think I know why. I've walked that way myself and I've a book here on the Coast Path by a chap who's an expert. The hilltop gives the best view there is of the whole coast down to the Start. It was dark, I know, but recall, you're explaining to people who use shore and off-shore lights to navigate by. The beach down below there was a classic place in historic time for running in contraband – Saint Gabriel's. Further east at Seatown or West Bay might be easier, but more obvious. We'll probably find that local notables, among whom Martindale and Sevenhampton can be said to figure, have a line upon coastguard activities but that's a wasps' nest I'll gladly leave to Armstrong. Meantime this guilty knowledge thing, I wonder if it's any – Pete!"

"Sir?"

"You might get on to the office and tell them I want names and addresses of all barbiturate deaths. I don't care if they're classed suicide or accident or whatever; I simply want the names of all the families concerned."

"Plenty of these cases have made headlines," said Castang. "Film stars, pop singers . . ."

"Right, it's common knowledge really, isn't it. And it doesn't answer our big question; why anyone should decide those two needed suppressing: that's worried me all along."

"Supposing . . ." began Castang hesitantly. "As you know I made only the most superficial check on those two. They had very different backgrounds. A very French conservatism – obedience to convention? – fixed patterns, and narrow – that the families have in common. Student rebelliousness, warmhearted hatred of injustice and bigotry; and then we get something further. They put all their resources into this boat. Often a symbolic refusal, would you agree, of all the corrupt and crooked values ashore – 'the sea is still pure.'"

"Ye-es."

"And if that were so what worried us is how they came to be mixed up in this squalid ideology of arms-for-the-people. Meaning the right people."

"Exactly. Fundamental contradiction there."

"But suppose they never knew."

"Never knew?" repeated Geoffrey, looking stupid. As Richard is fond of saying, the brightest ones are the most stupid.

"Imagine how it came about." Recklessly, Castang poured himself some more of Emily's whisky. "Sevenstar there arranges to buy arms, in Vienna or wherever, we'll find out. Arranges for transport across France; we'll find *that* out, too. Reaches a Channel port. Is stuck. Plenty of people in the market for coastguard dodging, but they're unreliable, or they're too obvious, or they're too greedy. Say he meets these two and thinks now there's a nice idealist innocent pair. Holds out some inducement – 'I've a friend in the boatyard business who'll do you good work at a nice discount' – say."

Geoffrey was beginning to nod encouragement.

"'You just bring me this parcel across and no questions asked' – not very bulky but compact and heavy: they'd probably think it was calvados. No objections. Spice of adventure. Arms never enter their heads.

"But it's just what splits all the pacifist-ecologist thinking: attain our means by violence, as against no violence whatever the cost. Both are fanatic. The non-violent have a holy horror of arms. Seen too much of the indiscriminate use of them. A syndrome seen perhaps more, in European countries. We're so accustomed to ruffianly cops, auto-defence leagues, brigati rossi, militias of every sort. I wonder whether English people realise yet, just what a menace weapons are."

"You think they'd be extremely shocked at finding out."

"And perhaps only did find out at this Christmas party. Somebody got a bit pissed and said, 'Let's drink to the next cargo of kalashnikovs'."

"Christ, Henri, I think you might have got it. They'd hardly say, 'We'll denounce you to the cops' since they've no use whatever for cops and, by God, they're right, but they might have turned damn awkward. Particularly if they'd had a lot to drink . . . And Martindale; wouldn't she be the one to decide that she could be as radical, as basic, as fundamental is that the word? – as they were!"

223

"Something of the sort."

"I no longer feel so wishy-washy," said Geoffrey, standing up and reaching for his stick. Adopting a heroic pose, he pointed it in the vague direction of Weymouth Bay. "As Marshall Murat used to say when the cavalry were about to charge, 'Troops, just follow my arsehole.'" Mr. Dawson too had had quite a lot of whisky.

It was like the last time – unlike only because of Peters' presence. A CID sergeant is a formidable figure at any time. A rugby player, one metre eighty-eight which is six foot three and broad with it, takes up a lot of room, as they found when they got into the lift with him. This lends stature (they agreed upon the word) to subsequent procedures. Miss Martindale would no longer treat them like small grubby schoolchildren with ears that stuck out.

"Miss Martindale is expecting you," said the black beetle in the hall.

"Is she though!" muttered Geoffrey.

As before, the companion was waiting, silent and colourless, in the passage. Frowned upon seeing Peters.

"My sergeant."

"Really! How ineffably sinister." Not a very good start.

The furniture had not been altered and the binoculars still stood on the occasional table but there was no one on the Empire day-bed; the big room facing the sea was empty. They stood around, in slight embarrassment, Castang holding his hat awkwardly. Geoffrey leaned on his stick and studied the view. Peters took up stance like the Grenadier of the Old Guard outside Napoleon's bedroom at Schönbrunn. The companion, flitting about, said nothing and offered no help. The door to the bedroom opened and Miss Martindale made her entrance. Very like Napoleon.

Dressed more or less as they had seen her: clothes didn't interest her and the longish skirt with an uneven hemline varied only from being dark brown to dark blue: the cardigan with its hand-knitted look from dark blue to dark brown. No jewellery, a crumpled silk scarf tucked in the neck of any-old-blouse. It was the head that was impressive. Large and square and formidable.

The hair as she had worn it in 1928 and never bothered changing; parted, brushed straight across, ear-ring length at the sides and short at the back, same as Gertrude Lawrence, any beauty of the time. Traces of beauty, even now: flesh might sag and crumble but big grey intelligent eyes looked out as they had then; the broad thin mouth which had never worn lipstick unchanged. Something was added, in character – it is the carriage, thought Castang. Old as she is, upright, standing there in the doorway, examining the scene at her leisure, in perfect command. Something in the sideways lift of the head as she took them in, a little toss or twitch of shoulder. Not contemptuous, but superior. Has always been on top: is going to stay that way: whatever happens.

She wasted no more time than had Sevenhampton. Like him aggressive? Aggressive, but not in the least like him.

"You may sit down," sitting herself straightbacked. "You have come, no doubt, having scraped together courage, and you will have imagined bits and shreds of evidence, and feel able to affront the horrible old woman. the queen bee. Cheville ouvrière don't you call it, you? Forgotten all my French. Got taught it as a child, and of course German. About all we were taught. Threw all that away promptly. Never was of the slightest use. I am listening – cat got your tongue, Dawson?"

"Your summing-up is accurate. There is evidence. Circumstantial, I grant. Close enough, pointed enough to give rise to questioning. Of an official nature."

"Tcha, accusations. Through my life I have been accused of so many things." An idle tone, almost of merriment.

"Not perhaps hitherto of behaviour meriting grave criminal charges." Dawson sounding stung. Sensing an over-reach he took pains to qualify. "I make no accusations, Madam. To determine whether there is a case to answer is not my function."

"But you propose to assess me. Like some auctioneer looking at a piece of furniture." Dawson wasn't going to get stung a second time; kept quiet. This is the sort one gives rope to, thought Castang. Paying it out. And hoping one doesn't run out of rope!

She looked at them clear-eyed. Leaned sideways to a box on

the table, chose with care a medium-sized cigar. The cutter snicked. She put it in her mouth and looked for a match. The companion, sitting silent at the other side of the room, tossed a box of matches which she caught deftly. Cuban-smelling smoke drifted. She hadn't offered them any cigars.

"There are two sorts of accusation," looking to see if it drew evenly. "I have known both. One factual: on such a date in such a place, drunk in charge of a car. It is worthless to contest direct police evidence. A magistrate utters nonsense to which nobody listens. One pays the price: there is no need of talk. And the other is suggestion, gossip, damaging innuendo, or what is thought to be such. When I was younger it was said that I was lesbian. How does one defend oneself against such tittle-tattle? Angry denials and explanations? To sue? Or to disregard? A person of character will disregard such things.

"I am old. I have seen many winds blow. I was born before 1914. Into the class called privileged. That rather tiresome young man Waugh invented the Honourable Agatha Runcible. Wasn't me. The nickname stuck awhile. I wasn't an Honourable. Saw no need for it. A crowd of lords and ladies. Weak in the knees for the most part, as well as deficient in wits. I moved among them, knew them. Young women the world called elegant, or witty, or beautiful. The two Dianas, Manners and Mitford, or the Lygon girls. And the men – few now survive. Many mediocre and vain, others for ever drunk. Birth, upbringing, money and privilege; oh yes, those things counted, at the start. But towards the end of a long life, one has found one's level by intelligence. But far more, by character. What have I to fear from the nervous worryings and imaginings of a young police officer?"

"The prospect of going to prison."

"I fear it no more than I do death. I have faced both."

"Well, well," Geoffrey said. "They're both puddings one will eat when the time comes, and then one will know the taste." That's well answered, thought Castang, and seemingly the old lady thought so too. She drew on the cigar, studying him; nodded slightly.

"So we'll see, shall we? If you have questions, put them."

"I think you know a Mr. Sevenhampton?"

"As a neighbour. Where d'you dig him up?"

"The village doctor, up yonder."

"Cackling old hen," she said amicably.

"You have been a guest in his house?"

"Upon occasion."

"The last occasion would have been on Christmas Eve?"

She put the half-smoked cigar on an ashtray.

"Take this away, Dorothy, would you, before it begins to stink? Well, young man; want to put your cards on the table, for me to have a look at?"

"That you were concerned in the illegal traffic of contraband arms is obvious. In view of your intelligence no court would accept a disclaimer of foreknowledge. Seeing you to be a masterful person it might likely tend to the view that you had the major hand in the planning if not the carrying out. Ross is your servant, Sevenhampton your creature. There will be others. Relatively minor and hardly worth arguing about.

"The further imputation is the graver. The Commissaire, here present, at this point enters the scene. He is concerned with the manner in which at least one cargo of arms crossed France, and will be examining that in detail, very shortly. Two young people of French nationality who owned a boat, but didn't perhaps have much money left were contacted – induced into running the cargo. And it can be established, I believe, that they shared this Christmas Eve dinner party."

"Why don't you let this Commissaire speak for himself?"

"You don't mind if I light a cigarette?" asked Castang.

"I shall not complain."

"I don't have the right to interrogate you, Miss Martindale. And Mr. Dawson can tell the story, which we believe to be accurate in the main features, in English. I have a word to offer, if you will allow."

"I'll allow you."

"Many whom the world and the police call criminal are not punished. Many are not even pursued. They rest comfortably, protected by privilege, or influence, or their well-placed friends. While many more, who are pursued with great zeal, and punished heavily, are guilty of bad judgment, brought on by fear and unhappiness and suffering. They have not had strength to resist wrongs, or the skill to turn them aside."

"Is this an exercise in French logic?"

227

"I am wondering; in which category you prefer to find yourself."

"Young man, if you hope to trick admissions out of me with dialectic of this sort you're much mistaken. Whatever you imagine you can lay at my door. Any allegation you make you'll have to prove it up to the hilt. That's the law here. And when you can't, I'll make you eat it."

"I shall not run away," said Castang politely.

"Much good may that do you," she replied sarcastically. Policemen watch for sarcasm: he smiled. He pointed to the binoculars upon the little table.

"You watch the sea."

"I do."

"In the Channel, in the shallow waters, there are sudden violent storms."

"There are indeed."

"In such a storm, last autumn, a French fishing boat was overturned, between Newhaven and Dieppe. English men risked their lives to save those sailors, because at sea there is solidarity. A thing we hear much of but see little. Nationalism is put aside, among sailors."

"The anecdote is edifying, but I fail to see the point."

"Here too we have French sailors, who lost their lives in England. I am here because I have confidence in your people."

"If people choose to kill themselves in an access of romantic sentimentalism . . ." – shrugging.

"Sailors do not have much trouble sleeping," said Castang mildly. "It is the waking up that worries them."

"The question seems academic."

"Perhaps it isn't. Mr. Dawson?"

"You have said," remarked Mr. Dawson, exceedingly colourless, "that I should put questions to you. As Mr. Castang remarks – in passing, the sentiments he expresses are my own – this question poses itself. The young people concerned, it has been suggested, poisoned themselves with barbiturates generally prescribed as narcotics. We don't need to be French to use a bit of logic there, do we?"

"As I understand, such things circulate freely, and there is a market in them."

228

"Quite so, but you'll allow me to follow a natural line of reasoning before the far-fetched. If we eliminate the one," friendly, "we can always fall back upon the other. You wouldn't object to giving me the name of your physician?"

"In London. And he will respect professional confidence."

"Let me assure you, Miss Martindale, that he will answer questions shown to be relevant. Elderly people often find it difficult to sleep well, and sedatives are frequently prescribed."

"Since it is a normal state of affairs why labour the point?"

"And the village doctor? A fool, as you remark. Perhaps handy sometimes, to renew the prescriptions made for you in London? These prescriptions are filled by pharmacies who are obliged by law to keep careful account of dates and quantities. Since, as you justly say, there is a traffic in such things. You will help in accounting for those you possess? – or have possessed? In the final months of last year, say?"

"I see no obligation whatever to encourage prying into my personal affairs."

"I take note of your reticence, Miss Martindale."

"Ridiculously far-fetched, to quote you out of your own mouth."

"Really? Even a magistrate – let alone a judge – might find it more far-fetched that two people in their twenties should come to England carrying a stock of drugs large enough to be fatal, for the express purpose of committing suicide upon English soil while taking the precaution of plenty to drink at a Christmas Eve dinner in friendly and congenial company. However, let's come a little closer to realities. Sergeant Peters?"

Peters, who had stayed still as a mouse, reached into his inside pocket as though for a big gun in a shoulder holster, and produced a grubby piece of paper. Unexpectedly he turned to the other silent witness.

"Isn't it Miss McCallum?" in a gentle friendly fashion.

"Yes," said the companion – secretary? – it had never been very clear. There was no surprise in her voice.

"Miss Dorothy McCallum? Sorry to sound pedantic. My information is that you had a sister."

"What nonsensical rubbish is this?" asked Agatha in her deepest tones.

"It's quite a common name, McCallum," apologised Peters. "We want to be sure we have it right. This information I have here concerns a Miss Alicia McCallum. That would be your sister? Your elder sister?"

"Yes."

"I'm sorry if I touch memories that are bound to be painful to you. Miss McCallum – a couple of years ago – put an end to her life – according to official findings – while of unsound mind brought on – citing evidence given at an inquest – by a painful disease: terminal stage, agreed her medical adviser in testimony. This was actually your sister?"

"It's in no doubt I imagine," in the same placid voice.

"The method used was a mixture of alcohol and barbiturate. There was a comment from the coroner concerning your sister's knowledge of the dosage needed to induce death."

"There was a booklet in circulation about euthanasia."

"Quite so. And the higher the alcohol level . . . these facts were known to you at the time?"

"There was a suggestion that I had put this information in my sister's way."

"The suggestion at one moment went further, I think."

"Yes. It was said that I had actually administered the dose."

"Which would legally have been murder, since the law does not officially admit euthanasia. However, the coroner directed that the findings exclude an open verdict since the matter was by no means proved. In consideration moreover of your pain and your close share in your sister's suffering.

"This is not a matter we wish to drag up, Miss McCallum. Two questions only, in regard to this other enquiry. You had in fact learned the quantity of barbiturate needed, in combination with a high alcohol level, to induce death? It's a formal question."

"I had, yes."

"And following upon that, have you spoken of this knowledge to another person?"

"Yes I have."

"Can you name this person?" There was a silence. One used phrases (yielding to cliché as usual) like a 'battle of wills' taking

230

place. It is both more simple and more complex. One will is always stronger than another, but the weaker can revolt. The how and why could be a lengthy matter. And pretty futile. The wide grey eyes, intelligent and alert, searched the dowdy blue eyes and got no answer.

"I am sorry, and I'm not sorry. But I won't retract it."

Agatha got up and stood by the French window, looking out to sea. Out there perhaps there was a vision of a medieval castle, so strongly placed and cunningly built that it could never fall to assault. There were several, and they all fell. Treachery is another cliché; a short cut, for the lazy.

Sergeant Peters did not fill the silence, so Geoffrey had to.

"You will not object," formal and courteous, "to accompanying us to the office? I believe that Superintendent Armstrong may wish to put further questions."

"We've been awfully inhospitable," said Emily. "I hate your rushing off like this. And now that the children are back at school at last ... Geoffrey will expect me to fuss over his wretched leg... Would you like to come into the town with me? I've no real shopping but we might look for somewhere nice for lunch ...

"Which way are you going home?" driving the car fast and expertly.

"London, I thought."

"Going back through London!" with as much horror as though he had suggested a stopover in Djibouti, "you can't possibly. But why?" like a child.

"Oh I thought something for Vera. The usual, you know; cashmere pullover to show off the Woolworth pearls."

"My dear boy, I'll get it for you here at half the price." Emily was rather bossy; but in a nice way ...

"Shall we have some coffee? I buy mine here and theirs always tastes nicer, I never can imagine why. Goeffrey does complain so. Can I have whipped cream on mine? Don't tell him for God's sake. You've hardly seen anything of the country, either. Not that one wants to, much, in January. Come again and bring Vera."

231

"Your turn."

"I haven't seen France since the children were born."

"Exactly like London."

"I suppose, but Geoffrey complains about my being so provincial. He gets terribly depressed, about here."

"You should see me, at home."

"So we have to cheer one another up."

They both came as far as the airport.

"Blasted leg," said Geoffrey irritably. "No need to go so fast, Em: we've loads of time."

At the gate she suddenly produced an enormous embarrassing carrier bag emblazoned with Union Jacks and heavy, as though filled with patriotic products by Mr. Sevenhampton.

"Only a few oddments," blushing guiltily.

"Oh, Emilienne, do stop apologising."

"Put her head foremost down in the bag," said Geoffrey, testy.

What a lot of work, thought Castang gloomily in the plane. That infernal boat. And Monsieur Bontemps. And funerals. And a doubtless tedious and unsatisfactory enquiry into those arms. One would try to shuffle that off on to SRPJ Rennes . . .

Did at least get that murder tidied up: I suppose that's something . . . Who does all the preliminary work in England, where there's no judge of instruction? The poor old donkeys of the CID no doubt. You go before a magistrate and reserve your defence, and Mr. Armstrong asks blandly for a remand in custody to complete his enquiries. Meaning a hell of a lot of work for Geoffrey Dawson and Peters.

He cheered up slightly, at the thought.

"I'm back."

"What's all this?" asked Vera diving instantly into the carrier. "Not all whisky surely? Oh marmalade, goody. And treacle! Something to be said for Olde Englande, right?"

At the bottom of the bag there was a woolly too for Lydia, put in as a surprise.

"And was it a homicide or a suicide, in the end?" looking at herself critically, in the glass. "Good colour this. Your choice, I hope."

"Certainly. No, homicide. Muddled up among three or more, so who thought it up, who did it – musical chairs, there."

"Oh dear. Like with Roger."

"Not a bit like Roger. Coldblooded, mean, and crapulous. And one will pursue them all the way to the Assize Court. And hope they get pegged good and proper."

"No way to talk," reproving.

"No sensible way to talk," he agreed. "Those were two innocents who got their heads caught in a fiddle."

"At least you had no part, in this one."

"I suppose not; no."

"Take it off now, Lydia, you have to keep it for best."

"Let her go on wearing it," pleaded Castang. "Best should be every day."

MORE ABOUT PENGUINS, PELICANS
AND PUFFINS

For further information about books available from Penguins please write to Dept EP, Penguin Books Ltd, Harmondsworth, Middlesex UB7 0DA.

In the U.S.A.: For a complete list of books available from Penguins in the United States write to Dept DG, Penguin Books, 299 Murray Hill Parkway, East Rutherford, New Jersey 07073.

In Canada: For a complete list of books available from Penguins in Canada write to Penguin Books Canada Ltd, 2801 John Street, Markham, Ontario L3R 1B4.

In Australia: For a complete list of books available from Penguins in Australia write to the Marketing Department, Penguin Books Australia Ltd, P.O. Box 257, Ringwood, Victoria 3134.

In New Zealand: For a complete list of books available from Penguins in New Zealand write to the Marketing Department, Penguin Books (N.Z.) Ltd, Private Bag, Takapuna, Auckland 9.

In India: For a complete list of books available from Penguins in India write to Penguin Overseas Ltd, 706 Eros Apartments, 56 Nehru Place, New Delhi 110019.

THE WIDOW

'Van der Valk's widow, Arlette, steps into her dead husband's shoes, and trips over herself, irresistibly' – *Yorkshire Post*

After the death of her husband, the late Piet van der Valk, life gets boring for his widow, Arlette. So she chooses to remarry, a decision which spurs her into setting herself up as an advisory agency.

Clients, though, bring with them not merely their own problems but also danger and threats upon her own life . . .

The background is Strasbourg – a regional capital with unusual riches and resonance which attracts the best from both France and Germany. And it is into this city of crossroads that Nicolas Freeling launches the resourceful Arlette.

ONE DAMN THING
AFTER ANOTHER

Nearly ten years after the murder of her husband, Piet van der Valk, Arlette is happily remarried to a phlegmatic Englishman and running a one-woman agency in Strasbourg which undertakes everything from detective investigation to the dispensing of tea and sympathy.

As she uncovers the activities of an illegal fur-trader, comforts an abandoned husband, undertakes a trip to the Argentine to retrieve a runaway delinquent, life for Arlette seems to be becoming just one damn thing after another.

And a cold voice threatening her on the telephone brings the last of Van der Valk's pigeons home to roost . . .

Also published
THE DRESDEN GREEN
GADGET
THE KING OF THE RAINY COUNTRY
A LONG SILENCE
THE NIGHT LORDS

PENGUIN OMNIBUSES

☐ *Victorian Villainies*   £4.95

Fraud, murder, political intrigue and horror are the ingredients of these four Victorian thrillers, selected by Hugh Greene and Graham Greene.

☐ *The Balkan Trilogy* Olivia Manning   £5.95

This acclaimed trilogy – *The Great Fortune, The Spoilt City* and *Friends and Heroes* – is the portrait of a marriage, and an exciting recreation of civilian life in the Second World War. 'It amuses, it diverts, and it informs' – Frederick Raphael

☐ *The Penguin Collected Stories of*
  Isaac Bashevis Singer   £4.95

Forty-seven marvellous tales of Jewish magic, faith and exile. 'Never was the Nobel Prize more deserved . . . He belongs with the giants' – *Sunday Times*

☐ *The Penguin Essays of George Orwell*   £4.95

Famous pieces on 'The Decline of the English Murder', 'Shooting an Elephant', political issues and P. G. Wodehouse feature in this edition of forty-one essays, criticism and sketches – all classics of English prose.

☐ *Further Chronicles of Fairacre* 'Miss Read'   £3.95

Full of humour, warmth and charm, these four novels – *Miss Clare Remembers, Over the Gate, The Fairacre Festival* and *Emily Davis* – make up an unforgettable picture of English village life.

☐ *The Penguin Complete Sherlock Holmes*
  Sir Arthur Conan Doyle   £5.95

With the fifty-six classic short stories, plus *A Study in Scarlet, The Sign of Four, The Hound of the Baskervilles* and *The Valley of Fear*, this volume contains the remarkable career of Baker Street's most famous resident.

A CHOICE OF PENGUINS

☐ **Small World** David Lodge £2.50

A jet-propelled academic romance, sequel to *Changing Places*. 'A new comic débâcle on every page' – *The Times*. 'Here is everything one expects from Lodge but three times as entertaining as anything he has written before' – *Sunday Telegraph*

☐ **The Neverending Story** Michael Ende £3.50

The international bestseller, now a major film: 'A tale of magical adventure, pursuit and delay, danger, suspense, triumph' – *The Times Literary Supplement*

☐ **The Sword of Honour Trilogy** Evelyn Waugh £3.95

Containing *Men at Arms, Officers and Gentlemen* and *Unconditional Surrender*, the trilogy described by Cyril Connolly as 'unquestionably the finest novels to have come out of the war'.

☐ **The Honorary Consul** Graham Greene £1.95

In a provincial Argentinian town, a group of revolutionaries kidnap the wrong man . . . 'The tension never relaxes and one reads hungrily from page to page, dreading the moment it will all end' – Auberon Waugh in the *Evening Standard*

☐ **The First Rumpole Omnibus** John Mortimer £4.95

Containing *Rumpole of the Bailey*, *The Trials of Rumpole* and *Rumpole's Return*. 'A fruity, foxy masterpiece, defender of our wilting faith in mankind' – *Sunday Times*

☐ **Scandal** A. N. Wilson £2.25

Sexual peccadillos, treason and blackmail are all ingredients on the boil in A. N. Wilson's new, *cordon noir* comedy. 'Drily witty, deliciously nasty' – *Sunday Telegraph*

A CHOICE OF PENGUINS

☐ *The Philosopher's Pupil* **Iris Murdoch**   £2.95

'We are back, of course, with great delight, in the land of Iris Murdoch, which is like no other but Prospero's . . .' – *Sunday Telegraph*. And, as expected, her latest masterpiece is 'marvellous . . . compulsive reading, hugely funny' – *Spectator*

☐ *A Good Man in Africa* **William Boyd**   £2.50

Boyd's brilliant, award-winning frolic featuring Morgan Leafy, overweight, oversexed representative of Her Britannic Majesty in tropical Kinjanja. 'Wickedly funny' – *The Times*

These books should be available at all good bookshops or newsagents, but if you live in the UK or the Republic of Ireland and have difficulty in getting to a bookshop, they can be ordered by post. Please indicate the titles required and fill in the form below.

NAME _____ BLOCK CAPITALS

ADDRESS _____

_____

_____

Enclose a cheque or postal order payable to The Penguin Bookshop to cover the total price of books ordered, plus 50p for postage. Readers in the Republic of Ireland should send £1R equivalent to the sterling prices, plus 67p for postage. Send to: The Penguin Bookshop, 54/56 Bridlesmith Gate, Nottingham, NG1 2GP.

You can also order by phoning (0602) 599295, and quoting your Barclaycard or Access number.

Every effort is made to ensure the accuracy of the price and availability of books at the time of going to press, but it is sometimes necessary to increase prices and in these circumstances retail prices may be shown on the covers of books which may differ from the prices shown in this list or elsewhere. This list is not an offer to supply any book.

This order service is only available to residents in the UK and the Republic of Ireland.

● ● ●